50 CLASSICS OF CRIME FICTION 1950-1975

A Garland Series
Chosen and Introduced by
**JACQUES BARZUN &
WENDELL HERTIG TAYLOR**

The Dead Past

JEAN SCHOLEY

GARLAND PUBLISHING, INC.
NEW YORK • LONDON
1983

Copyright © 1961 by Jean Scholey
Introduction Copyright © 1983 by Jacques Barzun
and Wendell H. Taylor
All Rights Reserved

This facsimile was made from a copy owned by
the Mercantile Library Association.

A list of the titles in the FIFTY CLASSICS
OF CRIME FICTION 1900–1950 and the
FIFTY CLASSICS OF CRIME FICTION
1950–1975 is included at the end of this volume.

Library of Congress Cataloging in Publication Data

Scholey, Jean.
  The dead past.

  (Fifty classics of crime fiction, 1950–1975)
  Reprint. Originally published: 1st American ed.
New York : Macmillan, 1962. (Cock Robin mystery)
  I. Title.
PR9399.9.S36D4   1983   823   81-47397
ISBN 0-8240-4964-0   AACR2

Design by Jonathan Billing

The volumes in this series are printed on acid-free,
250-year-life paper.

Printed in the United States of America

INTRODUCTION

Not long ago a feature writer for *The New York Times* opened his article by listing some of the things that leave one at loose ends; one was: "You've read all the good mysteries ever published." His meaning is easy to catch, but factually he was wrong. No one has access to all the good ones or would know which they were. And the supply keeps outstripping the eager reader's power to seize upon "all the good ones." As crime fiction of high merit continues to be produced, so does it continue to be rediscovered.

In a previous Garland series, *Fifty Classics of Crime Fiction*, covering the years from 1900 to 1950, these editors were able to introduce to the Anglo-American reading public at least half a dozen tales that reviewers and readers alike declared they had never heard of and that they rejoiced to find first rate. Side by side with these were samples of the work of well-known authors and peaks of achievement by the less well known but not obscure. These three categories—acknowledged classics, overlooked classics, and classics totally unsuspected—make up this second series, which takes the genre from where we left it to 1975. Both the starting and the closing date are approximate, for the sake of doing justice to authors whose best work would be excluded by the span of a few months or else by the vagaries of copyright here or in England. In short, the third quarter of the century has been represented as fairly as can be done in forty-nine full-length works and a volume of seventeen short stories.

To this confident statement—for the editors have cast their net wide and pondered long before their final choice—one exception must be made, which applied equally to the first fifty. One or two desirable titles are absent, owing to the unwillingness of the holders of copyright to allow reissue in a series. One has to say "holders of copyright," for it is extremely rare that an author himself or herself objects to the reissue of a work.

As one looks over the panorama offered by the present selection, what is striking to the connoisseur is not only the steadiness of the output in the two main producing countries, but also the continued preeminence of women writers and the stability of the subgenres. With the advent of the tough tale in the 1930s it was often said that everything done earlier would turn ridiculous and would perish. Ah, prophecies! People in their tens of thousands still read the old favorites with zest. Allingham, Sayers, Marsh, and the *prima assoluta*, Christie, keep reappearing in paperback like opera stars in one farewell tour after another. Equally notable is that they have worthy successors. One need only think of P. D. James, who takes her place in the present series with her first (1962) in the good old-fashioned and imperishable genre.

The tough (so-called, though actually a rather sentimental type of tale) have kept up their numbers too, like the police procedural and the story of menace and anxiety, to say nothing of the fact-laden report: region or town, industry, occupation, sea, air, underground, and so forth. This group, in which quite often the background becomes the foreground, is so instructive that with the decline of schooling we may perhaps rely on its popularity for the preservation of general knowledge. Nor has the "series character" died out. The inspector and his sergeant, the private eye, the lawyer or academic or insurance agent who is the same type under many aliases—all these are still flourishing in the flood tide of what the libraries perversely keep listing as "mysteries."

It is a misnomer, because the cliché that reading crime fiction feeds the taste for puzzles has long been discarded by thoughtful men and women and even by critics. Similarly, only publishers think that the term "suspense story" means anything. All good stories whatever have suspense, *are* suspense, and in all of them accordingly there are unknowns, which is to say mysteries: will they meet, love, hate, fight, win, lose, marry, die? It may be that the modern novel has in some instances abandoned suspense and lifelikeness, but that does not change the definition of story telling, and crime fiction stands in its central tradition. It is literature because each sample is a *tale*, like one of the *Arabian Nights* or *Don Quixote* or *Candide* or *The Three Musketeers*.

A tale does not profess to go deep into human psychology or comment on contemporary social problems—that has been the province of the novel since 1750. Even so, good crime fiction does tell us something about life. Whether as sheer information or as imagined behavior under extraordinary conditions, the tale depicts a real world—think of *The Odyssey* or *Robinson Crusoe*. Some of the best tales make the surprising come out of the ordinary, and the best crime fiction does just that.

For these very reasons the despised "detective story" has in the last fifty years overcome the prejudice that marked its beginnings. The novel itself in its nonage was similarly maligned: it was a waste of time and gave the young immoral ideas. Detective stories were never accused of teaching the young how to rob or murder, but they were thought the fated diet of the middlebrow—another cliché contrary to fact. The best detective stories, beginning with Poe's, have always been written by and for highbrows. Intellectual snobs therefore need not hide in the attic to enjoy *Done In At Dawn* or *The Stiff in the Skiff*.

Indeed, crime fiction in the last half-century has turned quite serious, yet without losing humor as one of its precious ingredients. What it has lost is the melodrama of the old French *roman policier* and the overreaction that followed, the self-conscious pose of "Murder, what fun!" Seriousness may in fact be on the verge of going too far. Book reviewers in London and New York have not merely vindicated the literary merits of the genre; they have begun to find in it symbols and allegories, as in modern literature. In England a famous poet has studied the oeuvre of Dick Francis. Over here college courses can be heard grinding out term papers. The worst is to be feared. One can foresee a Ph.D. dissertation on "Celtic Feeling in the Work of Agatha Christie." It would run like this: her protagonist's name, Poirot, sounds exactly like the French for *leek*. The leek is the emblem of the Welsh soldier. The Welsh are Celtic. Hercule Poirot's companion is named Hastings, who is clearly the dull Englishman defeated at the battle of that name (1066). Hercule, of course, denotes the all-powerful hero; so Christie's tales are actually the saga of the conflict between the intuitive Celt—in this case a Belgian—and the stolid Saxon. Poirot's superior mind avenges centuries of English stupidity—read Caesar's *Gallic Wars*, Shakespeare's *Henry IV*, and D. H. Lawrence, *passim*.

We say: No! Read Agatha Christie. Hands off Poirot. Douse the symbols and hush the footnotes pending the dissolution of the universities. Meanwhile, read the fresh set of *Fifty Classics* and enjoy them as simply as the old sultan enjoyed the imaginative works of Scheherazade.

JEAN SCHOLEY belongs to that small class of writers who make their debut in crime fiction with a splendid piece of work and never follow it up. One result is that the achievement, however striking, never gets widely known, for nowadays, more than ever before, it takes repeated blows of one's work on the public consciousness before that work begins to be recognized and associated with the right genre, let alone with a particular product. As a further result, the biographical facts about the diffident author do not come out. All that is known about Mrs. Scholey is that "she lives with her husband in the area about which she writes so vividly." Such at least was the report in 1961, the year of publication of *The Dead Past*.

The book tells of dramatic events in Tanganyika that concern the district commissioner, Geoffrey Hallden. It is his task to find out how the murdered stranger came by his end. In fiction as in real life there must be obstacles to purpose, and in fiction they must be picturesque as well as plausible. Tanganyika is ideal for supplying the physical difficulties, and one takes them just as they are told. As for the moral or psychological kind, the author being free to invent, one is grateful when they are anguishing but not agonizing. Jean Scholey sees to it that Hallden's doubts about the bearing of the crime on his own private life disturb him to the right degree; they do not tear at his vitals to the point where we feel like telling him to buck up and be a man. There has been too much masochism in recent fiction generally, and it is an insult not only to one's sensibilities but to one's intelligence. *The Dead Past*—like that earlier classic from the same corner of the world, Elspeth Huxley's *African Poison Murders*—stands firm as a model of sense and suspense.

THE DEAD PAST

I

KILIMANI – or, to give it its full name, Boma Kilimani, 'the fortified place on the hill' – is unlikely to be marked on any map of Tanganyika. Once, when the Arabs came down the coast, it was an important strongpoint for their inland trade with the southern part of the country, and a channel for slaves and gold and food for the dhows' crews. The dhows still come in every year on the north-east trade and leave on the south-east, but they bring only carpets and tiles and dried fruit and go away loaded with mangrove poles and cachou nuts and copra, and perhaps sometimes, hidden away, a more precious load of illegal ivory. The old Arab fort on the point has vanished, and only the ruins of the ancient mosque and the tombs of some of the conquerers still stand at the base of the headland that runs out into the sea.

The Germans came and went, and left a square honey-yellow fort on the hill, where it commanded the whole sweep of the bay, and a scatter of stone bungalows along the ridge where they would catch the breeze from the sea. Then the British took over, and the fort became the Boma, the seat of Government, and the Union Jack was run up every morning for the hours of daylight. Occasionally it hangs upside-down, for old Swedi, the ex-*askari*, who has outlived the Arab and the German invasions, is getting old now and his eyesight is dim. The British have built a few permanent buildings around the quay'and on the hill slopes, and tarred the main street, and the Indians who followed them in have built rows of blank-faced shops with roofs overhanging the dusty pavements. But in spite of these superficial changes things go on much as they have always done. The countrymen come in from their smallholdings with produce heaped up in baskets on the back of their bicycles or carried on the heads of their wives. The fishing boats put out to sea, the curved sails all leaning together against the wind, and on their return the fishermen chaffer under the casuarinas beside the blanched shells of their outriggers, while the women in black body-cloths and loose turbans spread the catch of small fry to dry in the sun. The smart town traders in their check skirts, shirts and white caps, or the enveloping white *kanzu* of the Swahili African, trade and idle in the market or the beer shop, joking with the girls in their brilliant *kangas* and black head-veils. Occasionally an Arab from the dhows swaggers through the town, small and wiry under the weight of his great turban, fingering the crescent dagger at his belt; and there are always the quiet Indian traders sitting outside their ever-open shops, with their wives and big-eyed children. But the town has decayed, slowly and inevitably, as the water flowing down the creek has silted up the harbour. Now and again one of the old Arab houses with their carved doors falls down into a pile of dusty rubble, but nobody much cares, except perhaps the district commissioner. The ruins lie there for the children to play in or the herds of goats to shelter from the sun.

On this March evening the district commissioner himself, Geoffrey Hallden, M.C., stood on the steps of the Boma and looked down on the little town and the harbour at his feet. He had just got back from ten days' safari in the outlying areas of his district, and he savoured the familiar pleasure of being back once more in his own place. For he felt that Kilimani was his, in a special sense. He had been stationed there for five years now – an exceptional time for this Administration – and he had come to identify himself very closely with its troubles, its people, its small triumphs. The position of a district commissioner in a small place, far even from his provincial headquarters, is still a powerful one. He stands as the symbol of Government and the Crown, and his word is law in his own little parish. Hallden was a man who took his responsibilities seriously, and it was a deep satisfaction to him to feel that he had come to know the town now, the temper of its people, its needs and its shortcomings, and because of this was perhaps able to build something useful and permanent here. The peace and order of the town in the evening light, the smooth bay, the fringe of palm and casuarina behind the beach, all were familiar and reassuring. He picked out the small changes that had come about in his absence – a new building started by the market, road repairs finished below the Boma, the crimson blossom starting to break out on the flamboyant trees, a couple of dhows lying at anchor that had not been there before. Then his gaze moved along the ridge to his right, to the cluster of bungalows that crowned the point. There lived the small Government community, the district officer, the medical officer, the veterinary officer, the public works department district engineer, and so on; and, of course, in the largest house, in the best position on the headland, lived the D.C. with his wife and baby daughter. He frowned faintly as he studied the house. That morning he had arrived back from safari and gone with all his staff and baggage straight to the Boma. He had phoned Mary as soon as he got in, and he thought she had sounded less welcoming than usual. Perhaps she was annoyed that he had not made the time to call at home, but he had been desperately busy. And Lois had been crying in the background. Probably Mary had been harassed, poor girl, and everything would be all right when he got home. He looked down at his dusty shorts and shirt and thought longingly of a bath, a drink with ice in it, and a quiet dinner by candlelight for the two of them – all the things he had been missing in the last ten days.

He started to walk towards the gate but paused at the approach of old Swedi, the Boma messenger and general factotum, who clicked his heels and saluted smartly.

'*Jambo*, Bwana Mkubwa!'

Hallden liked the old boy with his rheumy eyes and toothless grin, and returned the salute with a smile. Swedi should really have been pensioned off long ago, but he loved the prestige of working at the Boma and Hallden had promised himself he would see that the old man at least stayed out his own time as D.C.

They exchanged the formal Swahili requests for news and the assurance that it was good, then Swedi was pointing to the tall columns of cloud forming over the outlying islands.

'There is much rain coming. It is fortunate that the Bwana D.C. came back from his safari today.'

'Truly, Swedi. The tracks were very bad today after the rain. Tomorrow I should not have got through. Has all been well here?'

The old man spread out his hands. 'Fairly well, bwana, fairly well. But with the rain comes trouble.'

Hallden laughed. 'You are not afraid of a little mud, are you? We need the rains badly this year.'

They exchanged good-nights and the D.C. set off along the ridge.

His house was a German-built bungalow set on a plinth above ground-level and with a deep veranda along the front facing out to sea. The main drive curved round below the veranda, but approaching on foot one could pass through a gap in the hedge into the garden and enter the house by a side door that opened into the sleeping quarters. Hallden usually took this way, and did so tonight, letting the screen door bang behind him.

'Is that you, Geoffrey?' his wife's voice called from the baby's nursery.

He put his head round the door and saw Mary with her back to him, changing the infant's nappy at the table. Mary looked up and gave him a quick smile. He kissed the back of her curly head and stayed for a moment with his hand on her shoulder, watching her deft movements.

'How was the trip?' she said. 'You look pretty muddy.'

'The roads were shocking. It was worth it, though. I think I just nipped in the bud some trouble up at Dali. It might have been too late after the rains. And how have things been here?'

'Oh, all right. Just the usual. But look, darling, we've got visitors. Can you go and pour them some drinks while I get Lois to bed? It's the Chambers and Tom Griffith.'

'The eternal triangle? Oh, hell! I want a bath, and I don't feel like coping with company tonight, particularly those three.'

'I'm sorry, but you know what they are. Pauline just doesn't grasp the fact that there might be other things we would rather do than entertain her, and the others won't budge till she wants to go. I did the polite hostess for a bit, hoping you would come, then Lois got hungry and started to yell. I had to take her in with me, hoping Pauline would take the hint, but she just grabbed her and cooed about what a sweetie she was. Then, of course, sweetie started yelling again and wet all down Pauline's frock. . . .'

'I bet that started a scene.'

'Oh, the usual. Pauline shrieked with horror, and then said it was really a marvellous idea as Dudley would have to buy her a new dress now, and she hadn't had a rag for ages. I told her it would wash out, and fled before the next explosion.'

Geoffrey grinned at her exasperated tone and ruffled the back of her hair. 'Poor old thing. You've had a trying time. I'll get into some slacks and a clean shirt and go and ply them with drink. You come when you are ready.'

He touched his daughter's downy head carefully with the tip of one finger. 'Don't be long.'

'And don't give them too much to drink or they will never

go!' Mary called after him. 'You know Tom – and Pauline!'

Geoffrey did know them, with the intimate knowledge unavoidable in members of a small community, where your friends are ready-made, not chosen. He rinsed off a bit of the dust and put on slacks, a shirt and a tie. A quick look in the mirror showed him he badly needed a shave and a haircut, but there was nothing he could do about that now. He sighed, straightened shoulders that ached from days of jolting over bush tracks, and went towards the front room.

The guests were sitting out on a spacious veranda that looked over the sea. For a moment they were silhouetted against the evening sky, all three silent and motionless, as if, Geoffrey thought, they had nothing left to say to each other. Then Dudley Chambers turned his head, saw his host, and jumped to his feet to shake hands with him.

'Glad to see you back, old man.'

Tom Griffith, the young veterinary officer, half turned in his chair and said, 'Hallo, Geoff. Good safari?'

The veterinary officer was a dark-browed, stocky young Welshman serving his first tour in the territory, and Geoffrey had had a good deal to do with him in the short time he had been in Kilimani. There had been trouble over compulsory cattle dipping in the area, and the D.C. had been called in more than once to settle a near-riot among the African smallholders. He was convinced that half the trouble was due to Griffith's inexperience and his hasty temper. He had tried to bully where he should have explained and persuaded. The Africans, as always suspicious of anything new imposed by Government, had scented a plot to deprive them of some of their precious cattle. Rumours of cattle dying, being made sterile, or confiscated after dipping had blazed around the district, and Geoffrey had been compelled to drop all his other work and trek from village to village, trying to bring the angry peasants back to a reasonable frame of mind. The veterinary officer had gone beside him, muttering under his breath about pampering the so-and-so's and visibly resenting every moment of the tour.

Geoffrey was not, therefore, particularly glad to see the young man at any time, and tonight he was almost the last person he wanted to entertain. The final straw was to be hailed as 'Geoff' by a junior officer, some fifteen years younger than himself. So he merely nodded very briefly, said, 'Good evening, Griffith,' in a cool tone, then turned to the third member of the party, who was sitting with her back half to her husband and looking up smilingly at him.

Pauline Chambers made an attractive picture with the evening light catching the ash-blonde streak in her carefully arranged hair and softening the contours of her face. She was thirty-five, as Geoffrey knew from vouching for a passport application, but she would pass for ten years younger in this light. Her figure was perfect, its curves emphasised by a low-cut silk jersey dress that clung most of the way down. As always she was beautifully made up, in spite of the heat, and wore her usual collection of dangling earrings, rings, and a charm bracelet – each one designed to draw attention to her head or her pretty hands and arms with every movement she made. Her voice was deliberately pitched low, with a faintly stagey huskiness.

'We came to welcome you back, darling,' she said. 'You must be dead after that foul trip in the rain. We all so admire your devotion to duty – leaving Mary so long and everything. Tom, go and pour Geoffrey's drink so he can sit down and put his feet up.'

'Thanks,' Geoffrey replied briefly. 'I'll pour. Another for you, Dudley?'

He was not a man who bothered himself much about atmospheres, but he was uncomfortable tonight with this trio. Pauline with her restless movements and constant demands for attention he always found wearing, but he thought he had got used by now to her trailing her young men round in a threesome wherever she and Dudley went. At first it had surprised him that Dudley did not object, or, indeed, appear to realise that there was anything unusual about it. He could not like the young men for themselves. The choice of unattached males in Kilimani was limited, and in the past year there had been Bates, the rather crude youth from public works department, Derek Shotter, his own district officer, and now Griffith.

Geoffrey took his time mixing and handing round the drinks, listening idly to Chambers talking to Griffith.

Dudley Chambers was a well-preserved fifty, with fairish hair going thin on top and a small, stubby moustache. He was a little precise about his diet, exercise and physical fitness generally, and was made fun of by a number of people in Kilimani (including his wife) in consequence, but possessed, Geoffrey thought, a lot of those solid virtues that used to be implied in the old-fashioned term 'gentleman', and one could not help liking him, and even respecting him. He had been born to prosperity and educated at a good public school, but there had seemed no need for any training to earn his living, as a niche was already prepared for him in the family business. He had settled in there comfortably enough until the outbreak of the war when he had volunteered at once for the infantry. The army suited him, the ordered life, the discipline and the masculine company, and he did well in an unspectacular way. He left the army a lieutenant-colonel, with a fair private income, and at this peak of prosperity he met and married Pauline, fifteen years younger than himself and the spoilt daughter of suburban parents. When they met she had been trying to make a name on the London stage, with very little talent and no liking for hard work, and was beginning to realise she would never make a success of it. She had made a great fuss about the sacrifice of her stage career to marry him but her friends noticed she never afterwards made any attempt to go back to it when opportunity offered. Her family had considered Dudley quite a good match, and so had she at first. But things had gone badly for Chambers ever since. The family business had been absorbed by a large concern which was not prepared to create a comfortable sinecure for him. He had left England for East Africa soon after the end of the war with the idea that he would find more scope for enterprise there. Certainly there was enterprise enough, as he found to his cost. His money, invested in various attractive schemes, gradually melted away, until with the last of it he had bought a small papain estate near Kilimani. He acquired it, with his usual optimism, unseen, in Nairobi, from an enterprising Greek who had pressing reasons for leaving it. Chambers and his wife had lived there for about a year, and it did not look like being more successful than any of his other ventures.

Dudley was burbling on about the rains that had come so suddenly two days before.

'I suppose we shall be cut off for the duration,' Griffith grumbled. 'Doc. Slater knew what he was about when he went up to Dar for a conference at this time of year.'

'He can still get back by sea, even if the road is closed,' Hallden answered. 'Schmidt would go and pick him up in his schooner.'

'If Slater can get a message through. I tried to ring Dar myself today and was told the line was out of order – as usual.'

'I know,' Geoffrey replied. 'The post office say it is elephants again, knocking down the poles.'

'That means a couple of weeks, I suppose, before they'll get a chap with the nerve to go out and fix it. What a lovely damn country.'

'Oh well,' Geoffrey pursued peaceably, 'considering the line crosses miles of the most god-forsaken bush and has worked pretty consistently since the Germans put it in, it doesn't do so badly. And with the rains on——'

'Just about in time for my paw-paws.' Dudley had obviously been following his own independent line of thought. 'Plays the devil with the plantation, you know, the rains coming late like this. And now they've come I suppose all the boys will go off to their own *shambas* and there'll be no one to do any planting or tapping.'

'You wouldn't get much done anyway now Ramadan is here,' Hallden replied. 'When they are fasting all day and making up for it half the night you can't expect much from them. Is your road still all right?'

'Sticky. Not too bad.'

'I hear the bridge on the main road just north of you is under water already. The town Jumbe sent me a message this afternoon that a Land-Rover was stuck out there. I thought it might be you.'

'Land-Rover? No, I haven't been out there for weeks.'

'Who was it?' Pauline put in.

'I don't know. I can't think why the Jumbe didn't organise a team of Africans himself to pull the chap out for the usual consideration instead of sending half-baked messages to me. I couldn't get hold of Bates, so I sent Shotter out with a gang to see what he could do.'

Griffith was saying something about clots who got stuck in Land-Rovers and his own wide experience of safari in the rains, so Geoffrey did not have to listen. He leant back thankfully in his chair, stretched his long legs and sipped his drink. Beyond Dudley Chambers' head the sky was darkening to a cloudy copper and a faint peal of thunder echoed across the water. Tomorrow was Good Friday, he thought suddenly, for no particular reason. Dudley would go to the early morning service because it was the thing to do, and Pauline would accompany him because it was her only chance to wear a new hat. . . . He himself ought to go, he knew, but he was feeling lazy. The safari had been full of problems: a dispute over the allocation of some land to an Indian farmer; a campaign against the new agricultural programme that he suspected of having political backing from the local 'Black Africa' party; the usual nonsense over payment of poll tax, cattle dipping, road work . . . His mind slipped back into the channel it had followed all day. He was hardly aware that the others had stopped talking.

Into the silence came with unnatural loudness the whine of gears changing as a car came up the slope to the gate of the house. Pauline's bracelet jingled sharply as she leant forward.

'I wonder who that is?'

They all turned to look out into the darkening driveway. A Land-Rover swung into view and pulled up jerkily by the veranda. Geoffrey got up as soon as he recognised the Boma vehicle. A slight young man climbed hurriedly out. He looked like a schoolboy at first sight in his white shorts and shirt and with mousey hair spiking up a bit at the crown. His narrow face was pale and sticky with sweat, and the line of moustache he cultivated to make himself look older trembled rather ridiculously as he came towards them.

'What's up, Derek?'

'That Land-Rover . . .' Shotter's voice came out in a high squeak and he pulled himself up and started again. 'I found the Land-Rover, Geoffrey, but there's a – a chap in it. He's – he looks as if someone had attacked him with a *panga*. I think he's dead.'

The first thought that came to Geoffrey was that this explained the Jumbe's odd behaviour. He must have known there was a dead man in the car but he wanted someone else to have the onus of finding him officially. But that could wait. . . .

'Who is the man?' he demanded.

'No idea. I – well, he was face down over the wheel, so

I couldn't get a proper look. . . .' Shotter gulped and cleared his throat. 'I didn't recognise what I could see of him. And the car has a Dar es Salaam registration.'

'You left him there?'

'Yes. I thought I had better fetch you. I left the gang there to see no one touched anything.'

Suddenly a new voice spoke.

'What is it? What has happened?'

Mary had come into the shadowy room behind them as Shotter talked. 'Is someone hurt?'

'A man in a Land-Rover, stuck on the creek bridge,' Geoffrey said quickly. 'Derek says he has been attacked with a *panga*. Probably dead. I am going out now.'

'I'll come, too.'

'No, darling. It will be a nasty business.'

'Who else will you take, Geoffrey? Dr Slater is away, and I am a trained nurse. If he should still be alive . . .'

Geoffrey looked at the slim figure in the yellow dress, and for a moment he saw, not the Mary he knew as his wife, but the nurse, impersonal and efficient, whom he had first seen in a Dar es Salaam hospital three years ago.

'I'm sorry, Mary. Of course you must come. Get some things and go straight there in our car as soon as you can. I'll go with Derek in the Land-Rover. We'll have to pick up the police sergeant on the way, Derek, if we can find him.'

'Can I help?' Dudley asked.

Geoffrey shook his head. 'No thanks, Dudley. We'll be able to cope. Sorry I've got to leave you like this. . . .'

He nodded to the other two and climbed quickly in behind the wheel of the car.

2

THE CREEK BRIDGE was about three miles from the centre of Kilimani and on the fringe of the African settlements that straggled out along the main coast road. The sandy, winding road had dried out during the day but there were still pools in the grass at each side where a chorus of frogs kept up a monotonous 'bink-bink'. In the dry season the creek was a trickle of water in a waste of sand, but as soon as the rain came all the connecting channels up to its source filled and a brown torrent swept down, reaching or flowing over the bridge, which, like most country bridges in Tanganyika, was a basis of stout timbers with planks nailed roughly across to the width of a car. Darkness had fallen by the time the district commissioner arrived, but the headlights shining down into the dip where the creek lay showed that the water had receded a little, leaving a muddy pool at each end of the bridge. The stranded vehicle was over on the right of the road, facing into town, and leaning sideways with its off-wheels in a patch of mud.

Hallden took in quickly the position of the Land-Rover, the dim huddle of labourers squatting on the opposite side of the road, and his own car, pulled up clear of the mud with its headlights shining over the area. Mary was already standing beside the Land-Rover. She turned round when she heard him approach, looking pale in the harsh light.

'Sorry I am late. We had a job finding the police sergeant,' Geoffrey said quickly, then stood beside her looking into the vehicle.

'We are both too late,' Mary said.

Geoffrey did not need to reply. She was obviously right.

The Land-Rover smelled of mortality. Gently he pushed Mary aside.

'Go back to the car. I shan't be long.'

Geoffrey had become inured to death during the war. He had learnt then that it helped to tell himself that the scene in front of him was just a picture, something which bore no relation to reality or the emotions. Tonight, as well, he had something else to think about. This was a problem which had to be dealt with like any other, and he was the man who had to deal with it. After the initial shock of the discovery he found he was able to study the scene before him quite calmly.

At first the reflected light of the headlamps filled the interior of the car with deep shadows. Geoffrey switched on his torch and directed the beam on to the man who lay over the driving-wheel, face downwards, as if he had fallen asleep there. The light showed a broad back, a khaki bush shirt stained with dust and blood, and the back of a head with straight hair bleached on top by the sun and cut too long. Geoffrey turned and beckoned to the police sergeant to approach.

William was a magnificent specimen of an African from one of the up-country tribes with a long history of breeding warriors. His height and extreme slenderness were emphasised by the tall *kepi* on his head and the black sash wound tightly round his waist over the khaki uniform. His boots rang importantly on the ground as he paced over to the car and saluted.

'You had better see, William,' Hallden explained in Swahili. 'I am going to move him, and you must know how the body was found.'

Together they lifted the man gently back in his seat. The head rolled back against the upholstery. He was a youngish man, a bit younger than himself, Geoffrey thought – say thirty-three or thirty-five. The face had been handsome except for a weakness about the mouth and lines of strain or hard living etched in the cheeks and round the eyes. It was a face that could have been reckless, and probably gay, but was now set in an expression more of surprise than fear. The *panga* wounds were over the chest and body. There was no doubt what they were; William had seen too many cuts and slashes from the wide-bladed great knives to have any doubt.

'But little blood, bwana,' he added, touching the stained shirt.

It was true. The car was barely marked.

'Perhaps he was killed outside and put back in the car later,' Hallden suggested. 'He doesn't seem to have put up much of a fight.' He lifted one of the arms to show the hand, faintly coloured with reddish dust but showing no sign of a wound.

William murmured agreement, then stood rather helplessly looking at the body and the car and fingered his belt.

'Here! Hold this.' Geoffrey handed him the torch and got into the seat beside the dead man for a closer examination.

The pockets of the bush shirt and shorts were empty – as he had expected them to be – except for a crushed pack of cigarettes. There was a pile of bedding, a primus stove and other bits of camping equipment in the back of the Land-Rover, but on a quick examination they gave no clue to the identity of the owner. Even the licence disc was missing from the windscreen of the car, Geoffrey noted, although a ring on the glass showed clearly where it had been. There was nothing else to see – no weapon, no papers, and the bare minimum of clothing and personal possessions.

Hallden climbed out of the car with relief and beckoned to Shotter, who had been standing a short distance away with Mary.

'Get your gang to tow the car out and take it into town,'

he said. 'There is no more we can do here. William,' (turning to the sergeant) 'will you put stakes of wood in here, and here, to show where the car stood? There is not much good looking for tracks at this stage.'

He indicated the muddy area around the Land-Rover, which by now was marked by a number of feet and by the tyres of at least one other vehicle.

'I turned the car there,' Shotter admitted guiltily. 'I never thought . . .'

'No. Of course not.' Hallden cut off his apologies. 'And it must have rained anyway since the Land-Rover came here. Get the gang pushing the car out and I will go on in my own bus and get the dispensary opened up. He had better go there until we decide what to do with him.

'Oh, by the way———' he turned back to the district officer '– that camera of yours might come in handy, Derek. We must have some evidence for the Dar police when they do get here, and photographs are the best we can do. Could you fetch your kit round as soon as possible and we will tackle it tonight?'

Derek's face brightened. He was an impassioned amateur photographer. 'Oh, splendid, Geoffrey! Yes, of course I'll do it. Pity we can't have proper floodlighting, but I think I can manage something with flash-bulbs.'

He strode off, his brow creased with the weight of responsibility, to marshal his reluctant team of labourers.

Geoffrey and Mary drove in silence to the dispensary, which was right in the middle of the town. When they arrived he put his hand over hers. 'You had better get home, Mary. I shall be some time, I am afraid.'

'There will be some food for you when you come in.' Her voice sounded empty and tired. 'I am sorry you have got mixed up in all this, Geoffrey.'

'It's my job.' He was deliberately dry and unemotional. 'Unfortunate we are cut off like this with no doctor, and no

European police within reach. It's the sort of thing they always threaten new D.O.s with when they first come out. Cue for initiative. The administrative officer must be prepared to be the law and the medical profession and all the rest of the official hierarchy rolled into one. Derek and I will just have to go on coping as best we can until we can make contact with Dar and get the experts in. It's going to be a nice Easter!'

When Geoffrey did get home it was after nine. Mary was sitting alone on the veranda with a light beside her and a book in her lap, but she did not look as if she had been reading. Mohammed, the chief houseboy, brought in a tray of food without being asked and set it on a table by the D.C.'s side. Hallden looked at it without enthusiasm.

'I can't honestly say I feel much like eating.'

'I'll get you a drink. Whisky?' She moved over to the table and measured out the spirit and water as he liked it.

'Is there anything new?'

'About the poor devil in the Land-Rover? Not much. Derek and I took a lot of photographs for the police, and checked over all his belongings and the car as well as we could. It's not the sort of investigation the police would make, but it is the best we can do at present.'

'Have you still no clue who he is?'

'No. It's odd, isn't it? All his papers have gone – pinched with his money, I suppose – and there is nothing in his luggage or in the car to give us a hint. He was carrying very little stuff with him, and what clothing and so on we found is the sort of thing you can get anywhere.'

'Perhaps all the personal things were stolen?'

'Perhaps. But I think they were just after money. It didn't look as if his baggage had been touched. And I wonder why a stranger should come to Kilimani at this time of year, just at the onset of the rains. Even if he reached here, the road

farther south is hopeless after heavy rain. He's not a hunter
– at least he had no kit for it.'
'No guns, you mean?'
'No. Just ordinary camping equipment, a few tins of
food and some clothes. Of course, it is only a matter of
time before he is identified. Probably someone here was
expecting him and will get in touch with us as soon as the
news gets round. If not, as soon as we get particulars of the
car registration and check on the photographs and fingerprints . . .'
'Prints? How on earth will you manage those?'
'William turned up a set of equipment and seemed to
know how to use it, so we took the corpse's prints. I'll send
them up to Dar es Salaam with the photos and other dope
tomorrow by runner and the police can get going on it.'
'But surely you can't send a man off on foot all that way?'
'I don't know, darling. They travel longer distances on
their own concerns. But it is not as bad as it sounds. He'll
only have to get through to the first place that is in touch
with Dar by mail or telephone and hand the stuff over to
someone in authority to forward. And we'll give him a
bicycle.'
'I see. How long do you think he will take?'
'A couple of days, I should guess – so long as he hasn't too
many relatives and friends to visit on the way. That means
the C.I.D. may get someone down here in about a week –
by sea if necessary.'
Mary sighed faintly. 'And in the meantime? It looks as if
it was just a local robbery, doesn't it, for his money and
things?'
'It looks like it. I am calling the Jumbe up tomorrow for
a straight talk about how the body was found, and William
and his constables are getting down to enquiries about our
local bad hats. It doesn't sound like any of our old faithfuls,
but you never know. One thing I am sure of, though – most

of the facts will be known by tomorrow in the *pombe* shop and freely discussed by all the African populace down to the youngest *totos* . . . all except the police, of course. If only we could put a microphone in and tap the information at source we should be saved a lot of trouble!'

They sat in silence for a moment. Mary's eyes were fixed seawards, as if she was thinking over what he had said. The storm still threatened. A thin moon, the moon of Ramadan the month of fasting, was high in the sky, but below it columns and scrolls of black cloud hid the stars and were outlined from time to time by blazes of lightning. The sea reflected back the sky sullenly and the sound of the waves breaking on the sand was very faint.

Conscious of his eyes on her she turned and met his glance with a look he could not quite fathom.

'I wish you weren't mixed up in all this, Geoffrey,' she said. 'I don't like it.' She seemed about to say something else, but instead got up with a rustle of skirts, and came to stand behind him, her hand resting against his cheek.

'Your omelette will be cold. Do eat something if you can. I must go and get Lois's bottle ready.'

Geoffrey put his hand over hers for a moment, warmed by her touch. 'All right. Food, then bed. Are you going to early morning service tomorrow?'

'I had forgotten all about it. I suppose I ought to, but it is difficult with Lois. I'll think about it.'

She drew her hand away from his and turned to go. Geoffrey watched her walk down the long room to the door. She was wearing a housecoat of printed cotton, ground-length to give some protection against mosquitoes, and he thought she looked as pretty as she had ever done, with her slight, erect figure, curly dark hair and neat features. But with the clarity of extreme tiredness he saw that she had changed a lot in two years of marriage. He tried to think back to when they had first met in Dar es Salaam, three years ago. He had been a patient in the hospital with a bad attack of typhoid. As soon as he was well enough to notice anything at all he had noticed the young sister. She had seemed so alive, so quick in all she did, and with a spark of laughter in her dark-lashed blue eyes. He was a reserved man who had always been a little afraid of women and kept his distance from them. During the war there had been one or two passionate but short-lived interludes, but they had only touched one side of his nature. It was difficult to stay aloof now, though, when he saw so much of her, and she was so friendly, so teasing and gay. First he found himself liking her, then imperceptibly he fell in love with her. He had struggled against it for a while, because loving her would mean he would have to share his life with someone else, and he had never learnt to do that. But when at last he gave in the surrender was complete and overwhelming. And he had never regretted it. During the first year of their marriage she had been the same person, alert, full of laughter, with a fresh enjoyment of life that had swept him along with her. Then, when Lois was on the way, she had become ill, and it had been necessary to send her away to Dar es Salaam to be within reach of a hospital and expert medical care. Those three months of separation, or the birth of the child – perhaps both combined – had changed her. She was quieter, less impulsive, less ready to laugh, and though he knew she was still in love with him he had sensed a withdrawal. Or perhaps it was he who had changed? Without her he had got used again to a bachelor existence, to working all hours at his exacting job and devoting to it most of his energies and thought. Then when at last Mary returned she was so tired out and so occupied with the baby that he had been disappointed, and perhaps a little resentful, and had allowed the distance to remain between them. Perhaps, he thought cynically, all marriages were like this after the first honeymoon year. . . .

Unwillingly he dragged himself to his feet. He had eaten his food without tasting it, but that and the drink had made him sleepy. Surely it was only tiredness that was making him exaggerate any slight difference in Mary's manner, and after a sleep he would see there had been nothing really to worry about. The thing he should have on his mind at the moment was this murder at the bridge.

The D.C. reached the Boma late after a disturbed night. The storm which had been building up the previous evening had broken at about two a.m. and the constant peals of thunder had kept him awake on and off till four. Lois had been restless, too, and in the end Mary had to move into her room to try and keep her quiet.

What sleep Geoffrey had was disturbed by peculiarly unpleasant nightmares. In all of them the dead man was there, always a figure of vague menace, though Geoffrey could not recall ever seeing his face clearly. Sometimes he was dead, lying in the shadows of the Land-Rover, and sometimes he seemed to be alive. Waking from one of these dreams he lay for a while listening to the thunder echoing and re-echoing over the sea and the rain driving down in sudden, vindictive bursts. He felt oppressed by the dream and also by a nagging sense of worry over the whole of the previous evening's events. Had he missed something in the investigation? Had he bungled somewhere? He remembered now the things that had seemed incongruous at the time — the look on the dead man's face, the lack of blood, the unwounded hands. If only he knew more about these things!

At last he decided that this vague worrying was not going to get him anywhere. Grimly he set himself to go over in his mind all the things he must do in the morning and then tried to dismiss the whole business from his thoughts. He was only partly successful. Sleep came at last, but it was a shallow sleep, broken by more dreams, and he woke feeling tired and unrefreshed.

As Good Friday was a public holiday the Boma was officially closed and only a skeleton staff was on duty. Hallden was thankful to be spared the stream of phone calls, visits and minor interruptions that made up his normal working day. In the businesslike atmosphere of the Boma a lot of his uneasiness vanished, and he settled down to put into effect the various actions that had suggested themselves to him during the night.

It was just his bad luck, he thought, that this affair had not happened three months earlier. Then there had been a European police officer stationed in Kilimani, who would have coped with it all. But the always chronic shortage of police had become acute, and as a temporary measure the officer was withdrawn and the small post administered from Dar es Salaam. Even the radio link-up which connected most of the stations in Tanganyika had been postponed until the full complement of police could be posted to Kilimani. Hallden had agreed to all this at the time because there was little crime in Kilimani, and what there was followed a regular pattern of thefts and small outbreaks of drunken violence that could usually be dealt with by the African constabulary. But there was no good cursing his luck now; he would just have to get on with it as best he could.

In his career in the administration he had worked a good deal with the police force, and he thought he had an adequate idea of what their procedure would be in a case like this. The first thing was to get the African constabulary out to make as wide enquiries as possible. He had already arranged for Sergeant William to report early at the Boma that morning, and together they worked out a rough scheme of enquiries.

William's intelligence was limited, but he had a good deal of shrewdness and was well grounded in police routine.

He said he had already detailed his most useful officer to visit the area round the creek and try to find someone who had seen the Land-Rover or noticed anyone or anything suspicious in the neighbourhood.

'But it is Ramadan,' he added with a resigned shrug. 'If, as you think, bwana, this man was killed after dark, it is likely that all the people were in their houses and saw nothing.'

'Well, we can only try,' Geoffrey replied. 'And now about the town . . .'

There was always the likelihood that a criminal or a gang of criminals would make for the town. A stranger was news in the small villages, but in Kilimani he might mix unnoticed with the crowds at the market or in the little native hotels and drinking places. And if there was money to spend, that would be the place to spend it. Geoffrey had never known an African thief who could resist blowing his cash at the first opportunity – on flashy clothes, drink, watches, bicycles or women. William agreed to alert his uniformed policemen and sound out his usual chain of informers to see if any strangers had been noticed recently about the place or anyone was spending heavily at the *pombe* shops or the dukas.

He left at last, his brow furrowed with worry. An ordinary murder in the African community always meant a frightening amount of work, but the murder of a European – that was something much worse. Like the D.C., he was wishing earnestly that the European assistant superintendent of police was still at Kilimani.

But Hallden had no time for regrets now. He rang at once for his district officer, and Derek Shotter burst into the room almost as soon as he had put the phone down.

'I've got the prints, Geoffrey,' he said, laying a fat bundle carefully on the desk. 'Took me most of the night to do them, but they're not bad. Look.'

He took up an enlargement and passed it across the table.

'This is the best one.' He watched anxiously while the D.C. studied the print.

'Yes, it is good,' Hallden said at last. He had no eyes for the merits of the photograph at first. The face of the man in the Land-Rover had leapt up at him out of the picture with a ghastly illusion of life, as it had in his dreams the night before.

'Yes. They should be able to identify him from this,' he added slowly. 'It must be the lighting. He almost looks as if he could speak, doesn't he?'

Shotter did not seem to be aware of the repulsion in the D.C.'s voice. 'It is the lighting,' he said eagerly. 'I was afraid it might not come off, but I hit it exactly right. Some of the others are not at all bad either. . . .'

Geoffrey smiled. Shotter's eagerness was hard to resist. He leafed slowly through the bundle of prints, and after a moment's thought selected four and laid them aside.

'Those should do to send up to the C.I.D.,' he said. 'They can identify the fellow from the first one and the others will give them about all we know of the crime. Thanks, Derek. You've done a good job.'

'Are you sending them off this morning?'

'Yes. Rashidi is just finishing typing my report, and I've got a messenger standing by.'

'Who is it?'

'Maulidi.'

'What, the bandy one with the grin? Good Lord, Geoffrey! Do you think you can trust him to do it? I always thought he was the most clueless of the lot . . . and that's saying something!'

Geoffrey smiled. 'Swedi recommended him, and I trust the old boy's judgment over a thing like that. He says Maulidi is too stupid to get into trouble, and he has been a game scout in the past, so he is not scared of going off into the bush on his own.' He leant forward to press the buzzer on his phone. 'Let's get him in now and see what you think.'

The messenger came after a short pause, preceded by Swedi, who seemed to regard himself as official sponsor and kept up a muttered stream of exhortation as they entered the D.C.'s room. For once Maulidi's grin was in eclipse, and he shuffled his broad, splayed feet nervously.

Hallden greeted him gravely.

'Are you afraid of lion, Maulidi?'

The African hesitated and glanced uncertainly at Swedi.

'N-no, bwana.'

'Elephants?'

He hesitated again. 'Well . . .bwana . . .'

'Snakes? Leopard . . . ? Monkeys, perhaps?'

The grin broke through at last, wide as a slice of melon in the black face. 'With a gun, Bwana D.C., I fear nothing. I am a man of many safaris. . . .'

'Good. Then you are just the man we want. But what *I* am afraid of, Maulidi, is not the lions, the leopards, or even the elephants. I am afraid of the little siesta in the heat of the day, the bowl of *pombe* in the village at night, the little visit to your blood brother five miles off your route. . . . You understand me? This is an important message you must carry.'

'*Ndio*, bwana. *Ndio, ndio.* I swear to you I will be very diligent, very quick. I shall let nothing delay me.'

Swedi nodded his head approvingly in the background. 'I have told him, Bwana Mkubwa,' he said in his cracked old voice, 'if he does not do as he is told the Government will deal very hard with him. I have told him.'

'Good. Rashidi will give you the names of the places you are to go to. If the officer of Government is there you will hand over my letter to him and get a receipt – is it clear? If he is on safari you will go to the next place. You will not leave the letter with a clerk who says he will send it when the rains finish, eh? Good. And you will return here as soon as you have the chit for the letter. The chit will say the time you handed it over, so Bwana Swedi here will have words to say to you if you delay on the way home. Is it understood?'

Maulidi shuffled his feet and shot a sideways glance at the old man. The smile widened appreciatively.

'It is understood, bwana.'

He backed out of the room still beaming.

'Phew!' Geoffrey said as the door closed behind the two Africans. 'It's like talking to the Cheshire cat! Let's hope Swedi is right about him. The sooner those papers get through and the C.I.D. get down here the better I shall be pleased.'

As he finished speaking, Rashidi, the D.C.'s clerk, came in with some papers and stood by the desk while Hallden glanced through them.

'Those will have to wait, Rashidi,' he said, tossing an assorted heap across the table top. 'I shall be tied up with this police case most of the day, I am afraid.' He picked out his report to the Dar es Salaam C.I.D. and read it through, frowning. 'Mm! Not very impressive, but it will have to do.' He slipped the photographs he had selected into the envelope and sealed it carefully. 'Give this to Maulidi and tell him to get off at once with it.'

'Yes, bwana.' The clerk took the envelope, and after a sideways glance at the other photographs spread out on the desk, went quickly out of the room.

Hallden picked a cigarette out of a packet on the desk and tossed one to his D.O., then leant back in his chair and smoked silently. Derek Shotter fiddled with his lighter, then perched on the edge of the desk watching the D.C. He recognised the symptoms. Hallden was worried, and in that mood it was wiser not to disturb the train of his thoughts. The room was very quiet except for the creak of the big fan in the ceiling and the faint sound of traffic on the road below the Boma.

At last Hallden stirred, picked up the prints lying on the desk and spread them out like a hand of cards.

'You know, Derek, there is something wrong about this. . . .'

'The pictures? What. . . ?'

'No. Not the pictures. What they show. A man with those wounds should have bled like a pig all over the car. And he was a big chap; he should have put up a fight. He was obviously struck from in front. He ought to have seen it coming.'

'If he was asleep . . .'

'Perhaps. But I wish to heaven the M.O. hadn't chosen this time to go to Dar es Salaam. I'd like somebody to have another look before we put the body away for good. Perhaps there was a blow on the head that knocked him out before he was killed. . . .'

'What about one of the African dressers. . . ? No, I suppose not. Or a nurse could. . . . I say, what about Mary?'

'*No!*' Hallden was emphatic. 'Not Mary. Last night was quite enough.' Suddenly the D.C. leant forward. 'I've got it! Tom Griffith! Is he at home, Derek?'

'No. He was leaving just after I did. He's going down to the beach to sail that *ngalawa* of his.'

'Damn! That means going to look for him. Derek, will you stay here? And will you do something for me? Try and get hold of Padre Simons. He is over from the Mission for the Easter services, probably staying with the Jillsons – he usually does. I was going to ask him to bury the fellow this afternoon. Tell him I meant to see him myself about it but was called away, will you? We don't know anything about the chap's religion, but the Padre's a good sort and I expect he will be willing to do what he can. I'll be back in about half an hour. The Jumbe's coming in for a talk at half-past nine and I must be here to see him. I want you to sit in on it too. O.K.?'

3

THE BEACH was very quiet as Hallden walked through the belt of palm trees and came out on the sand. The sea lay flat and inviting, turquoise blue in the shallows and a deeper shade, almost purple, towards the horizon where the islands lay, each sharply outlined with its fringe of jagged coral and creamy line of surf. The tide was out and the light blazed up in the D.C.'s eyes from the white beach. Little pinkish crabs scuttled for their holes, and the dry sand sifted into his shoes. He saw Griffith almost at once, working on his outrigger in the shade of a group of casuarina trees. It was a peaceful scene – the weathered silver of the boat, almost matching the sand, the European, stripped to his bathing trunks and tanned a dark brown, bending over his task, and an elderly African in a loincloth squatting beside him. They were working quietly together without words, both apparently absorbed in the boat.

The African saw Hallden first and got to his feet, bringing his hands together in an old-fashioned bow of greeting.

'*Jambo*, Bwana Mkubwa.'

'*Jambo*, Mzee. *Habari?*'

'*Mzuri*, bwana.'

Griffith straightened up, flexing the strong muscles of his shoulders. He looked different today, Hallden thought: a healthy young animal, fit and relaxed. But as he recognised the D.C. his dark brows drew together.

'Hallo.'

'Morning, Griffith. Sorry to disturb your work.'

'Oh, we're just messing about. There's no wind for sailing yet. One of the outriggers is a bit loose and we were fixing it up.' He ran a hand lovingly over the rough, bleached timber.

'I've only once been out in one of those things,' Geoffrey replied, 'and I didn't enjoy it much. It must take quite a bit of sailing.'

'It's not yachting, if that's what you mean.' There was a faint note of resentment in Griffith's voice. 'The bay's not much good for that, and besides, I can't afford a decent boat. Mzee's teaching me how to handle this thing. Quite a bit of fun when you get the hang of it.'

Geoffrey looked down into the long narrow shell of wood with two rough planks fixed across for seats. 'Well, I admire anyone who can make this sail,' he said honestly. 'You must be something of an expert.'

'I was brought up in boats,' Griffiths replied shortly. 'My father is a fisherman. This is pleasure cruising to Cardigan Bay in winter, I can tell you. But you didn't come here to talk about *ngalawas*. . . .'

'No, but I'd like to hear more about them some other time. I came down to ask your help – rather urgently, I am afraid.' He explained briefly what he wanted.

'But I can't do that!' Griffith exclaimed angrily. 'I'm a vet, not a doctor. Cows are my business, not men!'

'You know enough about it to be able to do the job, though, don't you? We'll explain to all the proper people eventually that you only took it on in an emergency. Besides, you did start training as a doctor, didn't you, before you changed to veterinary work?'

'Yes, and ploughed my exams,' Griffith snapped. 'How did you know all this, anyway?'

'Your department sent me details of you when you were posted here,' Hallden answered calmly. 'It's quite usual, you know. Look, Griffith, I appreciate that you don't like the idea, but I am asking you to help out in a crisis. There is no one else to ask. It won't take long, and besides, I don't think you'll get much sailing today. It looks as if the rain is going to start fairly soon.'

Griffith picked his shirt up off the sand and started to struggle into it. 'All right. But don't expect too much.'

'I'll wait and run you up to the dispensary.'

'Don't bother. I've got my own transport. Here, Mzee . . .' He turned abruptly to speak to the old African in his bad Swahili and Geoffrey, dismissed, retraced his steps along the beach. Griffith was infuriating, but he supposed he would have to put up with it.

He had to hurry in order to reach the Boma in time for his appointment. It would never have done to be late. Jumbe Abdul bin Mohamedali had a proper idea of his own importance, and would have considered it a slight to his dignity if the D.C. had not been there, waiting with proper formality for the consultation.

Jumbe Abdul was a typical coastal Swahili, with a good deal of Arab blood mixed with the African in him. He might have been forty, but it was difficult to tell his age from his appearance. He was plumpish, leisurely in his movements, with a big mouth always ready for talk of laughter. Like most of his type he was practical, shrewd, and rather cynical in his outlook on life, ready for a jest on any subject, but no fool in spite of his lack of formal education. He arrived with proper dignity, on a bicycle, carrying a big black umbrella. He wore a navy blue tailored jacket over a green and black checked skirt, sandals and a finely embroidered white cap. He refused a cup of tea and a cigarette on the grounds of the Moslem fast, but settled down comfortably to the obligatory exchange of greetings as if this were a purely social occasion which he was ready to enjoy. Hallden knew that matters could not be rushed with the Jumbe, and discussed the rains, the crops and the state of the copra trade with apparent interest for a quarter of an hour. When he did broach the question of the dead European in the Land-Rover he did it indirectly, assuming the Jumbe possessed as much knowledge of the affair as himself. Abdul was voluble on the subject, but still managed to give remarkably little information. He said that news of the stranded car had been brought to him by *shamba*-owners in the neighbourhood of the bridge, but, alas! he could not remember who they were. Nobody had said anything to him about a dead man being in the vehicle, and he had reported the matter to the Boma simply because, being Ramadan, he could not persuade any of the usual volunteers to go out and get the car out of the mud. He met Hallden's eye blandly as he said this, and smiled.

'Perhaps I myself was a little tired too. You know how it is, Bwana Hallden!'

He was not more helpful on the question of who might have made the *panga* attack. There were bad hats in Kilimani, as everyone knew, but not, he thought, men who would take a *panga* to a European just to get his money. It just was not worth it. Here Hallden had to agree with him.

The D.C. asked had there not been strangers in the town lately. No, none to his knowledge, but of course, in these matters even the Jumbe was not infallible.

Hallden returned to the question of who had reported the presence of the car. Abdul pondered, cursed his bad memory, and at last said he had a feeling it was one of the *shamba*-owners beyond the bridge, but he did not know these people well. They lived outside the town boundary, which, as the Bwana D.C. knew, made them not really his affair.

The only clue (if it was a clue) which he gave came at the end of the interview, when leave-takings were ceremoniously exchanged.

'Now, if I were the Bwana D.C. with the Bwana D.C.'s well-known wisdom,' he smiled slyly, 'I would not bother the poor ignorant Jumbe. I would ask of the Indians. They know everything, the Hindis, is it not so? Sitting in their *dukas* like the crab in his hole on the beach, the eyes looking hither and thither!' He laughed heartily at the picture. 'But of course the Bwana D.C. does not need to be told his business.'

'And the Jumbe does not need to be told his, either,' Geoffrey said dryly after he had gone.

'The old devil knows something,' Derek said. 'Can't we force it out of him?'

'Of course, he does. But how?'

'Well, threaten him with the police, or prosecution or something. Damn it all, this is a murder case!'

As he looked at the younger man, red with emotion, Geoffrey recalled his own days as a junior district officer. He supposed he must seem just as hidebound and cautious to Shotter as some of his seniors had done to him. But he had considerably more sympathy for their attitude now.

'Look, Derek,' he explained patiently, 'we have no powers to force him to talk, just on a suspicion that he knows something; and besides, it just wouldn't be worth it. Old Abdul is a wily bird, and like all of them litigation is in his blood. I'd back him to be better at the legal ins and outs than we were, and to tie us up in knots if we tried to charge him with concealing evidence. And even if we did succeed in forcing him to talk, it would mean we had made an enemy of a man who carries a lot of influence for good here, and I am not prepared to risk that, for Kilimani's sake. Besides, though I don't trust the Jumbe on everything, I do think he is shrewd enough to tell us if he knew who had done the murder. He's got a vested interest in law and order as much as we have.'

'Well, what are we going to do, then? You aren't just going to let him get away with it?' Derek demanded.

'Yes,' Geoffrey said concisely. 'I am. But I am also going to go out to the village myself and have a talk with the elders.'

'But the police are already making enquiries. . . .'

'I know that, Derek. But it is worth trying. We are at a stalemate at the moment. This is our only lead. Possibly I shall be able to exert a little more influence than the local police.'

An hour later Hallden was driving out of Kilimani on the coast road, seated beside the uniformed driver in a police truck, with Sergeant William close behind him and leaning forward to talk over the D.C.'s shoulder.

'All the people say the same, bwana.' The deep voice carried clearly above the rattle of the truck on the rough surface. 'They see nothing; they hear nothing – no car, no fight, nothing. There have been no strangers; everyone was at home. They eat their food when it becomes dark, then they go to bed.' He made a gesture of extreme disgust.

'And nothing in Kilimani so far, either . . . Sergeant, does your man believe they really saw and heard nothing, or does he think they know something and don't want to talk?'

'He thinks they don't want to talk, bwana. But he is young, and he is from Dar es Salaam. He thinks they are silent because he is an outsider, to show their contempt for him.'

'Yes. I see. They are not easy people to deal with at Nguvumeni. There was the trouble over their cattle last year. . . .'

William grunted expressively. He remembered the trouble well.

They were leaving the town now and talking was difficult. The sandy track wound through flat country, among small bushes, occasional patches of cultivation, or coconut plantations. To the west a low range of hills filled the horizon. To the east were mangrove swamps, the fringe of trees lining the beach, and occasional glimpses of dark sea under a threatening sky of cloud. It was lonely country. Occasionally they passed a mud and wattle hut, or a solitary African walking back from the market. Once a troop of monkeys ran across the road ahead, and now and then a bird swooped down after insects brought out by the rain. The heavy truck lurched from rut to rut, the driver wrestling energetically with the wheel and crashing his gears cheerfully when it became imperative to change down. Then they came to a greener patch on the left, the neat rows of young paw-paw trees that marked the edge of the Chambers plantation. As they neared the turning to the house Geoffrey saw a small grey car come out on to the road ahead, slide in a patch of mud, then lurch out again with a tremendous jerk.

'Look out, driver,' he said quietly.

'*Ndio*, Bwana Mkubwa.' The driver pulled the truck over to the left and the grey car passed with inches to spare, drenching the side of the vehicle with muddy water. Geoffrey caught a glimpse of Pauline grimly hanging on to the wheel.

'*Ah-la!*' the driver said, with a world of meaning, and rolled his eyes heavenwards.

Geoffrey grinned. All Kilimani knew the Memsahib Chambers was a shocking driver. He wondered idly where Pauline was heading for in such a hurry. If she was hoping to join Tom Griffith on the beach she was going to be disappointed. . . .

In a few moments they came to the creek, and he asked the driver to stop while he got out and had a look round. The sergeant joined him and stood a pace or two behind, looking very out of place in his neat uniform.

The creek was running deep and brown with flood water today. Its banks were steep and covered with thick scrub that now trailed its fringes in the stream. On the higher ground, out of reach of the water, the scrub thinned out into patches of stunted trees, tufts of ragged grass and bare sandy soil. In all this, as far as one could see in either direction, there was no sign of human habitation.

'Well, no one is likely to have seen anything here,' Geoffrey said.

'No, bwana. No one lives nearer than the village. There is

the fishing over there, and the grazing, and coconuts. Here there is nothing.'

'No. Nothing.' A slight shiver passed up Geoffrey's spine as he looked at the muddy patch where the Land-Rover had stood. It was a lonely place to die.

The truck lumbered across the wooden bridge and lurched and slithered its way through the pool of flood-water on the far side. Geoffrey thought they were not going to make it, but at last the tyres gripped on firmer ground and they roared over a slight rise. The track here turned sharply towards the sea, and headed for the belt of trees that marked the shore. They came quite suddenly upon Nguvumeni. At one moment there was the empty road, and the next they swung right along a side track and emerged through a screen of mango trees and coconut palms into the village.

It was nothing but two irregular lines of mud and wattle huts, built closely together and facing each other across an open patch of trodden earth. Here and there one had fallen into decay, a framework of bare mangrove poles and a litter of fallen thatch and mud. Goats were wandering among the trees and scrawny little fowls pecked for food among the houses. A fruit vendor sat under a mango tree with neat piles of peeled oranges, big golden mangoes and green bananas laid out before him.

At the approach of the truck, goats, children and chickens scattered wildly, and the women gossiping at their doorways called out in high, shrill voices.

The D.C. was expected. A messenger had been sent in advance and a small group of men was standing apart watching the arrival in silence. Hallden climbed out of the truck and went towards them.

'*Jambo*, Bwana Mkubwa.' The murmur of greetings rose, then died into complete silence.

Hallden surveyed them. They looked a motley collection, the younger ones in ragged shirts and shorts and the elders in checked skirts and loose jackets. All had the same expression – a wary sullenness that Geoffrey had come to know well and to dread.

He looked round the group carefully, then picked out one he knew, a bigger man than the rest, and one of the leaders in the trouble over the cattle dipping.

'*Jambo*, Bwana Rehani,' he said. 'What is the news of the cattle?'

The African dropped his eyes. 'It is well, Bwana Mkubwa.'

'I hope so.'

The other men shuffled slightly away from the one thus picked out, as if to disassociate themselves from him. At the same time Geoffrey became conscious that the women and children were drawing closer, forming an outer circle of listening dark faces and bright watching eyes.

'As you have been told,' he said clearly, in his correct, clipped Swahili, 'I have come here to hold a *baraza*. It is on police business, business of a killing near here. I am seeking information, and I have come to ask the people of Nguvumeni to give me their help. This killing is a business of the greatest gravity, and the Government cannot rest until the guilty ones have been brought to justice.'

There was silence for a moment, then one of the older men stepped forward. If the Bwana D.C. would be pleased to come into the shade and be seated . . .

The procession moved towards a roofed enclosure with walls reaching about three feet from the ground – the market, meeting place and social centre for the little community. Chairs were placed at one end for the D.C. and Sergeant William, and the men grouped themselves before them in a silent phalanx. Gradually the ring of women and children closed around outside the wall.

Geoffrey knew before he began what he was up against. He had met the same silent front again and again all over the country. It was the African's main defence against a

Government that exacted taxes, imposed alien justice, and enacted strange laws that turned upside-down the simple existence of the peasant. And here, in this coastal community, he had not even the framework of the chief and the tribe to build on. Here he had just a mass of people living in a group, people of mixed tribes and beliefs, held together only by their common occupations and interests and by a community of feeling against the outsider. But these people were also his charge and his responsibility.

He went over the ground slowly, patiently and clearly. The European had passed this way on Wednesday and his car had been discovered and reported on Thursday. The village was only a few hundred yards from the road, and there must have been very few cars passing that way owing to the rains. Who had gone in towards Kilimani to sell fish or to buy food? Who had been herding the cattle and goats that grazed near the road? Who had come to the village from outside? What vehicles had been seen?

It went on and on. Short of sleep and still weary from his safari, Geoffrey found it hard to control his impatience with them, but it had to be done. Gradually he began to get answers instead of complete silence, then a little information instead of blank denials. And at last the field was narrowed down a little.

A child of about twelve had been herding cattle near the road most of Wednesday. He had noticed a van belonging to an Indian trader going north and then returning during the morning. A car had passed towards Kilimani in the afternoon, but he was sure it had not answered the description of the Land-Rover. He had brought the cattle home when the sun was low – about five-thirty, so far as Geoffrey could make out.

Several of the men had gone into Kilimani on the Wednesday, on foot or on bicycles, but oddly enough no one appeared to have crossed the creek bridge on the Thursday.

There had been no strangers in the village, the only visitor being the son of one of the fishermen, a youth called Joshua, who worked in Kilimani as a clerk and who had come on Wednesday afternoon to spend some time with his family. Geoffrey had picked him out already – a flashy youth in white trousers and a tight tweed jacket, who lounged against the wall smoking cheap cigarettes. But no, even he had seen and heard nothing.

4

THE SUN had moved far past the meridian when Geoffrey climbed wearily into the truck. At the first sign of his departure a noticeable change had come in the atmosphere. The older men had escorted him from the *baraza* in a body, talking readily about the rains and the fishing and the price of food. In common politeness he had been bound to listen and to reply, but all he wanted now was to get home, to have food and rest, and try to shake off some of the depressing aftermath of failure. But at last he was in his seat and the truck was moving off. Some of the children danced alongside, laughing and waving, and one woman, bolder than the rest, called out '*Kwa heri*, Bwana D.C.!' then giggled and buried her face in her *kanga*.

'Well, Sergeant,' Geoffrey said with a sigh, 'we got little news from Nguvumeni.'

'It is so, bwana,' William agreed solemnly. But Geoffrey suspected he was not displeased at the D.C.'s lack of success where the police had already failed.

They had just breasted the rise before the creek when Geoffrey noticed a figure standing by the bridge, leaning against a bicycle. It waved as they approached, and the sergeant snorted.

'Ha! He thinks he will get a lift in a police car, truly!'

'Wait a minute, driver.' Geoffrey had noticed something familiar about the figure, and as they slowed up he recognised the neat white slacks and tweed jacket. It was Joshua, the fisherman's son, the smart boy from town.

The youth grinned, laid his bicycle carefully down and came forward to the side of the truck.

'*Jambo*, bwana.'
'*Jambo.* You wish to speak to me?'
'Yes, bwana.' He glanced uncertainly back towards the village. 'I did not wish to say anything there. The old men, you know, they are afraid of trouble for the village. But I – I am educated, you understand, and I realise we should help the Government.' He paused a moment to allow the speech its full effect, then looked quickly over his shoulder as if to make sure he was not observed.

Geoffrey followed his glance. The road was clear, but someone might come over the rise at any moment.

'Put your bicycle into the back of the truck,' he ordered, 'and get in yourself. We can talk then.'

The African complied with alacrity and William grudgingly made room for him in the corner of the truck immediately behind the D.C. At a nod from Hallden the vehicle started to move again.

'Well? What is it you want to tell me?'
'The car, Bwana Mkubwa, the blue Land-Rover . . .'
'You saw it? When?'
'On Wednesday. After I finished my work in Kilimani I was riding my bicycle towards Nguvumeni. It was just getting dark – perhaps half-past six or a little later – when I passed the car. I saw the man in it, the tall European, driving alone. . . .'
'Where was this?'
'On the road a little further than this.'
'Towards Kilimani?'
'Yes. I can show you the place. Beyond the next corner, there, where the road runs straight. It was lucky I could see him. He was driving fast, and the light was not good. . . .'
'Towards Kilimani? You are sure?'
'Yes, bwana.' Joshua was a little less confident now. 'Why should I lie? It is the truth I tell, of my own free will, because I believe we must help the Government. . . .'

'Yes, yes. I am not disbelieving you. But the car was found back by the bridge. You did not see him again? The car did not overtake you coming back from Kilimani?'

'No, bwana. Nothing else passed. There was only the one car. That is why I remember it.'

'Thank you.' Geoffrey swung round to see the youth's face more clearly as he asked the next question.

'And no one else in Nguvumeni saw the car or the man?'

The African's eyes dropped. 'I only know what they say, Bwana Mkubwa. It is as they told you.'

'Someone saw the car on Thursday and reported it to the Jumbe in Kilimani. When people do not tell the truth in these things the police wonder what they have to hide.'

'They are foolish people and not educated. They are frightened it will bring trouble on them, that is all. I am sure that no one in the village has done anything wrong.'

'I am ready to believe that,' Geoffrey said, 'but until the killer is found there will be trouble for everyone, I am afraid.'

'Yes, bwana. But my people say this is not an affair of the Africans. It is nothing to do with them.'

There was no more to be got out of Joshua, and after getting his name and address in Kilimani Geoffrey put him and his bicycle down on the road well outside the town boundaries. The truck left him behind, taking off his smart, tight jacket and rolling his trousers up to the knees so that their whiteness would not be sullied by the mud.

'Well,' Hallden said as the truck moved off, 'this makes things look a bit different. If the man was driving towards Kilimani at dusk, how far did he get? And how and why did he go back to the bridge?'

'Yes, bwana. You think we should ask more questions in Kilimani.' William's tone was resigned.

'The Land-Rover should have been seen if it came into the town,' Hallden mused, 'although it is a pity there are so many like it around, and it must have been fairly dark by the time he reached Kilimani . . . if he got that far.

They were entering the town as Hallden remembered the task he had given to Tom Griffith.

'Take me to the dispensary first, driver. You had better come with me, Sergeant. It shouldn't take long.'

The dispensary was closed officially, but a drowsy African dresser appeared in answer to the D.C.'s knock and let them in.

'Bwana Griffith has left,' he said. 'He told me to give you this chit.'

Hallden took the torn-off prescription form on which Griffith had scrawled a brief message.

'Nothing there. I should have gone sailing.'

The D.C. screwed the paper up into a ball and flung it into a wastepaper basket.

'Damn! I wish we had a doctor here. There must be some reason. . . .'

'You said, bwana. . . . ?'

'Nothing, Sergeant,' Geoffrey replied in Swahili. 'I was just thinking. I hoped Mr Griffith would find why the dead man lost so little blood, but he says there is nothing to explain it.'

'You said perhaps he was killed outside the car, bwana. . . .'

'Yes. That may be it. And then wrapped in something that absorbed the blood. . . . We left his clothes here, didn't we?'

The clothes were in the small room in which the body lay, concealed under a sheet. It was not pleasant in there, and Geoffrey felt a moment's sympathy for Griffith. He took the heap of garments back into the waiting-room and the sergeant and he spread them out on a table for closer examination.

Suddenly William gave an exclamation.

'Look, bwana! Here in the shirt!'

'What is it?' Geoffrey bent closer and followed the black finger, pointing.

In the middle of the largest stain, where the fabric had been slashed by the *panga*, there was a small frayed edge. Carefully Hallden fitted the two sides of the material together. There was a round hole, its edges brittle as if they had been burned.

'Good God! What a thing to have missed!'

Hallden picked up the telephone and jiggled the rest impatiently. 'Bwana Griffith, veterinary officer,' he snapped. 'Quickly! Oh, Griffith, Hallden here. I am at the dispensary. Yes, I got the note. I want you to come down again at once. No. It is very urgent. I think the man was shot.'

Half an hour later Tom Griffith was peeling off his rubber gloves and washing his hands. He looked pale under his tan and was making a very thorough job of the hand washing.

'Did you examine the wounds before?' Geoffrey was demanding of his turned back.

'Briefly. You were talking about blows on the head, you know, not bullet wounds.'

'Lucky I wasn't altogether happy about him, wasn't it?'

Griffith swung round. 'Are you trying to say I missed it on purpose? You might remember I didn't want to do this job at all.' He jerked a towel down angrily and dried his hands. 'Anyway, you've got your answer now. I hope you are satisfied.'

'Satisfied? This just means I have to start all over again. If the man was shot and then struck with a *panga* . . . It's not the sort of thing African thugs do, is it?'

'That's your problem, not mine. All I can say is that the bullet must have killed him outright. A pretty close shot, too.'

Geoffrey was studying the small object resting in a pad of cotton-wool in his hand. 'A .22 by the look of it. There must be several of them in Kilimani. I've got one myself. Not a weapon an African is likely to possess. . . .'

Griffith broke in on his thoughts. 'Can I go now? I've got other things I want to do, you know.'

'Yes, of course. Thanks for your help.'

'Don't mention it.' The other's tone was bitterly sarcastic. 'Let's hope the fellow can be safely buried now.'

It was after two o'clock when Geoffrey reached home. He had gone straight from the dispensary to the Boma, where Derek Shotter was still waiting for him, getting a bit restive without lunch or a drink. He listened in astonishment to the D.C.'s account of his discoveries.

'A bit of a bloomer by Tom!' he exclaimed.

'Yes. I can't quite make up my mind whether he just scamped the job because he didn't want to do it at all, or . . .'

'Good heavens, Geoff, you don't think he spotted the bullet wound and said nothing about it?'

'I don't know. I suppose it was easy enough to miss if you weren't looking for it. How well do you know Tom Griffith, Derek?'

'Well . . . we've shared the house since he came here, about six months ago. He's a prickly sort of cuss – Welsh temperament, I suppose. Oh, we get on all right, Geoff, but we don't see an awful lot of each other, especially since . . .'

'Since he took over Pauline?'

Derek flushed darkly. 'Oh well, it was fair enough. He met her with me, and I suppose she just liked him better. I don't blame Tom . . .'

'No. And you know I think you were well out of that. But apart from the complication of Mrs Chambers, what is he like? What makes him tick? Is he ambitious, keen on his job?'

'N-no. Not exactly. The only thing he is ever really enthusiastic about is sailing that *ngalawa* of his. He's got a tremendous chip on his shoulder, you know. Thinks he never had a chance in life and everyone's out to do him down. He's always on about all the advantages I had – a decent education, parents with a bit of money and so on. Though, Lord knows, on an Army pension my father found it pretty hard going bringing the family up. . . . But I think Tom's sound enough, when you get down to it.'

'I hope so. Look, you had better come home with me, Derek, and have some lunch. I suppose your boy will have gone off hours ago.'

'You're right – and he can't cook, anyway. Thanks, Geoff. If you don't think Mary will mind . . .'

They found Mary on the veranda with Pauline Chambers.

'Oh, there you are!' Pauline cried. 'Oh, hullo, Derek. Geoff, I've been sitting here drinking and drinking, just waiting in the hope of seeing you!'

'I'm flattered.' Geoffrey gave Mary a quick look and she replied by pulling a face. 'Have another drink with us now, then, Pauline.'

He poured beer for himself and Shotter and replenished the women's gin and fruit juice. Derek sat down close to Mary and as far as possible from Pauline. It was common knowledge (Pauline had made it so) that she had 'run' him and then dropped him after a few weeks. He had gone about looking like a whipped dog for a while, and Geoffrey had seriously thought of getting him moved to another station. But he decided it would do him more good to face things out in Kilimani. Derek seemed to have got over the worst by now, though he kept away from Pauline if he could.

'And why were you waiting so anxiously, Pauline?' Geoffrey asked.

Her eyes opened very wide at him. 'But for news, of course! I want to know what is happening.'

'The rains have come . . . if that is news.'

'Don't be infuriating, Geoff! About this mysterious dead man, of course.'

'He is being buried at three-thirty,' Geoffrey answered discouragingly.

'You are a maddening man! Doesn't he drive you silly, Mary, with all this official discretion and nonsense? I have been trying to pump Mary, but she seems to know even less than I do. Why, everyone at church this morning was talking about it, how he was murdered out by the bridge, and you having a round-up of suspects . . .'

'You probably know as much about it as I do, then.'

'But who was he?'

Geoffrey lit a cigarette. 'We don't know yet. Nobody has come forward to say they were expecting him in Kilimani. He seems to be just a bird of passage. But we shall find out his name, of course, as soon as we can get through to Dar and check the records of the car and so on.'

'But what on earth was he doing here? Did anyone see him? Don't you know yet who shot him?'

'*Shot?*' Geoffrey stopped with the cigarette half-way to his mouth. 'Where did you hear he was shot, Pauline?'

She looked vague, avoiding his eyes. 'Oh, I don't know. Just around. I mean, one assumes a person was shot . . .'

'Does one? You heard Derek say last night that the man was attacked with a *panga*.'

'Did I? Oh, really, Geoff, don't make a mountain out of nothing! I just say casually . . .'

'Not casually, Pauline.' Geoffrey's voice was hard. 'We had better get to the bottom of this. You see, the man *was* shot, but nobody knew that until about two hours ago – nobody, that is, except the person who shot him.'

Pauline had gone quite pale. 'The . . . ? You don't think . . . you don't mean that *I* . . . ? Geoffrey, this is really too much!'

Suddenly Derek emerged from the background. His moustache twitched a little and he stammered over the words.

'This is serious, Pauline. It's no good putting on an act about it. I expect Tom told her, Geoffrey. She must have called in on her way here – didn't you, Pauline? I know Tom asked if I was going to be late back this morning . . .'

'I don't see that my movements are any business of yours, Derek,' Pauline said angrily. 'Or yours, either, Geoff. I've told you, I don't know anything. I was just guessing.'

'I see.' Geoffrey's mouth was still grim. 'Well, you had better tell Tom Griffith to keep his mouth shut on this business, Derek. And you too, Pauline.'

Pauline got up, twitching her skirt straight angrily.

'I'd better go, Mary. If this is your idea of a nice friendly chat among friends it is not mine. Come and see me out, Derek.'

He obeyed the command meekly.

'He *was* shot, Geoffrey? Are you sure?' Mary's voice sounded loud in the silence.

'Yes. We spotted it this morning. Tom Griffith made an examination. Looks as if someone had made an attempt to cover up the shooting by hitting him with a *panga* after he was dead.'

'How horrible! You found the bullet?'

'Yes. I haven't checked yet, but it looks like a .22.'

'I see.' Mary moved over to a table and picked a cigarette out of a box. She did not very often smoke.

'Can't you tell from a bullet what gun it was fired from, Geoffrey?'

'So all the detective stories say. I expect it is true enough. All bullets get marks on them in firing. I am keeping this one for the police to check on.

'By the way, what was Pauline really here for? Just a girlish chat?'

'I don't know. She came about one – said she didn't want any lunch but would adore a drink. And after that she just sat, nattering about this and that, and saying were you always as late as this without telling me where you were. . . . You know the way she does.'

'I know. Sorry about being so late. I'll tell you all about it later. Do you think she came here from Griffith's place?'

'She might have done. She murmured something about shopping in town this morning. I didn't ask. It doesn't pay with Pauline.'

'I'll bet she wouldn't have hesitated to ask you, though.' He finished his drink and put the glass down. 'I'll have to go to this funeral at half-past three. Can we have lunch now? I hope you can manage to feed Derek as well.'

'Why yes, of course. There's plenty. I'll tell Mohammed. Do you want me to come with you?'

He looked surprised. 'To the funeral? Do you want to?'

'No. I don't want to in the least. But I feel . . . well, somebody ought to be there, not just officially. If he has any family . . .'

On a sudden impulse Geoffrey pulled her to him and laid his cheek against her dark hair. She was a little stiff in his arms at first, then she relaxed against him.

'You are a strange woman, but I love you very much,' he said.

She looked up at him as if about to say something, but at that moment Derek returned from seeing Pauline drive off.

5

THE BRIEF service in the little European graveyard was depressing in the extreme. Rain started to fall as the small cortège arrived—not a shower, but a sudden deluge that poured off the Padre's bald, bowed head and sent the mud oozing down the open grave. Geoffrey, sweating inside his raincoat, thought of what Mary had said. If the poor devil had any family he hoped they would never know what a sad farewell had been his. The rain drowned most of the words of the service, and his thoughts wandered from the scene back to the events of the day. He turned over in his mind once more the few small shreds of evidence that he had collected. The man in the Land-Rover had come right into Kilimani, or else had stopped somewhere near it and turned back again. Where had he gone, and why? Visualising the bare stretch of road, the scatter of African huts and the meagre beginnings of the town, he was suddenly reminded of what the Jumbe had said about Indians in general, and the owners of *dukas* (the ubiquitous general stores) in particular. There was one such store, and only one, between the town centre and the bridge. In fact it stood at a point quite near where Joshua had passed the Land-Rover, in the middle of an African settlement. It was just a small place, with a mainly African trade, and was owned by an Indian called Gulamhusein Ismael. Hallden knew him quite well, and in fact had had several brushes with him in the past over price controls and the attempts of various Africans in the neighbourhood to dispose of land rights to meet the bills they had been allowed to run up at the *duka*. He knew he was wily and not too scrupulous and had a feeling that there were a lot of things Mr Ismael got away with that were quite unknown to the Administration.

It occurred to him now that if the Jumbe had really intended to convey anything by his hint, this would be the place to look for information.

When the burial was over and the wet mud heaped up on the grave Geoffrey walked back to the cars with Mary and the Padre.

'Sad business,' the old man said, buttoning his raincoat over his soaked clothes. 'I am thankful that I get more christenings than burials to do in this country.'

'I'm very grateful . . .' Geoffrey began.

'No need, my boy, no need. I am happy I was here to do it. And now I must be off and get dry, or I shall be kept in Kilimani with pneumonia.' He squeezed the D.C.'s arm briefly. 'You've got the worst end of the job. I shall be glad to get back to my nice quiet mission. Nothing but an occasional rape there, or a breaking of heads.' He chuckled. 'Good-bye, Hallden. Good-bye, Mary, my dear.' And before they could reply he had whisked into his shabby car and driven off with a reckless disregard for the muddy road.

'I wish I had his energy,' Geoffrey said as they got into the Austin. 'Look, Mary, I've just thought of something and I must be off on the chase again. I'll drop you at home on the way.'

'All right.' Mary sounded tired and subdued. 'Have you any idea when you will be back?'

'I don't suppose it will take long. All I really want is a warm bath and a chance to sit down somewhere and think. Keep some tea for me, won't you?'

The *duka* was a box of ochre-painted brick with a sloping corrugated-iron roof. The windows were small and heavily barred, but the door stood open for trade at almost any hour.

The owner and his family lived at the back of the premises. Everything about the place looked shabby and run down; the only sign of prosperity being a very large new car, parked in the yard among the empty boxes and stacks of Coca-Cola bottles.

The little shop was very dark and it took Hallden a moment or two to get his bearings among the stacks of materials, cooking pots, bicycles, ornaments and food that crowded the place. Then he saw a movement in the corner and a slight, quiet woman in European dress, but with her hair in long black plaits down her back, came forward and murmured a greeting in Swahili. He answered her in the same tongue and asked for her husband. A small child who was clinging to her skirts was sent running, and in a moment Ismael himself arrived, stout, smiling, expressing himself in excellent English as delighted by the honour of entertaining the D.C. Hallden found himself pressed into a chair, a cigarette lit for him, and a bottle of mineral water with a straw in it thrust into his hand. He abominated the stuff, and it made him feel rather foolish sitting there holding a bottle of pop like a child at a party, so he took one polite sip then put it down on the counter.

Ismael could not have been more than thirty-five, but at first sight he looked much older. The jovial face was set on a crescent of double chin, and his stomach bulged over the grey cotton trousers. But the black eyes in their pads of fat were clear and shrewd, his hair was thick and black, and the teeth that showed in his constant smiles were only touched with gold fillings.

'And now,' he said, 'I am not so foolish as to think the D.C. honours me just for a social call. What can I do for my friend Mr Hallden?'

'I have come to ask your help,' Geoffrey said, beginning on his carefully prepared approach. 'I am in search of information, unofficially of course, at present, and it seemed to me this might be a good place to start looking for it.'

'Information? Oh . . . anything I can do, of course . . . but I am afraid, out here in the bush, I hear very little . . .'

'You know a European was found out at the bridge last night, dead?'

'I had heard. Yes, I had heard. A bad business. Not a friend of yours, I hope, Mr Hallden?'

'No, fortunately. No one seems to know just who he is. Of course, we shall find out as soon as the telephone line to Dar es Salaam is back in action, but at the moment we do not know his name. Now we have reason to believe he may have passed here on Wednesday evening. The Land-Rover was fairly new, long wheel-base pattern, dark blue, with a D S K registration number; the man youngish, tall, fair-haired, in khaki bush shirt and shorts and brown suède safari boots. Do you remember seeing him?'

Ismael pondered deeply. 'Your sergeant, William, was in here this morning asking,' he replied. 'I could not say I had noticed this car. . . .'

Hallden let his eyebrows rise faintly. 'Oh? But I heard the Land-Rover was seen, actually parked outside here . . .'

The Indian's eyes flashed to his face, then dropped. He laughed heartily. 'And who saw this, I wonder, Mr Hallden?'

'Oh, "information received".' Just a shade of officialdom had been allowed to creep into the D.C.'s voice. He knew that there was something to be told after all, but all he could do now was to wait and watch while the other thought it over.

Suddenly Ismael swung round to his wife, standing behind him in the darkness of the shop.

'Of course! How foolish!' he cried, then switched to Swahili. 'Why did you not remind me? The European – you remember, the one who came in for a moment on Wednesday evening? For cigarettes, was it not?'

He turned back to the D.C. 'My wife is very forgetful. She

served him with the cigarettes. It had slipped my mind absolutely, absolutely!' He slapped his open palm on his forehead.

'I see. And he just bought some cigarettes?'

'Yes. Let me see. It was ten of the cheapest kind we have. My wife offered him the better kinds that Europeans usually smoke but he said no, he could not afford them.' Ismael laughed again.

'About what time was this?'

'Oh . . . perhaps seven o'clock? I was thinking of closing, but in Ramadan, of course, the Africans come late for their food.'

Hallden had a feeling there was something more, if he could only dig it out.

'He did not buy anything else? No food? Did he ask his way anywhere or mention where he was going?'

Ismael pondered again. 'It is two days ago now. I am so busy here . . .' Then a thought appeared to strike him. 'But of course! He asked if he might use the telephone. . . .'

Hallden's pulse quickened. So he was on to something!

'Whom did he telephone?'

'That I do not know, Mr Hallden. He made two calls – but I do not listen, of course.'

Hallden gave this the benefit of a smile – a slightly dubious one.

'May I borrow your phone?'

The instrument was in a gloomy corner at the back of the shop. Hallden got the African operator, who recognised his voice at once, and asked him to check from the records to whom two calls were made about seven p.m. on Wednesday night, from this number, and call back as soon as possible.

He turned back to Ismael. 'This may be a great help. I am very grateful for your assistance – you and your wife.' He smiled at the woman as he said it. She was a nice-looking creature, gentle in voice and manner, and Geoffrey felt she did not have a very easy time with her husband, nor often get a word of praise. She smiled back at him, then glanced at her husband and said something in an undertone in Gujerati. Now Geoffrey had served with Indian troops during the war, and had picked up enough of the language to recognise the one word, 'paper'. He broke in before Ismael had time to say a word.

'He left a paper?'

Ismael smiled but his eyes were hard as he looked at his wife.

'You are very quick off the mark, as you would say, Mr Hallden! Yes, my wife has reminded me now that the man left a scrap of paper – just an old envelope, nothing important.'

'But I should like to see it, none the less.'

Ismael recognised the tone of authority in the D.C.'s voice. Without a word he went to the little cash drawer, fumbled in a note-clip and extracted an old envelope, roughly torn open at the top.

'I thought he might come back for it,' he explained.

Geoffrey took it over to the light. It was post-marked Nairobi and addressed to 'P. Shane-Hamilton, Esq., c/o the New Era Hotel, Dar es Salaam'. Hallden knew the hotel, a cheap pub run by a Greek in the centre of the city. He turned the envelope over to see if there was any return address on the back, and his eyes lighted on two numbers scrawled in pencil. He looked again to make sure the first glance had not misled him.

The phone rang suddenly in the silence. He went over and picked it up, and heard the operator's voice repeat two numbers that he already knew.

'The first is Mr Schmidt's, sir, and the second, of course, you will know.'

Yes, he knew it. It was the number of his own house.

That phone number was in Hallden's thoughts all the way

as he drove home. He told himself that he was being unreasonable, that any man arriving in a strange town (and apparently broke) might want to ring the D.C., and at seven at night where else would he phone him except at his home? But Mary had said nothing about a call on Wednesday evening. He found himself remembering her face as she looked up from the body in the car. 'We are too late,' she had said. And then there was her unexpected request to come to the funeral that afternoon. She had looked very pale in a dark waterproof and black hat, and had stood silently beside him, not looking at the coffin or the padre, but straight in front of her. He had had to rouse her at the end of the brief service by touching her arm, and she had looked round at him as if a stranger had laid a hand on her. Of course it was ridiculous to think of any connection between his wife and the murdered man, but none the less, instead of returning to the Boma he drove straight home.

He found Mary on the veranda, but she was not alone. Lois was having her evening playtime, and lay happily on a rug waving her feet and arms and making vague gestures at the toys dangled in front of her. And squatting down beside her, playing with the rattle and string of beads and laughing at the baby, was a short, brown, bald man in his late fifties.

He got to his feet with the agility of a much younger man.

'Hullo, Hallden! Your daughter is enchanting, enchanting! She will be as lovely as your wife one day.'

'Hullo, Schmidt. I didn't know you were back.'

Mary was bending over the baby, slipping a cushion back under her head, and Geoffrey could not see her face. Schmidt went on in his deep, slightly accented voice:

'I got in this afternoon. The storms off Mafia held me up. I could not make it out of harbour for two days. But I am safely back and all is well.

'Your wife has been telling me of the excitements here with mysterious strangers and bodies in cars.'

Willy Schmidt seemed only politely interested in the subject, but then it was always difficult to tell what he was really thinking or feeling. He was a German who had fought the British in the first world war, here in Tanganyika, and been taken prisoner by them. But he had liked the country and stayed on, to be naturalised and to run a freight service up and down the coast with a small motor-driven schooner. There was some speculation, in Kilimani and elsewhere, about Schmidt's business. He never seemed to lack for money, in spite of the small scale of his trading. But he had never been caught out in anything illegal, and as people found him likeable and amusing he was on friendly terms with both the business and the Administration communities all along the coast. He lived in a small house near the beach, below the D.C.'s own. A series of African 'housekeepers' looked after his comfort there, and as he never invited Europeans to his house and did all his generous entertaining at the club, even the strictest of the English wives found it convenient to ignore his domestic arrangements. Hallden mistrusted him officially but could not help respecting his ability and liking him. Because of this he decided to tackle him direct about the mysterious phone call, instead of working round to it as he might have done with a different type of man.

'Do you know anyone called Shane-Hamilton, Schmidt?'

Watching the other's face Geoffrey could see no reaction beyond a slight frown of puzzlement.

'Shane-Hamilton? I cannot place it, no, but it has a vaguely familiar sound. Is it someone I should be expected to know?'

'He appears to know you.'

Schmidt shrugged. 'I am known to many people. In my business it is necessary. I may know this man, I may not.' He shot Geoffrey a shrewd glance. 'Something tells me, you know, that this is not my friend Geoffrey Hallden asking idle questions. This is the Bwana D.C. interrogating a suspicious character! Come now, what is it all about?'

He sat down comfortably and crossed his legs. 'I deduce a connection with the mystery of the dead stranger. Am I right?'

'Quite right.' Geoffrey found it easy to relax, too, and sat down opposite Schmidt. 'Shane-Hamilton appears to be the name of the man we found by the bridge. We have also found out that before he was killed he came into town, bought some cigarettes at Ismael's store, and from there made a phone call – to your number.'

'And I was away in Mafia, alas, or we might have been able to solve this interesting mystery. I can only suppose this gentleman wanted to see me in a way of business – perhaps he wished to go somewhere by sea, as all the land roads from here are blocked. My name is well known as the person to get you anywhere on this coast, you know, even as far as Dar es Salaam.

'And this is your only clue? Did he not see anyone, or phone anyone else?'

Geoffrey had been conscious while they were talking of Mary sitting silently on the floor beside Lois, although he had not looked in her direction. But now it was an effort to keep his eyes on Schmidt while he answered his question. He tried to keep his voice even and matter-of-fact.

'Yes,' he said. 'He phoned here.'

'I see. And you were on safari.' Schmidt's eyes moved casually to Mary, and Geoffrey found his glance following the other's. Mary was sitting back on her heels with the rattle still in her hand as if she had forgotten it. Her glance met Schmidt's smiling gaze and then her husband's, and there was nothing for anyone to read there but polite interest.

'Yes,' she said. 'Someone did phone for you that evening, Geoffrey, but when I said you were on safari he rang off.'

'So,' Schmidt summed up, 'he tries me first and finds I am away, then tries the D.C. and he is away . . . so in despair he goes off and shoots himself.'

'And then cuts himself up with a *panga?*' Geoffrey interrupted sharply.

Schmidt twinkled at him. 'I apologise. I am being frivolous on a serious subject. You know, I still am not sure, after thirty-odd years, when you English (or *we* English, I should say) require the light touch and when it is to be serious. But I see now that this is serious. Yes, the *panga* wounding is odd.'

'Did Mary tell you about the shooting?' Geoffrey asked, surprised. His wife was usually very discreet on official matters.

Mary herself answered. 'No. Mr Schmidt seemed to know all about it. He asked me if it was true, and I said it was.'

Schmidt chuckled. 'My grapevine. Most efficient, Hallden. You should employ it more at the Boma. The house-boys, the clerks and the messengers – they all have flapping ears, and they know I like to hear things. But this shooting – it looks as if it was not just an African after money, eh? They do not usually play with guns in this part of the world.'

Geoffrey had to agree that was correct.

'And there are not so many revolvers in Kilimani, either. The bullet should have an interesting tale to tell when the police see it.' He got up as if the subject was exhausted.

'I must go now. Thank you for the drink, Mrs Hallden, and for the delightful chat with Miss Lois. I hope I have not bored you with all this talk of murders. You look a little tired, if I may say so without offence. But still very charming.' He clasped Mary's hand warmly in both of his. 'Good-night, my dear lady.'

As they walked to the car together he turned to Geoffrey.

'You are conducting this investigation by yourself, Hallden?'

'Until the police get here.'

'But it may be some days before they get down from Dar by sea.'

Geoffrey explained what he had done.

'I could go and fetch them,' Schmidt suggested. 'My ship would be quicker than your black on a bicycle, and I might not even charge the Government for my services.'

'I would rather you stayed in Kilimani for the present.'

'You are still worried about the phone call, then?' Schmidt laughed out loud, showing his strong teeth.

'All right. I will stay. But do not forget I was not the only one this Shane-Hamilton telephoned!'

Geoffrey had not forgotten. He stood watching Schmidt's Volkswagen go down the drive, trying to remember exactly how Mary had looked and sounded when she had spoken of the phone call. Normally she would have got the caller's name and tried to help them or put them on to Derek Shotter. Why had she not mentioned this particular call?

Into his thoughts broke a tentative voice.

'*Hodi!* May I come in?'

Geoffrey swung round to find Dudley Chambers standing just behind him. He was wearing an Aertex shirt and white shorts and carried a tennis racket. He held the racket up apologetically.

'Didn't mean to startle you, old chap. Just been down to the club for a game. Felt the need of a bit of hard exercise, you know. Then I thought I'd drop over and see you, but as I came through the garden I saw you had someone here and didn't think I should interrupt, so I just waited till he had gone.'

Geoffrey knew Dudley was not fond of Schmidt (he had referred to him more than once as 'a bit of an outsider', which was the strongest of criticism from him) and he was not surprised that he had avoided meeting him.

'I didn't hear you coming in those tennis shoes, Dudley. But come in now and have a drink. You must have sweated a lot of liquid out of you at tennis today.'

'Oh, not bad. I'm still in fair trim, you know. Ah,

Mary! Forgive me bursting in like this, not changed or anything.'

'Oh, good heavens, Dudley, you don't have to worry about that with us! But you will have to forgive me if I go in a moment. It is more than time for Lois's feed.'

'Don't go just yet,' Dudley begged. 'Fact is . . . er . . . I had a reason for calling in like this. Pauline told me she . . . er . . . dropped in this morning, and from all I can gather she seems to have . . . well, put her foot in it a bit, with you both . . .'

He waited anxiously for them to deny it, but when they were both silent his face clouded.

'I say, you don't seriously think that Pauline is . . . well, mixed up in this business in any way?'

'She seems very interested in it,' Geoffrey replied non-committally.

'But you know what women are! (Forgive me, Mary.) She's got little enough to think about here, and anything like this, well, she's bound to want to know what it is all about. That doesn't mean she's involved in any way.'

'I know that, Dudley. But to be quite frank with you, I thought there was a bit more to it than just normal curiosity. Why didn't she just explain, instead of denying everything and going off in a huff?'

Dudley looked down at the spotless white shoes which he was prodding with the tennis racket. 'You know what women are,' he repeated. 'They like to know things before anyone else does . . . and of course, Pauline is . . . friendly with Griffith. . . .'

'She told you she heard about the shooting from him?'

'Well, not exactly. She was upset, you know. But I gathered from what she said . . .' Dudley floundered, then stopped.

They were still all standing uncomfortably on the veranda. Geoffrey caught a look of appeal from Mary, asking him to do something to end the awkward situation. He pulled the envelope Ismael had given him out of the breast pocket of his shirt and passed it to Dudley.

'You might have a look at this while you are here,' he said.

Dudley took it and swung round to get the light on it. 'What is it?'

'This was in the dead man's possession a little time before he died. Men don't usually carry round letters addressed to someone else, so it looks as if it identifies him.'

Dudley looked up. 'It wasn't actually on him, you say? Where did you get it?'

'I can't tell you that at present, I am afraid; but we have proof that he actually came into Kilimani before he was killed.'

Chambers hastened to protest. 'My dear chap, forgive me. I don't want to seem to pry into official secrets. But this whole business . . . well, naturally it has upset me a bit. I just wanted to put things right with the two of you . . . old friends . . . don't want misunderstandings.' He ran a hand over his thinning hair. 'I must go. Pauline will be expecting me. No, don't come with me, old man. I'll just walk to the club and pick up the car. Exercise is good for me, you know. Good-bye, Mary. Good-bye, my dear fellow.' And he was gone.

'He seems in a bit of a state,' Geoffrey said.

'I expect Pauline has been taking it out of him.' Mary bent down to pick up a fluffy rabbit that Lois had thrown on to the floor. When she straightened up, 'You don't really think Pauline knows anything about this business, do you?' she asked.

'I don't know. I admit she annoyed me this morning and I am not sorry if she is sweating a bit over it – but there was something odd in the way she acted, you know. It wasn't just girlish modesty over being caught having a drink with Griffith, whatever Dudley likes to think. I wonder if she did know this fellow? She got around a lot when they lived in Nairobi, I believe.'

'One can't help knowing a lot of people in East Africa,' Mary said. 'It doesn't necessarily mean anything.'

Geoffrey looked at her in surprise. 'I didn't think you would leap to her defence, darling.'

Mary smiled a little. 'No. I don't normally, I know. But you sounded awfully smug and . . . well, male. Women must stick together over some things.

'And now I must go and feed this starving baby.'

She picked the drowsy bundle up and tucked her into the crook of one arm. 'And I think I'll go straight to bed when I have got her settled, Geoffrey, if you don't mind. Mr Schmidt was right. I am tired after all that getting up last night. I'll tell Mohammed to bring you your supper here. Don't stay up too late.'

6

THE FOLLOWING morning there was the usual rush at the Boma, made more hectic by the holiday the previous day. Hallden warned his African clerk to keep everything he could away from him and settled down to try to clear some of the arrears that had accumulated during his safari. On reaching his office he had tried to telephone, but was not surprised when the operator told him there was still no sign of life on the trunk line to Dar. The local news on the radio that morning had announced the arrival of the rains all along the coast, and given the usual list of roads closed, railway embankments collapsing and towns cut off. It did not make cheerful listening for Hallden, who more than ever now felt the job of the European's death was one to be put in the expert and impersonal hands of the police force. He felt his own inadequacy, not only through lack of experience and equipment, but because he was far too close to the affair and to the people who might be involved in it.

He tried to put it out of his mind for the present and was concentrating on a Secretariat despatch when his clerk poked an apologetic head around the door.

'Sorry, sir,' he said in his precise middle-school English, 'but Mr Chambers has called and says he wishes to see you urgently.'

Geoffrey sighed and pushed the papers back. 'Send him in, Rashidi.'

Dudley looked hot and worried. He kept smoothing his hand across the top of his head or fingering the crease in his immaculate white shorts. His bush shirt clung to his back and wilted visibly away from the neck. He took a chair and lit a cigarette with quick, nervous movements, and for once omitted the apologies for disturbing a busy man which would normally have taken five minutes to get through. He plunged abruptly into the middle of his business.

'I thought a lot about our talk last night, and I talked a bit to Pauline when I got home. She doesn't see eye to eye with me . . . fact is, we had a bit of a row about it. But it seemed only fair play to tell you . . . I mean, let the dog see the rabbit, eh? You'd find out soon enough, anyway, and we ought to give you what help we can now. . . .'

Geoffrey was completely at sea. 'Just what was it you wanted to tell me, Dudley?'

'That fellow . . . Shane-Hamilton . . . Patrick Shane-Hamilton . . .' He paused.

'Yes?'

'I . . . that is, we knew him in Nairobi.'

'Oh. You knew him well?'

Dudley hesitated. 'To be honest with you, *I* hardly knew the fellow at all . . . not my type. Very smooth character, successful with the ladies, you know. I always thought him a bit shady. Good family, good war record and all that, but a man picked up rumours about him that weren't . . . well, not the things a gentleman gets mixed up in.'

'Pauline knew him then?'

'Ran around with him a bit. You know Pauline likes the gay life and a bit of admiration. Nothing to it, of course, but she did see a bit of him at one time. She was all against telling you after you thinking she had some stake in the business anyway, but I said you were bound to find out as soon as the news got around that he had died here, and it would look a lot worse if we kept quiet about it.'

'Very sensible of you, Dudley. Thank you for being so frank with me. But before we go any further, perhaps we had better make sure it is the same man.'

'You mean, identify him?' Dudley looked startled. 'But I thought the chap was buried and all that . . .'

'I got some pictures. Not very pretty, but I think they should give a recognisable likeness.' He pulled out of a drawer one of Shotter's prints.

Dudley studied it with distaste and dropped it back hastily on the desk.

'Nasty; but yes, that is him all right.'

Geoffrey drew a deep breath. 'Good. Now we can really get somewhere. What can you tell me about him, Dudley? You said there was gossip about him in Nairobi? What sort of things was he mixed up in?'

Dudley looked uncomfortable. 'Well, one doesn't like to repeat things about the dead . . . and is a lot of out-of-date gossip really relevant? After all, it seems pretty obvious that the chap was set upon and robbed . . .'

'Not quite so obvious as all that, Dudley, I am afraid. I thought so myself yesterday. But of course Pauline told you what we discovered?'

'About him being shot? Yes. Yes, she did.'

'We also have some evidence that he had little or no money on him before he was killed, which seems to rule out a casual murder for gain. A thug of the calibre that carries a gun doesn't usually attack a man until he is pretty sure he has something worth stealing.'

'No. No. I see your point. It does seem to make the whole thing more complicated. But, as I was saying, I hardly knew the fellow and didn't much like what I did know of him. It doesn't seem quite fair to tell you a lot of gossip which may not even be true. . . .'

'I hardly think the normal rules apply in a case like this,' Geoffrey put in dryly, 'but if you don't like the idea perhaps I had better drop in and have a word with Pauline . . .'

'No, no. Don't do that. I can tell you as much as she can about him, in that way – probably more. And she is pretty ratty about the whole business of my coming here. She might just refuse to tell you a thing.'

He stamped his cigarette out in an ashtray and automatically took another.

'As I say, I wasn't close to the chap – not much interested really – but I did hear things. You know how people gossip. The talk in Nairobi was that he was some sort of agent for all kinds of rather shady deals. He went round trying to get people to put money up for other chaps' schemes. Got me to invest a few hundred in some wildcat mine up on the Uganda border – folded up in about a year and I lost the lot. That was when I first met the chap. He had a kind of charm, you know. Very persuasive. You felt he was putting a good thing in your way because he liked you. All nonsense, of course. Just picked out the gullible types, I suppose. Then, of course, before that there was the diamond business . . .'

'Diamonds?'

'Yes. Everyone seemed to know about it. Chap was a flyer, you know. Pilot in the war, with D.S.O., D.F.C. and bar, and so on. . . . He had a job on a diamond mine for a while, flying passengers, supplies and so forth in and out. They were losing a lot of diamonds off the property at the time, and rumour had it Shane-Hamilton was kicked out for smuggling them in his plane. Nothing proved, you know, but apparently they were pretty sure of it. It was after that he came up to Nairobi – Tanganyika got too hot for him, I should think – and took up the other sidelines.'

'Was he well off when you knew him?'

'Threw a lot of money around, you know. Had a sports car and gave expensive parties. But I don't suppose he had much in the bank. By the time we left Nairobi he was in trouble with his *duka* bills, they said.'

'That would be about a year ago, wouldn't it? I wonder what he had been doing since?'

'I wouldn't know, my dear chap. He wasn't exactly a

friend, and we don't get much news of the world, buried down here.'

Dudley got to his feet with an air of relief. 'Well, now I've told you all I know I'll be getting along. Know you are a busy man, and I have got things to see to, after all this rain.'

Geoffrey went with him to the door.

'Paw-paws doing all right?'

'So-so, you know. Never knew the things were so hard to grow. Fellow who sold me the plantation told me you just put the pips in the soil and there you were. . . .' He laughed hollowly.

Left alone, Geoffrey walked to the window, gazing down on to the quiet harbour and the peaceful town in the clear light after last night's rain.

'Diamonds,' he thought. 'Diamonds! That might be the clue to the whole business.' As a young district officer he had served in the area of the big diamond mines in Tanganyika, and he knew a little of the business of I.D.B.– illegal diamond buying – of the network of small traders, go-betweens and agents who clustered round the diggings, buying the odd stones that workers smuggled out; of the dodges, old and new, worked to get stolen diamonds past the searchers at the gates or handed through the perimeter fence. He had also heard rumours of the bigger boys in the business, who lurked in the background negotiating the really important deals. There was talk of international gangs who were organised on a world scale, and of the huge profits made by them and the big rewards of the middlemen all along the line.

Suppose Shane-Hamilton had been mixed up in smuggling diamonds while he worked for the mine. He would know some of the contacts outside. Perhaps he had kept in touch while he was in Nairobi, or taken the business up again when he returned to Tanganyika. And if so, what were the possibilities of connecting it with this mad trip to Kilimani at the onset of the long rains? Geoffrey fiddled absently with the window catch as his mind turned the problem over. Suppose, for example, Shane-Hamilton's channel of disposal for the diamonds at Dar es Salaam had gone, or the police had got suspicious of him. Might he not then have brought his supplies to a second agent in Kilimani, someone who could get them easily out of the country and hand them over, on the high seas or in some other port, to the next man in the chain? With no European police here and a free and easy customs control Kilimani might be just the right spot for such a deal. And it would account for the fact that no one had come forward to say they were expecting him or to explain his business here. Or perhaps he was simply trying to get quietly out of the country to evade a pursuit which was getting too close to him? But on balance the former seemed the more likely. After all, apparently Shane-Hamilton had arrived penniless. He must have been expecting to get some more money in Kilimani.

Geoffrey's eyes rested on the small single-masted schooner lying peacefully by the jetty. That telephone call to Willy Schmidt! Of course, Schmidt would be the answer, either way! He was known, he came and went freely up and down the coast, to no fixed schedule. No one questioned it if he made a sudden trip to Dar es Salaam or even went as far down the coast as the Portuguese East Africa border. He was the ideal 'disposer'. Geoffrey remembered the interest Schmidt had shown in the details of the unknown's death the previous night. True, he had given no sign of any guilty knowledge at the mention of the dead man's name, but he had left the way open in case he had to admit later on that he knew him, by saying that the name of Shane-Hamilton sounded 'vaguely familiar'. And the phone call – he had a plausible explanation for that. But then, Schmidt would have. He was not a man to panic easily, and he had had plenty of time to think up a story before he talked to the D.C.

Suppose then that Shane-Hamilton had come to Kilimani

to see Schmidt. Why had he been murdered? Was it just robbery – some casual person who discovered the existence of the diamonds and killed him to get them, or could it be because he was dangerous to someone and was better out of the way? If the former, the murderer could be anyone in Kilimani. If the latter, Schmidt must surely be involved. But according to him his ship had been held up in Mafia at the time. Geoffrey cursed again the failure of the telephone line. He could only reach Mafia through Dar es Salaam, though the island lay much closer to him than the capital, and with the telephone out of order he would have to rely on sea mail, which might take weeks, before he could check Schmidt's alibi. Perhaps some of his crew could be persuaded to talk before Schmidt got at them. . . .

His thoughts were brought abruptly to earth by the door opening behind him and by a gentle *'Hodi!'* He swung round.

'Oh, come in.'

Old Swedi approached, carrying the tea-tray carefully in both hands and planting his bare feet splay-footed, like a caricature of an English butler. This was a daily ritual, cherished by the old man, who liked to stand for a few minutes while the D.C. tasted his tea and exchange some of the news of the day. Geoffrey was busy, but he could never bring himself to be abrupt in the face of Swedi's good manners and anxiety to please, so he sat down at the desk, poured out the tea as usual, and asked, 'Well, old man, what is the news in the *pombe* shop?'

It was an old joke, and Swedi laughed appreciatively, showing the wide gaps in his teeth.

'This and that, bwana, this and that!' he replied, as he always did. 'Much of it is not fit for the Bwana D.C.'s ears.'

They chatted about the rain and the price of maize and millet, and, as he often did, Swedi railed against the rapacity of the Indian traders and the shocking prices they charged, raising both his hands in despair. Then the old man bent forward solicitously to wave away a fly that was hovering over the sugar basin.

'The Bwana Ismael, now,' he said, elaborately casual, 'perhaps you saw the filth he is selling for maize meal when you visited his *duka* yesterday?'

Geoffrey grinned, imagining Swedi was amusing himself by demonstrating how good his sources of information were.

'Your eyes are everywhere, old man!'

The messenger acknowledged the compliment with a bow, and made as if to take his departure. But by the door he turned and said, still carefully casual, 'The Bwana Ismael must be worried, is he not, since he is known to have driven the car of the European?'

Geoffrey sat up. 'The car . . . ? Which European?' But of course he knew.

The messenger put on an elaborate face of surprise. 'The bwana did not know? But I was sure that the Bwana D.C. with all his sources of news . . .'

'No. I did not know, Swedi. Tell me now, quickly. This is important.'

The old man was serious at once. 'It is just a story in the *pombe* shop, bwana. It is said that someone saw him drive the car of the dead European, after dark, the night he died.'

'Towards the bridge, or towards the town?'

'To the bridge, bwana.'

'And who is this man who saw him?'

Swedi shrugged. 'That I cannot tell. It is just what I hear. Many men and their wives and families live near the *duka*, and of course all of them buy from the Bwana Ismael.'

Geoffrey knew perfectly well that he was being tactfully informed that the man who saw Ismael was in debt to the Indian and did not dare tell officially what he had seen. He was aware that Swedi would never betray the source of the information, but he had to go through the motions of trying to make him.

'But this is police business, Swedi. A man has been killed. Yet no one has come forward to tell the *askaris* about this matter when they questioned them about the night the man died?'

'What would you expect, bwana?' Swedi shrugged. 'That William is a foreigner from the uncivilised bush up-country, and his constable, though a good Swahili, was a boy brought up in Dar es Salaam, and he thinks he is unfortunate to be put among these ignorant countrymen who know nothing of the town.'

Geoffrey had to acknowledge the truth of the implied criticism. It was a constant headache to the police. But if you employed a local boy in his own district he came under all sorts of pressures of tribe, family and friendship that were hard for an African to resist.

He let Swedi go without thanking him for his news. It would, he knew, be a breach of etiquette to imply that the old man had deliberately passed on information. After a moment's thought he rang for Derek Shotter and told him what he had learnt from Chambers and the old messenger.

'Good Lord!' Derek exclaimed, eyes popping. 'It looks as if Ismael did him in for the diamonds he was carrying, then?'

'Don't go so fast, Derek. The diamonds are pure supposition on my part, don't forget! And then it isn't likely a foxy character like our friend Ismael would kill the man and rob him on his own doorstep, and then be seen driving the car away. We haven't a scrap of evidence we could hold him on, let alone bring up in court.'

Derek pondered, fingering his line of moustache.

'What about searching his house? He might have kept the papers and things – and the diamonds, of course.'

'Not legal. We haven't even a witness we can produce who

saw him in the car. Officially it is just a *pombe* shop rumour.'

'Oh damn! Couldn't we get away with a search? You're a magistrate, after all. . . .'

'My dear chap,' Geoffrey said kindly (and, he feared, a little pompously), 'as you remind me, I am a magistrate. I am meant to be the arm of the law and of the administration in Kilimani. And so are you. Apart from the ethics of the thing, imagine what a smart Dar es Salaam lawyer could do with a D.C. and a D.O. authorising a search by the police without *prima facie* evidence to justify it!'

'If we found something it would jolly well be justified!'

'I know. But I think we have to approach it a little bit more carefully. Let me think. He must have left prints on the Land-Rover. . . . Damn, I wish we had thought to fingerprint the driving wheel before half a dozen people handled it! I suppose the C.I.D. would have done it automatically. Just shows what a mess amateurs can make in a business like this!' He thought for a moment, then snapped his fingers. 'That's it! Get William up here, Derek, and tell him to bring the police car. He is to wait outside here until he is given the word, then drive out to Ismael's place, taking the main road.'

'To search the house?'

'No. To park the car outside then stand patiently by the telephone until I ring him. Then will you come back? I want you to phone Ismael and summon him at once to the D.C.'s presence.'

Derek looked at him then winked solemnly. 'I see. Bluff.'

'Yes. For want of any better means, bluff.'

7

'SIT OVER THERE and take notes,' Hallden said to Derek Shotter. 'And look official.'

They had just heard the big American car owned by Ismael drive in to the Boma entrance. In a few moments the merchant was shown in. He looked a bad colour and was perspiring, but then it was a hot day, and he had obviously come in a hurry. He took the chair offered him, directly opposite the D.C. and half-turned towards Shotter (who sat at one end of Hallden's desk with an open notebook in front of him) so that both of them could see his face. The Indian smiled with an attempt at ease.

'Good morning, gentlemen. Your wife and daughter are well, I hope, sir?'

'Thank you, yes.' Geoffrey lined up a batch of papers neatly on the desk in front of him. 'I am sorry we had to send for you in such a hurry, Mr Ismael.'

Ismael, whose eyes had been taking in the D.O.'s notebook and the serious faces of the two officials, essayed another smile.

Geoffrey went on. 'Some evidence has appeared, Mr Ismael, which leads us to believe you were not telling the whole truth yesterday about your contact with the European who was found dead by the bridge.'

The Indian's smile was almost a grimace now. 'But what is this, Mr Hallden? You thanked me yourself, yesterday, for all the help I gave you. . . .'

'That was yesterday.'

Geoffrey opened his desk drawer and took out the photograph of Shane-Hamilton which he had shown Dudley

Chambers. He held it out delicately by one corner.

'First, do you formally identify this as the man who came to your shop on Wednesday evening?'

Ismael took the photograph and turned it over in sweating fingers as if he might find some inspiration on the back.

'Yes,' he said cautiously, 'it looks like the man.'

'Thank you.' Geoffrey held out his hand for the print. Then he slipped it into an envelope and rang the bell on his desk.

There was a tense pause, then the clerk came in quickly, his eyes bright with interest.

'Take this to the police post, Rashidi, and ask them to check the fingerprints on it with the set they already have – at once.'

Ismael's eyes had followed every move. As the clerk went out he glanced down quickly at his hands and pushed them into his lap below the level of the desk, as if they might somehow betray him. But he said nothing.

'And now,' Geoffrey went on, 'I am giving you an opportunity to make a full statement about what happened that night – leaving out nothing.'

Ismael's eyes swerved round to the D.O., who was writing busily. There was no help there.

'I do not understand,' he began, and attempted another smile. 'I told you everything I could remember. If there is some small detail . . .'

'I see.' Geoffrey's flat statement stopped him in mid-sentence. He forced the Indian's eyes to meet his.

'I have given you a chance to volunteer a statement, Mr Ismael, because I thought it only fair to you. Had you done so it would have counted in your favour. But now I will tell you that there is a witness who saw you on Wednesday night, in the Land-Rover belonging to the dead man. . . .'

'Who was it?'

'That it is not necessary to tell you now. Do you deny it?

'It is a plot! Someone is saying this to harm me! I have enemies, Mr Hallden, people who do not like me because I am a business man and wish to be paid for my goods! I swear it is not true. I did not leave my house all the evening. My wife will tell you so.'

'Is there anyone besides your wife who saw you there?'

Ismael hesitated. 'I do not remember. A friend may have called in. . . .'

Geoffrey's voice was as cold as steel. 'You had better remember now, Mr Ismael. It was not very long ago. And I should warn you that you will be expected to sign an official statement before you go home and there will be no opportunity for you to amend it after you have, shall we say, refreshed the memory of any of your friends. There is no hurry. You can take your time.'

There was silence in the room except for the whirring of the fan overhead. Ismael sat with his head bowed, a long lock of greased black hair falling over his brow. Then Derek Shotter shuffled his feet slightly and gave a strangled cough. The Indian raised his head but did not look at the D.C.

'No. I do not think there was anyone . . . after the shop was closed. It was raining. . . .'

'And you still say you did not leave the house?'

'No. No. I was there . . . working on my accounts. My wife will tell you. It must have been some other person driving this car. Many Indians look alike to other races . . . to Africans. . . .'

There was a half question in his voice but Geoffrey ignored it. He arranged the papers on his desk again in a precise pile and spoke in an apparently casual voice.

'The fingerprints in the car should settle the matter.' Ismael was silent and he went on, still casually, glancing at his wrist watch. 'The police should have had a good half hour at your house by now. Will you ring, Shotter, and see what they have found?'

Derek dropped his pencil, stooped to retrieve it, and reached for the phone.

Ismael's colour had faded now until it was like wet clay. His eyes were glazed as if they could no longer focus properly on the D.O. as he reached for the receiver and lifted it. He licked his lips once, twice, as if about to speak. Shotter cleared his throat and asked the Boma operator to ring the number of the store. The room was so quiet that all three men could hear the metallic voice say, 'Yes, sir,' and repeat the number.

'Stop!'

Quite suddenly, with a wholly Eastern gesture of defeat, Ismael bowed his head on his hands and rocked himself back and forth. After the one word he did not speak for a moment. Geoffrey gestured silently for Shotter to replace the phone.

The words, when at last they came, poured out, as if Ismael wanted to make up for his previous silence and evasion by the fullness and speed of his confession now. His voice was high and harsh.

'I will tell you all. I did not kill the man. You must believe me. He was dead when I found him, shot here,' and he pointed to his heart. 'I knew he was dead. There was nothing I could do for him. But the car was in my yard. I heard it drive in. . . .'

'What time?'

'After half past eight. I am not sure. It was raining very hard. I thought nothing of it, but that a friend had called and was waiting till the rain grew less. Then no one came, so I went out. He was lying there, against the window of the car, and he had been shot. Someone had brought him there so the blame would be on me . . . someone who knew I had a gun . . . someone who hated me! And I thought, what can I do so that people do not think I kill him? Then it came to me that if he has *panga* wounds they will think an African has done it, to rob him. So I take his money and papers and I find a *panga* and I strike him where it will cover the wound of the gun. I . . . I was afraid. I did not know what I was doing. But he was still in my yard. I had to take him away. It was still raining, though not so hard, and I thought the Africans from the *shambas* would all be at home, so I drove the car out to the bridge with the man beside me. The water was up so I could go no further. I turned the car so it would seem that the man had not yet come to Kilimani. I took off the licence plate so that people would not know who he was and threw it away. I left him there, and I ran home.'

'And the things you took from the man? What did he have?'

'Some letters. A little money. Nothing of value, I swear.'

'You kept them?'

'Yes. The police will have found them. They are in my shop, with my money.'

'We will go and see them now.' Geoffrey got up and nodded to Derek. 'Ring Sergeant William and tell him we are coming, will you, Shotter?'

They went down in Hallden's car, with the D.C. driving and Ismael sitting in the back with Shotter. At the little *duka* a knot of curious Africans had gathered round the police vehicle and there was a murmur of interest as Ismael drove up with the district commissioner and district officer. His wife and two skinny childen were standing just inside the shop. The woman took one look at her husband's face and shrank back into the shadows, pulling the children against her skirts.

Sergeant William came forward and saluted.

'Put your constable at the door to keep these people away, will you, Sergeant?' the D.C. said.

'And now, Mr Ismael, please show me where the things are.'

The merchant hurried to the back of the shop and dug around behind the merchandise until he found a small cash-box. The key was hidden in another cache, and it was a minute or two before his shaking fingers got the lock open.

The D.C. motioned him back and himself took out the little packet and sorted through it slowly. There was a bill from the New Era Hotel, Dar es Salaam, a fountain pen and propelling pencil, an expensive cigarette lighter, and a notecase containing about five pounds in notes and change.

'This is all?'

'All.' The Indian had revived a little with the interval in the car and the D.C.'s milder manner.

Hallden looked at him sternly. 'I am giving you another chance, Mr Ismael. There should have been something else in Mr Shane-Hamilton's possession – something of considerable value.'

Ismael threw out his hands pleadingly. 'I am telling you the truth, sir. That is all there was. I swear it. I did not tell the truth before, as I was afraid, but now there is nothing held back.'

'All right.' Hallden picked up the wallet again. 'You said, I think, that the man was short of money when he bought the cigarettes from you? You still stick to that?'

'Yes.' Ismael was anxious to supply all the detail he could on this comparatively harmless point. 'He searched in all his pockets and found just enough for the telephone and for the packet of ten cigarettes, with a few cents over. He looked in the notecase and I saw there was nothing there.'

'Yet he had nearly one hundred shillings an hour later. . . .'

'Yes, indeed!' His eyes lit up and he cried excitedly, 'And does not that prove he must have seen someone else – the person who killed him? Perhaps killed him for this thing of value you say he possessed. . . .'

'It does not prove anything, I am afraid, Mr Ismael. And now I would like to see this gun of yours, unless you have already turned it in to the police?'

Ismael hung his head again. 'No. I must confess, when the

police asked this morning I said I had no gun. It is one I . . . received, in payment of a debt, some years ago. This shop is lonely at night, and I needed protection for my wife and children. . . .'

'But why was not the gun licensed?'

Ismael hedged. 'The way I obtained it was, perhaps, irregular. I did not know. I did not want any trouble.'

'I see. Bring the gun, then, and let me have a look at it.'

At one glance Hallden could see that this was not the weapon that shot Shane-Hamilton. It was a heavy ex-service revolver, in such a rusty condition that he doubted whether it would fire at all. He handed the weapon over to Sergeant William and asked him to give Ismael a receipt for it.

'That is all now?' Ismael asked hopefully.

'I am afraid not. You will have to accompany the sergeant and Mr Shotter to the police post to sign your statement formally, if you are willing to do so. Then you will have to remain in custody.'

'But I am innocent!' Ismael wailed hysterically. 'I confessed all! You cannot put me in prison! What about my business? I did not kill him! I swear it! I swear it!'

'That will do!' Hallden's voice was a command. 'There is not sufficient evidence at present to charge you with murder, but you have confessed to certain other very serious crimes – mutilation and robbery of a dead body, attempts to conceal the commission of a murder, possession of an unlicensed firearm – you could be held on any of these.'

'I will say nothing without a lawyer! You must let me have a lawyer from Dar es Salaam!'

'As soon as a lawyer can be reached you may certainly call him in. But in the meantime I must ask you to accompany Sergeant William to the police post.'

'This is British justice!' Ismael cried, almost beside himself with fear and rage. 'Because I tell the truth I am to be put in jail and my business ruined! Because I am a poor man and an Indian. . . .'

'You are doing yourself no good by all this,' Geoffrey rapped out. 'You knew perfectly well that what you did was a crime in law even if you did not actually kill the man. And so far you are the only person who we know had contact with Shane-Hamilton in Kilimani and could have killed him. . . .'

'What about those others . . . the telephone calls? He saw someone . . .'

'Have you evidence of that?'

'He said . . .' Ismael's eyes suddenly narrowed. 'He said he would be seeing someone – someone at your house.'

Geoffrey looked up, startled. 'I know he rang my house,' he said. 'He wanted me, but I was away. Did you actually hear his phone conversations?'

'I heard some. I could not help it.'

'Tell me all he said, as far as you can remember it.'

Ismael was thinking. Looking at his expressionless dark eyes Geoffrey wished he could see what schemes were hatching behind them. Clearly he thought he had found a way out, or a lever, and was wondering how to use it to the greatest effect.

'The first call . . . he asked for Mr Schmidt. . . .'

'Say it word for word, if you can remember it.'

'I will try. "Is Schmidt there?" he says, and then frowns and says it again more slowly, "Is Mr Schmidt there?" '

'He spoke in English?'

'Yes. He listened and then he said something like, "I wish to see him urgently", and then, "No, I will try again tomorrow. I will not leave a message." He spoke some more but that was all I heard.'

'And the other call?' Geoffrey felt the muscles of his cheeks tense trying to hold his expression without sign of the anxiety within him.

Ismael's eyes flickered. 'I did not hear much. He thought

I was listening and put his mouth close to the telephone with the hand over it. I went to the other side of the shop. But I know he spoke for several moments. And at the end, just before he rang off he took the hand away and I heard him say, "All right. I will see you then." '

The dark eyes watched the D.C.'s face. Ismael had recovered some of his composure and there was curiosity and a touch of malice in his glance. Geoffrey was very conscious of Derek Shotter standing just behind him, listening eagerly.

'Is that exactly what he said?'

Ismael shrugged. 'As I remember it.'

'He did not say, "I will be seeing you"?'

'Does it matter? It may be.'

There was an audible breath of relief from Shotter.

'It matters quite a lot,' Geoffrey snapped. ' "I will be seeing you" is just a conventional phrase of farewell, and certainly does not mean you intend to see the other person in the near future. I think you must have misunderstood.'

Some of Ismael's confidence had left him again at the sharpness of Hallden's tone. Perhaps he had been foolish to antagonise the D.C. at this stage. He allowed his shoulders to droop again and said meekly, 'No doubt, sir. But Mrs Hallden will be able to tell you.'

In the car Shotter gave a sigh of relief. 'Well, that seems to be that. I suppose the old devil bumped him off for the diamonds and then panicked.'

'I wonder,' Geoffrey replied slowly. 'There is the gun . . . and that matter of the five pounds. Why should Ismael lie about a thing like that? It seems so pointless. And there is the gap after Shane-Hamilton left the shop. How and where would Ismael have got hold of him again?'

'He might have come back to the *duka* for something. I say, you don't think there is anything in that business of the phone calls, do you? I thought it pretty obvious Ismael was trying to alibi himself by inventing a lot of cock. Odd he picked on Mary, though, as the victim!' Derek laughed with great heartiness.

'Yes,' Geoffrey agreed. 'Silly, isn't it? But it is the Schmidt angle I am interested in. I'd like to have heard the rest of that conversation. If he talked in English it couldn't have been just a houseboy who answered the phone.'

'No. But that woman of Schmidt's – what's her name? – I believe she speaks pretty good English.'

'Mm. It would bear looking into.'

But as Hallden drove back to the Boma his thoughts were not of Schmidt and his woman. A voice was repeating in his mind a brief phrase, with slightly different intonations and wording.

'I'll be seeing you. I'll see you, then. I'll see you, *then*.'

8

ALTHOUGH the Boma shut officially at twelve for the weekend the D.C. had such a pile of urgent matters awaiting action on his desk that he decided to work right through the day. He was in the middle of a major task at lunchtime and, telling himself it would be sheer waste of time to break off to go home for the meal, rang Mary and asked her to send down something cold to the office for him. She hesitated before answering. Normally she would have exploded and told him he must come home for a break and a proper meal. Now she said politely and coolly that she would see to it at once, and rang off. Geoffrey was left holding a silent receiver, feeling somehow relieved and disappointed at once. Then he pushed from his mind the personal problem, and the whole teasing business of Shane-Hamilton's death, and plunged back into his familiar district work, letting it absorb his whole brain and energies as it always had done in the past.

He worked with few interruptions until six o'clock, and got up from his desk at last, stretching and yawning, looking with satisfaction at the pile of paper he had shifted from the 'in' to the 'out' tray. The old messenger was still on duty at the door, and Hallden paused as usual on the step to exchange greetings. It had rained heavily during the afternoon, and the air was hot and steamy like a Turkish bath. But now the sky had cleared and the town, the bay, and the distant islands were brilliant in the late sunshine. The D.C. was reminded sharply of the last time (was it only two nights ago?) when he had stood like this and looked over his little world of Kilimani, congratulating himself on how well he knew it all, and its heart, the people of the town. And now –

how much could he really be sure he knew, not only about the town but about his own household?

Mary was feeding the baby when he got home and he called out to tell her he was back.

'Let's go down to the club for dinner tonight, when I get Lois settled,' she replied. 'I'd like to get a change of scene.'

Geoffrey's immediate thought was that it would postpone the talk they must have for at least a few hours, and he found himself agreeing almost eagerly.

The Kilimani Club was to the pattern of all the other clubs in small country settlements throughout East Africa, little centres created by the British population to enable them to meet together at their ease and do all the things they imagined they might have been doing if they still lived in England. They could play games, have tea, lean on the bar, or just sit turning over the pages of English publications several months out of date. Membership was open to any Europeans who lived in the place, and a few Greeks and Italians belonged, but the atmosphere, customs and décor were all unmistakably British. In a town without a cinema or an hotel it was almost the only place to go if you wished to get away from your own home, and the small bar and indifferent dining-room were well patronised on most evenings. It was run by a Goan steward, a quiet and discreet man, and a small African staff who had been there for years and were well known to all the members. The club was another of the old German buildings, on the top of the hill near the Boma, and its long open veranda looked over the sea. It was shabby, poorly equipped and badly lit, but it had a friendly air about it that more than compensated, in the eyes of most of the members, for its lack of smartness. Behind the building were a couple of tennis courts created by the energy of a long-past D.C., and a caricature of a golf course, a monument to Hallden's Scottish predecessor.

As tonight was a Saturday, and Easter Saturday at that,

the veranda and the bar were crowded. All the Government contingent seemed to be there, and a smattering of 'commercials' who operated agencies or businesses in the town.

The Halldens knew everybody, and normally would have spent the first ten minutes or so exchanging greetings and gossip with friends on their way to the bar. But tonight there was a certain constraint about the company. The buzz of conversation dropped as the D.C. came in, and people merely waved or nodded, or called out a 'good evening' as they passed.

At the bar they found Pauline Chambers surrounded by a court consisting of Tom Griffith, Derek Shotter and (surprisingly) Willy Schmidt. Pauline had been drinking, and as a result was playing to her all-male audience with exhausting vivacity. Her low-cut dress was slipping down off her shoulders, little beads of sweat glistened through her make-up, and her eyes were brilliant with excitement. The men were taking it differently. Schmidt leaned beside her, twinkling encouragingly; Derek Shotter was perched on the edge of his stool, dipping his face regularly into a mug of beer like one of those birds that used to perform on bar counters; and Griffith was propped sulkily against the bar on the other side of Pauline, getting mostly her turned back as his portion of the conversation.

Pauline greeted the Halldens loudly. 'Ah, the D.C. and his wife. Make way, make way! And you, Tom, buy them a drink.'

Geoffrey frowned at the greeting, and was just about to refuse the drink when Schmidt suavely intervened.

'That I cannot allow. I promised the honour to myself. What can I get you, Mrs Hallden?'

He steered Mary skilfully to a bar stool and had produced the drinks before Pauline had a chance to say any more.

'Where is Dudley, Pauline?' Geoffrey asked.

'Darling, can't I have a night out without him without

everyone being funny about it? If you must know, he's got some sort of tiresome tummy complaint and has gone to bed, feeling frightfully sorry for himself. He says it is a chill, but I think he ate too much curry at lunch. Anyway, I am a gay grass-widow tonight and making the most of it.'

'Is he really ill?' Mary put in. Like Geoffrey, she was fond of Dudley, when he did not irritate her to distraction.

'I don't suppose so. You know what he is . . . behaves as if he was dying over the least little thing.'

'I'll call in and see him tomorrow in case there is anything I can do for him.'

'Darling, what a pity he didn't marry you instead of me!' Pauline gave a cat's smile. 'He'd love to have a nurse perpetually hovering over him!'

'As Gilbert puts it so touchingly,' Tom Griffith put in with drunken deliberation, ' "She will tend him, nurse him, mend him, air his linen, dry his tears . . ." eh?'

'Perhaps he could do with a bit more of that,' Mary retorted.

Pauline opened her eyes very wide in mock surprise and purred, 'Darling, do you have to be catty?' She raised her glass to Geoffrey.

'Well, congratulations on the solving of the great Kilimani mystery, by the D.C. and his gallant assistant, the D.O.!'

Geoffrey looked at her and then at Shotter. 'So it is solved, is it? That's news to me.'

'Isn't it? But I thought you had arrested that dreadful Indian down at the *duka*?'

'We haven't arrested him for murder,' Geoffrey answered shortly.

'But you do think . . . ? I mean, Derek said . . .'

Derek, who had flushed and was biting his moustache worriedly, broke in. 'You must be fair, Pauline. I told you it looked as if he might have done it. I didn't say there was any proof.'

'Derek is entitled to his own opinion,' Geoffrey said coldly. 'There isn't a scrap of real evidence that the man killed Shane-Hamilton and you will be liable to get into trouble if you go around saying he did it, Pauline.'

Derek looked chastened, but Pauline just shrugged. 'You're always so damned official, aren't you? Well, *I* think he did it! He's just the slimy sort to bump someone off for money, isn't he, Tom?'

Tom grimaced sulkily. 'Don't drag me into this. I know nothing about the business.'

Willy Schmidt's calm voice broke in on the discussion.

'But, forgive me, Hallden, Ismael *has* been arrested? The rumour is correct then? And for something connected with the murder?'

'He has been charged with robbery, concealing the evidence of a murder, and for possessing an unlicensed firearm.'

There was silence in the bar, then a sudden murmur of talk. Geoffrey became aware that all the people around had been listening with interest to the exchange.

'That seems to be enough to be going on with,' Griffith said. 'Have you identified the gun yet?'

'Not yet. We haven't had a chance to test any of the ones the police have collected.' A sudden thought came to Geoffrey and he turned to his wife. 'By the way, Mary . . .'

'Yes?' She looked up from her drink, blankly, as if her thoughts were a long way away. He had been going to ask her about his own gun, but something warned him not to do so here.

'Never mind. Later will do.'

He ordered a round of drinks and the conversation switched to other topics. It was an uncomfortable evening. If Pauline had set out to make things awkward deliberately she could not have succeeded better. She ignored Griffith and Shotter most of the time and concentrated on Geoffrey and on Schmidt. Geoffrey felt that her attentions to himself were solely to annoy Mary, and discounted them accordingly, but he was puzzled by the change that had suddenly come over the relationship between her and Willy Schmidt. Pauline had been spoilt all her life, and she had a sure instinct for picking out men who would carry on the spoiling process – the young ones who were dazzled by her, and the ones passing middle age, who petted her and usually could afford to indulge her expensive tastes. The others she ignored or openly disliked. Now Willy Schmidt could never be suspected of spoiling a woman. They had a place in his life, but it was a very small and clearly defined one, and he had always adopted towards Pauline an attitude of amused indifference. She in turn expressed her dislike of him freely, and enjoyed telling spiteful stories about his odd tastes in women and the *ménage* down on the sea shore. But tonight she had apparently asked him to join their party and was paying him a flattering amount of attention. Schmidt in return was attentive enough, teasing her mildly and encouraging her flirtatiousness as if it amused him. Geoffrey could only surmise that Tom Griffith, sulking in the corner of the bar, had displeased Pauline, and she had picked on Willy Schmidt as the only unattached male available to play off against him.

When the Halldens decided to go for dinner Schmidt asked if he might join them, and Geoffrey accepted readily, thinking the other had probably had enough of Pauline for the evening. He admired the dexterity with which Schmidt headed off Pauline's suggestion of accompanying them and they left her with the two young men, still drinking at the bar.

Inevitably the talk at dinner turned to the murder.

'Have you any word from the police yet?' Schmidt asked.

Geoffrey replied that it was too early for anyone to have reached Kilimani yet in response to his message, and the telephone lines were still out of order.

'My offer to go up and fetch the police is still open,'

Schmidt twinkled. 'As soon as you are prepared to let me go.
'Thank you,' Geoffrey said, 'but I hope they are on their way by now. Perhaps if nothing happens this week . . .'

'I suppose,' Schmidt went on blandly, 'you cannot keep Ismael in jail indefinitely if you are not satisfied he did the murder. You are not happy in your own mind about it, are you? And I think I agree with you. Somebody took a big risk in killing this man. Ismael is a typical merchant type. He likes to see his profit before he makes his deal, and I do not think he would gamble on killing a stranger for what he might be carrying.'

'That depends what he was carrying – and if Ismael knew about it.'

Schmidt paused with a piece of bread half-way to his mouth and his shrewd eyes studied Geoffrey thoughtfully. Then he put the bread into his mouth and chewed it deliberately.

'And what was he carrying?' he asked.

Geoffrey took the plunge. 'What would you say to – diamonds?'

'Diamonds?' Schmidt grinned. 'Well, well! Did you find them on him?'

'No. But there is certain . . . evidence that he was carrying them when he came to Kilimani.'

'I see.' Schmidt apparently returned his attention to his food, but Geoffrey thought that he was weighing his words more carefully than usual. Perhaps his wild guess about the diamonds had something in it after all!

'But,' Schmidt was saying, 'if you have not got the diamonds how can you be sure he was carrying them?'

'He could have mentioned them . . . or shown them to someone. . . .'

'He could indeed. This is all very interesting. Quite a drama – diamonds, international crooks, eh, Mrs Hallden? And what do you suppose he was doing with these diamonds?'

'Getting rid of them, I should say.'

'In Kilimani?'

'There isn't much choice, is there? There is nowhere very likely further down the coast. And he had business here. He went to Ismael's store, and he telephoned you. . . .'

If Schmidt was aware that the gloves were coming off now he did not show it. His smile was pure amusement. 'Ah, but he also telephoned you, my friend, so where does that get us? And besides, I was in Mafia.'

'It is lucky you will be able to prove that, isn't it?'

If Geoffrey hoped Schmidt would rise he was disappointed.

'Isn't it?' the other said calmly.

Dancing had started on the veranda when they came back to the bar. Pauline let out a little scream when she saw Schmidt.

'There you are at last, Willy! Come and dance with me! It's an old-fashioned waltz, and I know you do them divinely.'

Schmidt bowed and submitted. Pauline had obviously had a few more drinks while they were gone, but she could still dance. At first the floor was crowded and there was little room to manœuvre, but gradually the dancers, by common consent, moved outward leaving the centre of the floor to Pauline and Schmidt. He danced in the old-fashioned way, holding his partner well away from him and steering her by a light pressure on her waist. Like many stocky men he was light on his feet and his balance and grace were surprising. At first Pauline was talking and laughing, but at something he said she stopped speaking abruptly and gave herself up entirely to the dance, leaning back, eyes half-closed and lips parted, oblivious to her surroundings. When the dance was over she was gasping, perspiration beading her upper lip.

'That was sheer heaven.' She flashed a glance at Tom Griffith as she opened her compact. 'It's a pity you can't dance like that, Tom . . . or any of you bright young men. You dance like a bear with its legs chained together, and of course Derek here hovers around like a duck on the edge of a puddle.'

It was cruel, but apt, and Schmidt laughed. Then he saw that Tom was genuinely angry and Derek confused, and with his usual tact he turned the jibe aside.

'And I dance like an elderly man who learnt thirty years ago,' he said. 'And Mrs Hallden here like a woodnymph, so light, so quick . . .' and he swept Mary off to dance with a laughing apology to Geoffrey.

Pauline bit her lip as she watched them go. Then deliberately she turned her back on the dance floor.

'Buy me another drink, Tom. I need it.'

Over the edge of the glass her eyes moved round to Geoffrey's face as he stood beside her.

'Aren't you drinking, Geoff, my pet?'

'Not at the moment. I've just finished dinner.'

'Come on. It would do you good. You look so stuffy and miserable . . . not that I blame you. It must be terribly difficult for you, sweetie, the way things are.'

Geoffrey was only half listening. 'The way what things are?'

'Well, you know . . . you being in charge of the investigation, all ever so official, and having to keep quiet about the dead man being an old boy-friend of Mary's . . .'

Geoffrey swung round. 'What did you say?'

Pauline's eyes were great innocent circles. 'Didn't you know? Didn't she tell you? Oh dear!' She gave an artificial little laugh. 'Well, I have put my foot in it, haven't I? But, sweetie, I thought you *must* know. It was all round Dar – before Mary met you, of course, but it was quite a thing, apparently. And then, last year when she was so sick, poor sweet, and had to be left in Dar all alone . . . well, you can't blame her, can you?'

Geoffrey was listening through a sort of haze in which the music of the radiogram, the chatter of the crowd behind him, and Pauline's husky, spiteful voice were all mixed. He knew he had to say something, to pretend to pass it off lightly, but the words just would not come.

Then suddenly a new voice broke in behind them.

'I've brought your wife back, Hallden. She says it is time to go home and feed the baby, so I have reluctantly agreed that Miss Lois must have first claim.'

It was Schmidt, his face the usual pleasant mask. But one look at Mary told Geoffrey that she had heard Pauline. Shock – or was it fear? – was written nakedly on her face. He moved quickly to get between her and the others.

'We must go. I hadn't realised it was so late. Did you have a wrap, Mary?'

'My . . . my scarf.' She pointed to the gauzy shawl lying on the bar counter. Geoffrey put it swiftly round her shoulders then gripped her arm hard and turned her towards the exit.

'Come on, darling. Home,' he said quietly.

Mary managed to call a good night to the others, but he could feel her arm shaking within his.

As he stood back to let her through the door he glanced back at the bar, where the crowd had thinned out. Pauline was sitting up on her stool, watching them go with a little, satisfied cat's smile on her lips. Derek flushed and turned away as he caught Geoffrey's eye. Griffith was looking morosely into his beer as if he had heard nothing. Schmidt was not watching the Halldens. His eyes were fixed on Pauline, and there was a very odd look in them.

9

IT SEEMED a long way home. A thin rain was falling, clouding the windscreen and making the dirt road slippery. Geoffrey drove carefully, concentrating on keeping the wheels on the firmer ridges of the road and refusing to let his mind dwell on the real problem: how did a man say to his wife, 'Was the man your lover? Did you see him when he came? Have you lied to me all along, deceived me?' and all the other questions that were at the back of his mind, which he did not dare put into words.

But this was Mary, his wife, loved and trusted, his heart argued; and instantly his mind replied. She had heard Pauline. Why did she not say at once it was a lie, before all those people who must have heard Pauline, too? He remembered then the silence that had met them when they entered the club, and the attempts to greet them normally, the quick, measuring looks that had followed them. Had Pauline been talking before they came in? Did everyone know but him, the husband? A gust of anger swept him as he thought what a fool he must look – the upright D.C., who had always held himself a bit above other people's weaknesses and follies. He half turned to Mary to say something then, but the look on her face stopped him. In the dim light reflected from the dashboard her face was set and pale, and she looked in front of her as if she was alone with her thoughts. Let her speak first, he thought. He was not going to beg her to tell him the truth. Let her find the words to begin.

At the house she got out of the car, still in silence, and waited for him to unlock the veranda door. Inside, the sudden glare of light seemed to startle her and her eyes flinched back from it. She dropped her evening bag and scarf on a table and began to move towards the door leading to the bedroom quarters. He had to speak, though he would not ask what he really wanted to know.

'Just a moment.' She paused by the door, half turned away from him.

'The police called in this afternoon about the gun. . . .'

'The gun?' The word did not seem to register.

'Yes. You remember, I left it out for you, in the drawer of the bedside table, before I went on safari. William said you couldn't find it. . . .'

'No. I . . . I looked today, when he came. I thought you must have taken it on safari with you after all.'

'No. I didn't. You haven't seen it since I left? Think. It is important.'

'Is it the same kind . . . the gun that . . . ?' and as she saw the answer on his face she cried out. 'Oh, my God! Not that!'

She groped towards the couch and sat down, her hands over her face. Geoffrey looked at her bent head, at the drops of rain still sparkling in her hair. He almost put his hand out to touch her, then he remembered.

'Don't you think it is time we talked about this?'

'I've tried so often, Geoffrey! Ever since I came back from Dar. But it hasn't been easy. It seemed as if I couldn't really get through to you any more. . . .'

But he had only heard the words that confirmed what he had dreaded and half expected. 'Ever since I came back from Dar.' So there was some truth in what Pauline had said.

'Surely you owe it to me to tell me the truth now, even if you could not do so before?'

Mary raised her head with a flash of her old spirit. 'Don't talk to me as if I was . . . was in the dock at one of your precious courts!' She made an obvious effort to control herself and speak calmly. 'Sit down, please, Geoffrey. I can't talk with you towering over me like that.'

He moved over and sat down at the other end of the couch.

'I know how all this looks, but I must try to make you understand. I have felt, ever since we were married . . . even before, perhaps . . . that your standards were so high that if I didn't match up to them . . . you would have no more use for me. You've never done anything to be ashamed of yourself – not really ashamed – have you? And you deserve a wife who has nothing to be ashamed of either. But I am not like that, Geoffrey. I like life and fun, and then suddenly I find I am in the middle of something I hate but can't get out of. . . .'

'You're not . . . What are you trying to say, Mary?'

She gave him a startled look, a new idea dawning behind her eyes.

'Geoffrey . . . you don't . . . you don't think I *killed* him . . . ?'

'In heaven's name, no, no! All I know is what Pauline said tonight, and that little things keep connecting you up with . . . with Shane-Hamilton. I have felt you knew something, but you were keeping it from me. I have tried just to believe blindly that it wasn't anything important, but after what Pauline said . . .'

Mary drew a little further away from him and looked down at the hands clasped tightly in her lap. 'If you need the assurance, Geoffrey, I can swear most solemnly that I didn't kill him. As for what Pauline said . . . I wish you hadn't heard it in that way and that I had had the courage to tell you first, before it really mattered. But will you let me tell you now, Geoffrey, in my own way, from the beginning? I'll try and be honest about it – but I want a chance to make you understand . . .'

He made a gesture for her to go on. He could not speak.

She told the story briefly, keeping her eyes on her hands,

trying to make her voice calm, as if it was someone else's story she was narrating. But now and then her hands tightened together and she hesitated over the words.

It began when Mary first came to Dar es Salaam, a nursing sister of twenty-five, escaping from the narrow life of a London hospital into what seemed a glamorous new world. But after the first excitement of coming to a strange tropical country she had been lonely. There was much to see and do, but no one to share it with. The other European sisters all seemed busy with social life and men friends, and she found the society of the sisters' mess irksome after a week or so, with no friends or family outside to break the monotony of living and working with the same people. Then one day she had met Patrick Shane-Hamilton on the beach, and life had changed overnight. He was gay, amusing, physically attractive. He seemed to have unlimited money to spend and time to fill all her spare hours with parties, sailing, dancing, picnics, impromptu midnight bathes – all the amusements that Dar es Salaam could offer a young woman eager for enjoyment. For nearly two months they had been constant companions. At the end of that time, after a long and expert pursuit, he had become her lover. About a week later he had been called to Nairobi on 'business' (he was never at all explicit about the nature of his business) and during his absence she had had time to think and to get back into touch with the normal world after the artificial life of excitement she had led with him. She realised then that, however much she was attracted to Patrick and amused by him, she did not really like him nor trust him, and being essentially honest she knew that for her it was impossible to love someone unless she could like and respect them as well. Once her eyes were opened she wondered how she could have been blind to so much about him that was doubtful or second-rate. There were the little evasions he practised about his job, about where his income came from, and where he went on his sudden absences from Dar. She realised that his friends were all as shallow as he was, and that none of them seemed to have known him for more than a few months. She began to hear hints about his past, too. When he talked about the past it was always the days of his war service that he recalled – the 'shows' he had been in, the places and the people he had come across – and there, apparently he had spoken nothing but the truth about a brilliant career as a pilot. But other people spoke of the recent past – the succession of jobs he had taken and lost in East Africa, the *shauris* over money, his numerous women friends around the territory, picked up, 'run', and dropped as quickly.

Mary had wanted to break things off as soon as he returned, and knew now that she should have done so. But she was afraid that he would laugh at her as immature and schoolgirlish if she made a scene and refused to see him again. So, although they never returned to the old intimate relationship, she still went around with him in public, and, to tell the truth, she had been a little piqued when it came to her ears that Patrick was said to be 'dropping' her. While she still hesitated he suddenly announced that he was taking up a flying job at a diamond mine up-country, and that seemed to settle the matter for her without the need for a definite break. After he had gone Mary settled down to her own work, found new interests in Dar es Salaam, and wrote him off, she thought, as an experience which she regretted but was the wiser for.

Some time later she met Geoffrey, fell in love with him and married him, and completely forgot about Patrick until she was sent up to Dar three months before Lois's birth. There, living on her own in a flat near the hospital, loaned to her by a friend on leave, she had been glad to renew some of her old acquaintanceships. Then at a sundowner given by someone who had known them both, she had met Patrick again, looking a little older, a little more dissipated, getting just a bit seedy.

He had told her he was back in Dar es Salaam for good in a 'job', but he was vague about its nature. He had seemed pleased to see her, highly amused at her respectable marriage to a district commissioner, at her pregnant state, and at her change in attitude to him. Mary thought that the fact that she so obviously did not want to see him brought out a streak of cruelty in his nature. He began to take pleasure in pressing his company upon her. He kept turning up at the flat at odd hours of the evening, offered her lifts if ever he saw her in town, and monopolised her attention if he met her at anyone else's house. At first she tried being polite and distant, but that had no effect. Then, when she became aware that gossip was starting about them she told him bluntly that she did not wish to see him again. But he was too vain a man to accept a dismissal. She had once admitted that she had never told Geoffrey about him, and he used that knowledge as a threat – a teasing threat, of course – to make her see him again. She had thought of writing to Geoffrey and telling him the whole thing, but when she started to put it on paper it seemed to be making an issue of something that was no longer of any real importance. Geoffrey had promised to come up at the first opportunity for a few days with her, and she intended to talk to him then, but one thing after another had cropped up to prevent his visit, and in the end he did not arrive until just before Lois's birth. Patrick was away from Dar at the time, and there had been so much else to think about that she had never raised the subject.

When she got back to Kilimani she had been exhausted and depressed, finding all her mental and physical energies needed to cope with the baby. Geoffrey seemed to have grown away from her during their separation, and Mary felt that the child was an added barrier between them. Though he was proud of Lois he had very little to do with her. His work came to absorb more and more of his time and attention, and Mary had felt that he would not be interested in revelations about Patrick

Shane-Hamilton, and that it would only stir up unnecessary trouble to mention him. So it had remained, just a small prick in her conscience that she was glad to forget.

Then, out of the blue, Patrick had rung her up on Wednesday evening. She could not believe it was he at first. He had insisted on seeing her against all her protests, and had implied that he could make things very awkward for her in Kilimani if he chose to spread the news of their past friendship around. And she knew he could. The district commissioner's wife had to be like Cæsar's. In the end she had agreed to meet him by the back entrance into the garden. He came about quarter past seven. By then it was raining heavily. It was impossible to talk outside in the streaming downpour, and she would have found it difficult to explain her soaked clothes to the servants, so, unwillingly, she had let him into the house through the bedroom wing. Mohammed had been tidying up in the sitting-room, so she had left Patrick for about five minutes in the bedroom until she was sure the coast was clear.

She had expected that Patrick simply wanted to borrow money, as he had done several times in Dar es Salaam. She had decided to give it to him straight away and tell him to go. But there was more to it than that. He took the money – about one hundred shillings in small denominations – but what he seemed more anxious about was a small package which he wanted her to look after for him, just for twenty-four hours or so, he said, until he could redeem it. It had been a linen envelope, roughly sealed, and when Patrick put it into her hands to try and force her to keep it she could feel it held some small, hard, irregular shapes. When she asked what they were he had said, 'mineral samples', and explained that he had to see someone in Kilimani about them and that it might be a bad thing if he actually had the 'samples' on him. No one would think of looking for them in the D.C.'s bungalow, though.

Mary had flatly refused to keep the packet. Geoffrey was

due back the following day, and she would not risk Patrick coming to the house while he was there. She told him she wanted no more contact with him and that nothing would persuade her to get involved in any of his shady schemes. Patrick had been furious, but he saw that she meant what she said, and in the end gave way. He had said he 'would have to try his luck elsewhere'.

The next time she had seen him had been in the Land-Rover by the flooded bridge.

'That is all,' she said.

Geoffrey had listened in silence, not looking at his wife, but aware of every pause, every variation in the tone of her voice. He was trained to listen to evidence in court and long practice had given him an instinct for the lies, the evasions, the skating over weak patches in a story. The way she told this one carried conviction at the time, and he believed it was the truth – but then, she was his wife, and he wanted so badly to be able to believe her.

He got up and began to pace up and down the long living-room.

'You realise that a lot of what you have told me may be important evidence about the murder?'

Mary looked up at him for a moment. 'Evidence of fact . . . or of my motive?'

He made a violent gesture of denial. 'You know what I mean as well as I do, Mary. You must realise my position. As your husband I can accept without question that you know nothing of Shane-Hamilton's death, but as the district commissioner in charge of the case . . .'

'I know. "I could not love thee, dear, so much . . ."'

'It does no good to mock at it, Mary. God knows, it is no laughing matter.'

'Laughing! No, I assure you, Geoffrey, I am not laughing about it!' Indeed, tears had come into her eyes. She tried to rub them away clumsily with the back of her hand, and the childish gesture suddenly moved him unbearably.

'My dear . . . don't! I . . . I know how difficult this has been for you – telling me all this.' He sat down on the couch near her and dropped his head in his hands. 'My God, what a mess! If only you had told me before! I'd give anything to be able to wash my hands of the whole business, Mary – but I can't. There is nobody else to do it, and whatever I feel about it, it has got to be done.'

'I know.' Her voice had softened. 'I do know, Geoffrey. You wouldn't be you if you didn't feel that way. I should never have put you into the position where you had to choose. That is why I shirked telling you these last few days. I was going to tell you about Patrick as soon as you got back from your safari. I knew if he was in Kilimani we might meet him, and at least you would find out that he knew me . . . and if he was up to something shady you ought to be warned about it. But then you went straight to the Boma instead of coming home, and when you did come the Chambers and Tom Griffith were here, and Derek came and told us . . .' She covered her eyes with her hands. 'I keep seeing him, there in the Land-Rover by the bridge. I thought I should go mad waiting for you to come. And after I came home here alone I was still going to tell you. Then I thought . . . Patrick was dead . . . it might not be necessary for you ever to know, or at least not until the case was over. If it was just a robbery – Ismael, or some African we didn't know – my evidence would not have mattered.'

'But when you heard he had been shot! When Schmidt was here and I asked you about the telephone call . . . !'

'I know. I lied to you. I couldn't say anything else while Schmidt was here, but I knew you would find that hard to forgive. After that I was in so deep I . . . I just didn't know how to begin to tell you. It has always mattered so much that we should trust each other. I felt if we lost that there would be nothing at all left . . . for us . . . for Lois . . . Can't you understand why I hoped you would never find out?'

'But it was bound to come out sometime, Mary. You must have realised that. Tanganyika's too small a place; people talk too much . . .'

'Yes. Yes, I suppose so. It was just a sort of . . . of hiding my head in the sand. I see that now. You think the story will be all over the country in a few weeks? "D.C.'s wife implicated in murder!" What a wife I am making you! You must feel . . .' She broke down then and started to cry, smothering the sobs in her handkerchief.

Geoffrey put out a hand tentatively to touch her arm. 'Don't, Mary. Don't. Please don't upset yourself so. It's not as bad as that. . . .'

To his own ears the words did not carry much conviction, but they seemed to help Mary to pull herself together. She sat up and dried her eyes, turning her face away from him while she struggled to regain control.

'I am sorry, Geoffrey. I am not making things any better, am I? Suppose we try and forget all that for a while and just pretend you are the D.C. and I am an unknown woman who has some evidence to give. Look, light me a cigarette and tell me what you want to know.'

Geoffrey pulled out his case and lit two cigarettes. He put one between her lips, then touched her hair gently with his hand as she turned her face up to him. He made his tone deliberately light.

'That's better. I am not used to taking evidence from weeping females.'

A little colour had come back into her face, and she looked more like the Mary he knew instead of the white-faced stranger who had suddenly seemed to take her place at the club. As she had suggested, he forced himself to think about her story as if it was simply another bit of evidence in the case – how important a bit he did not yet know.

They talked about the mysterious packet Shane-

Hamilton had been so anxious to be rid of. Mary had never seen uncut diamonds, but when Geoffrey described to her their probable size and shape she agreed that the packet could well have held them, and quite a number. So Geoffrey's guess had unexpected confirmation. The telephone call Ismael had overheard was explained, and the money which had appeared in Shane-Hamilton's pocket between his call at the *duka* and his death.

Geoffrey probed for a long time into what Shane-Hamilton had said about his future movements, but in the end all that Mary could contribute was an impression that he was going straight away to see someone else – whether to leave the diamonds with them or to negotiate for their handing over she could not say. Geoffrey mentioned his suspicions that Willy Schmidt was the agent he had hoped to deal with, but that he knew Schmidt was unlikely to return till the following day. He inclined to the idea that, failing Mary, Shane-Hamilton would have tried someone who might act for Schmidt. The only clue Mary could provide was that Patrick had said it might be 'a bad thing' if he kept the packet for the next twenty-four hours. He had not explained, and could have meant either that he feared some specific person might try to get hold of it, or merely that he was nervous of sleeping in the open in his Land-Rover with diamonds in his possession.

'Then there is the gun . . .' Geoffrey said. He looked questioningly at Mary.

'You think someone may have stolen your gun to shoot him with? But that would mean someone knew where it was and could get in. . . .'

Geoffrey shrugged. 'We can't rule out anyone yet, even our own staff. But I was thinking of Shane-Hamilton. You said you left him in the bedroom for about five minutes?'

'Yes. You think *he* took it then?'

'It sounds reasonable, if he was as scared as you say.

Most people out here keep a gun, and the bedside table is the most likely place for it to be. I don't suppose he had any scruples about exploring our bedroom. . . .'

Mary must have heard the return of bitterness in his voice, but she merely replied quietly, 'He wouldn't have had any hesitation.'

'Well, then . . . if he had the gun he may have got into an argument or a fight, had it taken from him and used against him.'

'It's possible. . . .' Mary sounded as if she still doubted it.

'I am afraid it is more than possible. The other .22s on the Arms Register all belong to people who seem to have no connection with the case, except for Schmidt, and he says his gun was locked up in the house while he was away. But we shall see tomorrow if any of the guns match up with the bullet. Derek and I are going to do some tests.'

There was silence for a moment.

'Is that all?' Mary's voice sounded very tired.

'I think so.'

'Will you want me to make a . . . a statement or something official, tomorrow?'

Geoffrey hesitated. Half Kilimani would know by now what Pauline had said in the club, and if he took no official evidence from his wife there would be plenty of people to think the worst. The local police and Derek Shotter had access to all the records of the case. . . .'

Then he made up his mind. 'No. It's not necessary while I am in charge. When the police take over you will probably have to sign a statement, but don't worry about it now.'

'Thank you.'

Mary got up, and with the slow movements of exhaustion picked up her bag and scarf. 'I've got to feed Lois now. Ayah will be wondering what has happened to us. Don't stay up late, will you?'

Geoffrey echoed her 'good night', but sat on in the familiar room for a while, trying to think about everything that had been said this evening. He attempted to fix his mind on Mary's evidence, and feel some satisfaction that his wild guess about the diamonds had been confirmed, but all he could think about was Mary. He remembered a lot of things now. Soon after they became engaged she had started to talk about herself and her past life while they sat in the dim light of a restaurant after dinner, and he had stopped her.

'As far as I am concerned, Mary,' he had said, 'your life began when you met me. I don't see any point in digging into the past.'

Partly it had been, he saw now, because he did not want to dig into his own past and talk about the few wartime affairs that now looked unpleasantly sordid in the light of his love for Mary; partly it had been a genuine feeling that nothing mattered but themselves and their coming marriage. She had laughed and said, 'Well, if you want it that way, darling . . .'

One or two people had dropped hints in Dar es Salaam about Mary's old flames, but he had snubbed them so firmly that they had gone no further. It had been all quite impersonal then. He had not been able to visualise a tall, muscular body, fairish hair cut too long, the face, showing the marks of charm as well as dissipation, that had looked out at him from the Land-Rover and from Shotter's photographs . . . Pauline's ex-boy-friend and Mary's ex-lover. And for fate to bring this man and kill him almost on his own doorstep, and then fix it so that he had to try to find the murderer!

But what hurt perhaps more was that Mary had not told him. That was hard to forgive. He had always felt that they shared everything important, and now here was a whole chapter of her life that he knew nothing about. Even when she had found Patrick Shane-Hamilton dead she had not trusted him enough to tell him, had hoped that he need never find out. Perhaps there was some truth in what she had said, that he had been difficult to approach the last few months, and that she had had little chance to talk to him when he got back to Kilimani. But afterwards, after they had found Shane-Hamilton dead, she had plenty of opportunity then if she had really wanted it, if she had trusted him enough to tell him the truth.

What was he to do now? Most of Kilimani would know by tomorrow that Mary and the dead man were linked, and the fact that she had seen and talked to him just before his murder was bound to leak out in time. There seemed to be only one easy solution – to resign from his job, ask to be relieved at once, and hand the whole thing over to someone else.

Then he remembered – the flooded road to the north, the sagging telephone pole and broken wire somewhere out in the bush that cut him off from anyone who could help him. He could see in his mind's eye the Boma messenger with his rifle and his precious papers dawdling with maddening deliberation on his way; mending a puncture, spending an evening drinking with his friends, falling asleep under a tree in the heat of the day . . .

For the first time in his adult life he longed to be able to dodge a responsibility, to dump it in someone else's lap. Perhaps if he did nothing for the next few days, let the whole thing lie until the C.I.D. arrived to take over . . . After all, he had done quite a lot already, found Ismael's connection with the case, practically proved that Shane-Hamilton had been carrying stolen diamonds . . . And Mary? Could he leave Mary to take her chance with the police, along with all the others . . . ?

For a long time he sat there, smoking one cigarette after another, getting up to refill his glass as he emptied it, staring out into the darkness beyond the veranda as his thoughts went round and round the same track. At last sheer exhaustion defeated him. He could no longer think. All he wanted to do was to lie down and fall into blessed oblivion. He almost stretched out on the couch where he was and went to sleep, but he thought of the houseboys coming in in the morning and finding him there, and forced himself to get up and go to his own room.

10

THE NEXT morning broke to a heavy downpour. The sea was a flat grey with columns of rain rising to the dark clouds above the islands. Outside the district commissioner's house water lay in great pools under the trees, and all the paths were muddy channels choked with débris of leaves and crushed flowers. Indoors the whole house steamed with heat and moisture. Geoffrey awoke and lay for a moment listening to the steady roar of the rain. His sheets were soaked with sweat and he felt as if he had hardly slept at all. His mouth was dry from too many cigarettes and too much whisky, and he was weighed down by a feeling that something had happened that he did not want to remember. The emotion was so strong that he turned over and hitched the sheet up over his shoulders and closed his eyes, although the bedside clock told him it was after six. But it was no use. His brain was awake, and brought back in vivid detail all the events of the previous evening from the visit to the club up to his late departure to bed. It was no good trying to push the thing away. He had got to come to terms with it.

He sat up and looked over to Mary's bed, but it was empty. She must have gone to give Lois her early feed. It was a relief not to have to face her immediately.

He had a bath, shaved, then put on fresh white shorts and shirt that immediately clung damply to his skin. But the effort made him feel a little better. His despair of the previous night was gone and now he was rather ashamed of some of the things he had felt and thought. This was a job – his job; there was no one else to hand it on to, so he would just have to do it as best he could. So far as the job was concerned he would have to act as if Mary was not his wife but simply a witness in the case of no more importance than any other. He went over her story of the meeting with Shane-Hamilton in his mind. Last night, in spite of his other doubts, he had believed that implicitly. He still believed it – but had she told him everything? Mary had kept from him so long the mere fact of her knowing Shane-Hamilton; might she not have kept back some more of the story last night, something more damaging than what she had told him? There was the business of the gun. It did not seem so plausible this morning, his suggestion of Shane-Hamilton finding it, taking it, and then losing it to the person who shot him. . . .

At this point in his thoughts Mary came in, and he looked up almost guiltily. She too looked tired and pale, as if she had slept badly.

'How is Lois?' he asked.

'All right. The rain woke her early, but I think she is going off to sleep again now.'

'Why don't you go back to bed and try to sleep for a while? I shall have to grab some breakfast and get straight down to the Boma.'

Mary ran a hand wearily through her tumbled hair. 'I shouldn't sleep now. It's far too hot. Anyway, I'd rather be up and doing something.'

'Just as you like.' Geoffrey bent down to lace up his shoes, conscious that his wife was watching him.

'Will you be in for lunch?'

'Yes, but I may be a bit late. I don't know just what will crop up today.'

'All right. You go on and have breakfast. I'm going to have a bath.'

On his way to the dining-room Geoffrey, on an impulse turned into the nursery and stood by the cot for a moment, looking down at his daughter. She looked relaxed and perfectly content, her eyes closed and her thumb tucked into the corner of her mouth. He pulled the little hand gently away, but after a moment it crept back again and he left it where it was. She seemed a little unreal to him, this small, fragile object. He and Mary had had great plans for their firstborn, but somehow things did not seem to be working out as he had expected. He and Mary . . .

He heard a movement behind him. The ayah padded quietly into the room, a plump, smiling woman with a white apron tied incongruously over her brilliant print frock. She greeted him softly, then stood by the door, waiting until he should be ready to leave. He could feel the curiosity in the bright dark eyes, and wondered just how much his household knew of what went on under their master's roof. Suddenly he felt he could not bear that silent, smiling presence behind him any longer, and though he told himself he was being a fool, letting his nerves get the better of him, he turned and went quickly past her out of the room.

The water in the road to the Boma lay in great puddles and the mud sucked hungrily at his car wheels. He had arranged to go out with Derek Shotter that morning and test the guns that the police had rounded up on an improvised target behind the Boma, but the rain was still coming down in sheets and it would clearly be hopeless to fire off guns and attempt to retrieve bullets in the deluge. As it was Sunday the Boma was officially closed and the empty rooms were bleak and cheerless under the battering of the rain.

Sergeant William was waiting in the D.C.'s office to report on his enquiries over the weekend. He had been trying to find the man who had seen Ismael driving the Land-Rover, but, as old Swedi had implied, the crowd in the beer shop or gossiping in the open market all became unnaturally silent when the sergeant or constable appeared, and they had got nothing but blank stares or voluble denials in answer to their questions.

William had tried to get more out of Swedi himself, but had no better success than the D.C. The old man had taken refuge in a convenient vagueness. Yes, he had overheard some talk, but could not recall what the men had looked like. He thought it was in the market, but he had also had a drink or two, and it might equally well have been in the *pombe* shop. The more the policeman questioned him the vaguer and more senile he became, and at last William gave up in disgust. He felt he should have got more co-operation from a member of the Boma staff, and hinted as much to the D.C., but Geoffrey only shrugged.

'I think the old man has told us all he knows, William. And even if he did remember the names of the men he heard talking, would it get you any further? They would simply deny it, and then Swedi would be in trouble for nothing. Let him alone.'

Geoffrey had the hopeless feeling that every lead in this case simply took him to another dead end. The information about Ismael had seemed to provide the answer to the whole business, but he felt more and more strongly that the shop-owner had intruded merely by accident. Chance had brought Shane-Hamilton to his shop and chance had led the murderer to dump the Land-Rover and the body in Ismael's yard. If the Indian had not panicked but had reported finding the body at once, he would not even have been suspected of causing Shane-Hamilton's death. Mary's story, too, had seemed about to give a vital clue, but was he any further now than he had been yesterday afternoon? He knew what had happened up to, and immediately after, Shane-Hamilton's death, but of the death itself, or who had caused it, he knew no more than at the start of the enquiry. There were a few pointers, it was true. Shane-Hamilton had been carrying diamonds, to be smuggled out of the country; Willy Schmidt must be mixed up in the racket, and was almost certainly the person who was to get the diamonds out and, presumably, pay Shane-Hamilton for his share in the deal.

At this point Hallden looked up and found William still standing in front of him at attention, his expression ludicrously like that of a fairly intelligent dog waiting to be told where to dig for the bone.

'I am sorry, Sergeant,' he said. 'I was thinking what we should try to do next. You know Bwana Schmidt?'

Yes, William knew of him.

'What do you know about him and his affairs? Tell me.'

He had often been surprised at the exact and detailed information about Europeans which the Africans living round them possessed, in contrast to the general ignorance or indifference of Europeans towards Africans, even those living on their own premises.

William was diffident at first of discussing one European with another, but in the end his training as a policeman overcame the inhibitions of the African. He seemed to know a good deal about Schmidt.

As Geoffrey was already aware, he had living with him a half Arab, half African girl called Fatuma. According to William she ran his household with the help of two houseservants, and, being intelligent and educated above the average, also helped with Schmidt's local trading business. Her brother was one of the crew on Schmidt's schooner, and she was also related to a number of well-placed persons in the town, including one of the Boma clerks and the wife of Hallden's own head houseboy, Lois's ayah. ('So,' Geoffrey thought, remembering how he had felt in the baby's nursery that morning, 'the "grapevine" that serves Schmidt has branches in my own house! Why didn't I find this out before?')

According to William, Schmidt was respected by the Africans as a hard man of business, bad to cross, but fair in his dealings. It was generally accepted throughout Kilimani that he did not rely for money only on the trading in local crops and staple imports that was ostensibly his business, but it was not thought wise to be too knowledgeable about the other things he was mixed up in. He was rumoured to be very rich and to keep a lot of valuables in his house, but it was well guarded and no serious attempt at robbery had ever been made. Schmidt was known to be the sort of customer who would shoot first and investigate afterwards, and there were some odd stories, dating back to the days of the German occupation, of his methods of dealing with thieves or employees who tried to cheat him.

Geoffrey asked whether *alamasi* (diamonds) had ever been mentioned as one of Schmidt's sidelines, but William looked completely blank and seemed hardly to know what the word meant.

It had occurred to Geoffrey that he ought to check as far as he could on Shane-Hamilton's conversation with Schmidt's household. Ismael might be telling the truth, or he might just have said what would involve him in the least trouble. He said Shane-Hamilton had spoken in English, and that at least was probably correct. So he asked William if he knew who in Schmidt's household spoke and understood English. William was quite emphatic that Fatuma was the only one. She had been to school in Zanzibar, he knew, and spent some time in Dar es Salaam as an ayah to a highly placed Government family, and her English was quite good. The two servants, on the other hand, were both up-country boys with no education and little intelligence, and would certainly not even understand English. Geoffrey gathered that William was a little in awe of Fatuma. It would obviously be useless, therefore, to send him to talk to the girl. He would have to go himself. It would be interesting to meet her if she was as exceptional as she sounded, and at least it would give him something positive to do.

As William's information now seemed exhausted Geoffrey put him on to enquiring from the crew of Schmidt's schooner the time of their departure from Mafia. Not that he expected to catch Schmidt out on such a simple point, but it would be useful to have an independent check if possible.

Altogether it was an unsatisfactory morning. When William had left, Geoffrey tried the telephone, but the trunk line to Dar was still dead. Then a call to Bates, the public works department man, confirmed that it would be some time before the main road would re-open for traffic, even if the rain stopped that day, which it showed no sign of doing.

'Better consider yourself stuck for the duration,' Bates added in his thick north-country voice. 'These roads aren't built to stand rain, as you know, but it's rain we are going to be having for a month or so yet.'

Putting the phone down on this prophet of gloom, Geoffrey looked up to see Derek Shotter's head poke round the door.

'I say, are you free?' he asked nervously. 'About the guns . . .'

Geoffrey gestured at the window still opaque with rain. 'We can't do it in this.'

'I think it's going off a bit. There's a clear patch over the sea.' Shotter had by now followed his head in the door and was hovering by the desk.

Geoffrey knew perfectly well what was on the boy's mind, but he was damned if he was going to open the subject for him.

'You can start as soon as it clears,' he said. 'I've got to go out on a job. I'll join you later, if I can. Get one of the police to help you.'

He picked up a paper and started to read it. There was silence for a moment, then the shuffle of feet and a nervous cough. Geoffrey liked his young D.O., but that did not stop him being irritated by him, and he slapped the paper back on the desk with unnecessary violence.

'If you've got something to say, Derek, for heaven's sake say it! I've got work to do.'

Derek flushed furiously and mumbled an apology.

'It was just . . . er . . . I wanted to say how frightfully sorry I was . . . about last night, you know.'

'What about last night?'

'Well . . . I know you thought I shouldn't have talked to Pauline about that Indian fellow. But she's so damned clever. She sort of leads you on, and says something stupid to make you contradict it, and then, before you know . . . well, you've said more than you should.'

'I thought you'd finished with Pauline.'

'Oh, I have!' Derek blushed again, more brightly. 'But I feel, well . . . it's bad form to be too rude. Small place like this . . . can't get away from people . . .' The words died away into a mumble.

Geoffrey spoke more kindly. 'Well, you know my views on Pauline, Derek. I think the woman's a menace. She's got no heart and precious few scruples, and you are a sight too good for her. I should keep out of parties like last night's, if you can.'

'I will . . . I mean, I wanted to last night, but I was in the club on my own, and it was difficult . . .' He paused, took an irresolute step towards the door, then blurted out suddenly, 'I say, I hope she didn't upset Mary. I . . . I thought what she said was pretty awful. If I hadn't already decided Pauline was no good I . . . well, that would have finished it.'

Geoffrey had expected something like this, but hoped he had succeeded in choking it off. He sat in silence for a moment, plucking at the ruler resting in his pen-tray.

'Yes. It was unfortunate,' he said at last. 'Pauline timed it nicely to do the maximum amount of damage. I suppose the story is all over Kilimani by now?'

'Well . . .' Derek's face admitted it all too plainly.

'Perhaps you can do a bit to put things right then.' Geoffrey silenced Derek's protestations with a gesture. 'It's not a very nice situation. You had better know how things stand. Mary did know this chap – Shane-Hamilton – in Dar, long before we met. He turned up again while she was up there before Lois was born, and made himself a bit of a nuisance. She told him she didn't want anything to do with him, and thought that was the end of it. Unfortunately she did not think it worth while mentioning the matter to me, and when he turned up here – well, I suppose she lost her head and thought of all the things that would be said about the D.C.'s wife if it was known he had been to see her . . .'

'Then he did go?'

'Yes. He tried to get her to keep the diamonds overnight for him. She refused, and that was the last she saw of him. Mary . . . well, I suppose I've been a bit unapproachable these last few days, and she hadn't had a proper chance to tell me about it. She didn't for a moment think that his visit to the house could throw any light on the murder, and as I say . . . I suppose she lost her head a bit and thought it might never need to come out . . .'

'It must have been pretty ghastly for her. I mean, going out there and finding him in the Land-Rover. . . .'

Geoffrey looked up and saw nothing on Derek's face but the most genuine concern. 'Yes,' he said slowly, 'the shock must have been tremendous. I don't suppose she herself realises how great.' He pressed his fingers over his eyes, which had begun to ache. 'Well, that is the story, Derek. I am not putting it down in the official records of the case as yet, until I have had a talk with the police. I'll rely on you to try and squash all the wild rumours that I am sure are circulating.'

'Of course, old man. I would have anyway, but I'm awfully glad to know just how it was. If there is anything else I can do to help Mary . . .'

'Thanks, Derek. I know she'll be grateful.'

It was a relief to Geoffrey to get out in the open air. The rain had stopped now, and the harsh sun was sucking up clouds of vapour from the earth. Geoffrey's shirt stuck damply to his body and the perspiration trickled down his temples as he walked down the steep road to the bay. He wondered how he should tackle Fatuma. He hesitated to go to Schmidt's house. If he was out there was a sort of underhandedness about questioning his staff about his affairs, and if he was in Fatuma would only say what he allowed her to say. In the end he decided to try the warehouse where Schmidt's official business was transacted.

At the bottom of the hill he turned towards the beach and the little wooden jetty that ran out into the harbour. The warehouse was one of a group of shabby, Arab-style buildings at the end of the jetty. They were built of rubble, plastered a pleasing creamy-beige, and each had a bossed and carved Arab door of great beauty set in the flat façade. The first house in the group was the customs office, and seeing the door ajar, on an impulse Geoffrey went in. It did not match up to the splendid door. Inside it was a typical Government office, its peeling walls stuck with out-of-date notices, the furniture rickety and ill cared for, and the stone floor worn and discoloured with the scraping of many feet.

The local customs officer, an Indian called Padar, was there, dapper in his white drill jacket and trousers. Apart from the uniform he was a typical clerk to look at, slight in build, bending forward a little as if to aid his weak eyesight, polite, meticulous in detail, and lacking completely in imagination.

He was quite overpowered to see the D.C., especially on a Sunday morning when the office was not officially open. He rushed for a chair, apologised for having no tea or soft drinks to refresh his guest, dusted off the furniture, and expressed his sense of the honour of this visit all in the same moment, and Hallden had some difficulty in persuading him that he had dropped in on an impulse and only wanted an informal chat. But at last Padar seated himself behind the desk and prepared to listen to his visitor.

Hallden asked permission to smoke, and chatted on general subjects for a few moments to put the other at ease, then asked casually if Padar knew whether the Schmidt office was open today.

'Yes, indeed. I had occasion to go down to the jetty half an hour ago and the door was open.' Padar had not actually seen Mr Schmidt there himself, but someone must be inside, as they were always very careful to lock up if the place was empty.

The little official was obviously bursting with curiosity, and to satisfy it Hallden concocted a story about having an idea some contraband (unspecified) had been brought to be disposed of in Kilimani. It had occurred to him that Mr Padar might be able to make some useful suggestions about the most likely channels. It would be something small, easily concealed, but of considerable value.

Padar was diffident of expressing an opinion. He had no evidence, the D.C. must understand. If he had possessed any it would, of course, have been put at the disposal of his superiors in Dar es Salaam immediately, so that action could be taken against the criminals concerned. It took Hallden some time to persuade him that it was not evidence he expected; all he wanted was the guesses of the man in Kilimani who was best informed on the subject. Reassured, Mr Padar gave his mind to the problem.

He had, of course, suspicions. Every customs official knew that a certain amount of smuggling went on in spite of all he could do, and often he had a very good idea of what it was and who was doing it. Proof was the difficulty. He had far too few men to examine incoming vessels properly, and often small craft had tied up and the natives were swarming all over them before he could get down for an inspection.

He repeated, rather hesitantly, the same rumours about Schmidt that William had heard, but apparently he thought that Hallden's enquiries were concerned with ivory, which is the favourite contraband of the East African coast. But he mentioned in addition an interesting point. Schmidt, he said, was tied up with the owners of several of the dhows plying up and down the coast.

'One of them is in port now,' he said, getting up to point it out from the window. 'The smaller one with the blue-painted prow.'

Geoffrey joined him at the window and studied the ship. She looked to him like all the other dhows that called here, though he knew there were, by ancient tradition, many differences between the craft built in Arabia or India or here on the East African coast, and that an expert could have placed this one to a single home port. It was a thing of beauty, lying in the calm water by the jetty, though the great curving sail was furled away and only the bare bones of the mast visible. From here he could see men moving along the crowded decks, taking on bales, hauling on spars and ropes, and in imagination he could smell the pungent stink of the craft – of ancient hides carried in the hold, dirt, too many unwashed bodies living at close quarters, Arab cooking, and many other untraceable nuances.

'She looks as if she is getting ready to leave,' he commented.

'Yes indeed. She should have gone several days ago, but her captain decided to wait for another load.'

'When was she due to go originally?'

'Thursday, I think it was.'

'Mm. Interesting. I wonder if she was waiting for something that didn't turn up? Perhaps for my little parcel? You say Schmidt owns a share in this one? Possibly they were waiting for him to get back from Mafia.'

'I think very probably,' Padar said carefully. 'The wind was good for them Thursday. I did not think the captain made a very convincing story about the goods that delayed them. Perhaps they had been told to wait for this . . . this consignment, and, Mr Schmidt being delayed, they awaited his instruction.'

'And now it is not worth their waiting any longer?' Geoffrey mused. 'I wonder. Do you think you could let me know when the dhow shows signs of leaving?'

He glanced at his watch, which said nearly eleven o'clock, and turned to the door.

'Thank you for your help, Mr Padar. If there is anything official I can tell you about this I will do so at once. But at the moment, you understand, I only suspect that this contraband was here and that someone was going to try to get it out of the country.'

Padar raised his narrow shoulders in an expressive shrug.

'If you find more I shall do what I can, of course, Mr Hallden, but with a small staff only, and myself, there is little we can do to stop these things happening. And, you appreciate, I am very busy always with the forms and returns and so on for headquarters.'

Geoffrey followed his gesture towards the pile of papers on the desk and smiled.

'You are not the only one, my friend,' he said.

11

GEOFFREY paused for a moment outside the customs house, wondering what his next move should be. The existence of the dhow, about to leave, argued that the diamonds were now in Schmidt's possession and would soon be outside the country. Or was he imagining too much on the strength of Schmidt's interest in the craft and the timing of its departure? He knew he could not get the dhow searched without far more definite evidence that diamonds were aboard, and even if a search was made, what were the chances of finding such a small needle in such a cluttered haystack? He decided to go ahead and talk to Fatuma. Perhaps something fresh would emerge, and it could do no harm. He turned towards Schmidt's office a few doors further away. It was like all these older houses, with small barred windows high up in the pale walls. Geoffrey had been in only once before, to collect some baggage delivered by Schmidt's schooner, and he had a confused memory of a single big, dark room used as the warehouse, and one small corner containing a table and a couple of chairs to represent the 'office'. The door still stood open, and without announcing himself he stepped inside.

The building was dark and cool. Vaguely he could make out piles of crates and hessian-wrapped bales in front of him, and the place was full of the smells of mixed merchandise; copra, hides, grain, rotting fruit, were among those he could recognise.

A movement drew his attention to the 'office' corner, and he saw a man get up quickly from the nearest chair. Geoffrey could not make out his features, but by his silhouette knew at once that it was one of the Arabs from the dhows. The short, wiry figure, the loose, sleeveless coat, a shawl flung over one shoulder, and the great turban swathed over the greasy curls – all were unmistakable.

'*Hujambo!* Is Bwana Schmidt there?' Geoffrey said.

As his eyes grew accustomed to the dim light he saw that, seated behind the table, was a woman. She wore the conventional dress of a Moslem African woman; a brightly printed cloth or *kanga* wrapped tightly round her body and tucked in above the breasts, and a black head veil that tied with strings under the chin for out-of-door wear but now was flung loosely back around her shoulders. The *kanga* was an expensive one, brilliantly coloured, and the headdress was of silk instead of the usual black cotton. She had heavy strings of gold beads round her neck, and elaborate earrings dangled from her ears. The clean-featured, golden-skinned face was beautiful with some of the impassive smooth beauty of a carving in wood.

She looked at Hallden for a moment, then got to her feet. Her greeting was conventional and perfectly polite. Mr Schmidt, she said, was out. Could she help the Bwana D.C.? The silent Arab was ignored, but Hallden was conscious of his bright black eyes following every move.

'Do you expect him to return here?'

Fatuma's eyes went instinctively to the Arab. Ah, Geoffrey thought, so the Arab was waiting for Schmidt!

'Later, perhaps,' the woman said. 'I do not know.'

'Perhaps you can help me then. May I sit down?'

'Certainly, bwana.' Fatuma did not sound very enthusiastic.

The Arab said something to her in an undertone, jerked his coat about him and strode to the door. In the shaft of light from outside Geoffrey noted the elaborate curved dagger gleaming in his belt, and the embroidery on the coat and shawl. Obviously this was no underling, but the captain himself.

Geoffrey took the chair Fatuma offered him and she sat down again behind the table, her eyes bent on the bare wooden surface. She did not look the conventional African woman, and from William's account she obviously could not be, but she observed most decorously the silence and self-effacement before strangers traditional to Swahili women both by tribal custom and Mohammedan teaching. Geoffrey asked if he might smoke, and as an afterthought offered his case to Fatuma. She hesitated, then took one and inhaled the smoke deeply.

'You speak English, don't you?' Geoffrey said in that language.

'Yes. Not very well.' She sounded fluent enough, but Geoffrey reverted to Swahili.

'You have heard about the European who was killed on Wednesday?'

'Yes.' Still the carved image, expressionless.

'I wished to find out a little more about a telephone call he made.'

'A telephone call? I know nothing of telephone calls. You had better speak to Mr Schmidt.' She was talking quickly now, betraying some unease.

'I think you can tell me more. He spoke to you, didn't he?'

The black eyes flickered. 'Who, bwana?'

'The European. He telephoned from Ismael's *duka* to Bwana Schmidt's house. We know he spoke to you. There is no harm in it. I just wished to hear from you exactly what he said.'

She lowered her eyes. 'She is going to play stupid again,' Geoffrey thought, and broke in before she could speak, using his sternest tone.

'You know this man was killed, Fatuma. Anything he did and said may be important, and I must know. Think back to Wednesday. About seven o'clock in the evening. Did you not answer the telephone?'

She hesitated only a moment, then shrugged. 'I had forgotten, bwana. The telephone rang and a European spoke to ask for Mr Schmidt. It happens very often. I said he was away, but would return the next day.'

'Did the man say who he was or what he wanted?'

'Nothing more. He would not tell me. I am only an African servant, bwana.' The mocking eyes contradicted the statement as she made it.

'And he did not come to the house at all? You did not see him?'

'No, bwana. He would not come if Mr Schmidt was away.'

And that was all Geoffrey could get out of her.

He was getting up to go when he heard a car stopping outside and recognised the sound of Schmidt's Volkswagen. So he was prepared while Schmidt was not.

He came into the dark warehouse from the blazing street and started towards Fatuma without seeing the D.C. standing in the shadows. He looked tired and frowning.

'Where is the fellow?' he snapped at Fatuma in Swahili. 'The idiot has not gone?'

He pulled up sharply and peered into the shadow. 'Who is it? Good lord, Hallden!' His brow cleared at once and he came forward smiling. 'Were you looking for me?'

'I wanted to get an account of that phone call to your house on Wednesday from the receiving end,' Geoffrey said, evading the lie direct. 'I understand Fatuma here talked to Shane-Hamilton, so I have just been asking her about it.'

Schmidt glanced at the woman, who was standing with lowered eyes. 'And what did you discover?'

'Nothing more. She confirms what Ismael had already told us.'

'So you have wasted your time? I am sorry. You must permit me to try and make good your failure by giving you a drink. It is hot and you have had quite a walk. Come along to my house and have something cold and long before you go back.'

He urged the drink so pressingly that Geoffrey could not refuse. In any case he had a curiosity to visit Schmidt's house, which he had never entered before. He had little hope that Schmidt would let drop any useful information; he was far too careful for that. But there might be developments with the dhow and its captain.

Schmidt flung down some keys on the office table and said casually to Fatuma, whom he had ignored completely, 'Lock up when you leave. If that fellow comes back tell him to wait until he has seen me.'

Fatuma nodded meekly and took up the keys.

'I do not think you have ever been in my house before?'

They had spoken little walking round the curve of the bay, but now they were going up the steps to the closed door.

'No,' Geoffrey agreed. 'You don't entertain people much here, do you?'

'It is not a home,' Schmidt replied. 'It is a living quarter – an office – a place for sleep and work.'

He was right, Geoffrey thought. The landward side of the house had a shut-in look. It was built on a stone plinth about six feet high, so that one could not see into the windows, which were small for the tropics and had business-like expanded metal guards over them. The building was four-square and the entrance led into a passage with a room each side, one of which appeared to be an office and the other a dining-room. Schmidt led the way to the back, into a veranda room that ran most of the length of the house. One end was screened off (for sleeping quarters, . Geoffrey assumed) and the whole was closed in again from floor to roof with expanded metal. A chubby stone balustrade was the only break in the cage wall. There were no curtains and only three or four basket chairs and a few small tables scattered about. The only touches of individuality were two very fine Persian carpets on the stone floor and two deep shelves the length of the inside wall, one holding books and the other a collection of good African carvings.

Schmidt made a gesture towards the bare walls. 'You see – no pictures, no trimmings.'

'You don't need pictures with that in front of you,' Geoffrey replied, nodding towards the view of the sea that filled the open wall. The house was built just above high water mark and, raised as it was, gave the effect of being almost on the sea. A few coconut palms threw their graceful curves across the sky and their long fronds made a continual whispering background. Beyond them were only the water, the sea-birds, the low dark islands on the horizon and the banked blue clouds of the rainy season.

Schmidt excused himself to fetch the drinks and Geoffrey heard him shout to the outside kitchen and servants' block for the boy before he went into the dining-room. There were the small sounds of cupboards being unlocked, a refrigerator opened, glasses and bottles clinking, and his host's voice upbraiding the servant for clumsiness. Geoffrey strolled over to admire the carvings and glanced, as one does, at the books to see what they told him of his host. They were mainly in German – philosophers well represented, Geoffrey noted with surprise, as well as manuals on navigation and seamanship, and accounts of early exploration in Africa – and there were one or two volumes in English, including a well-worn Shakespeare.

Schmidt came in, followed by a sulky-looking, low-browed African who seemed to bear out Sergeant William's comment on the poor intelligence of the German's servants. He served the drinks in silence, barely replying to the D.C.'s conventional greeting. Schmidt's quick eyes had noted Hallden's interest in the books, and they talked for a while of the early German travellers who had done much to open up the country. Schmidt was most interesting on the subject, and normally Geoffrey would have found the conversation absorbing, but today he could only wonder when Schmidt would get to the object of the visit – for he was certain this was not just idle hospitality, however much Schmidt might like his company.

They were interrupted by the phone ringing in the office, and Schmidt excused himself briefly to answer it. He closed the door after him, so Geoffrey could hear nothing. Was it Fatuma telephoning to say the Arab had returned? The houseboy had disappeared. Evidently the servants kept to their own outside quarters except when summoned, and Geoffrey could imagine that they would therefore have little opportunity to know who came or went, or what took place in the house.

Schmidt returned, brisk and smiling.

'As you see, this is an office, simply an office, where people can bother me on business even on a Sunday morning.' He filled up Geoffrey's glass again with iced beer. 'And how are your enquiries progressing, my friend? Not so well, eh, if you have to bother my poor Fatuma about telephone calls?'

Geoffrey took a long drink before he replied. 'You seem very interested in my investigations, Schmidt. Just idle curiosity?'

'No. Shall we say a rather well-developed sense of self-preservation? We can be frank here, you and I, Hallden. Clearly you think I am involved somehow in this affair of Shane-Hamilton. You cannot suspect me of killing him, as I was fortunately elsewhere at the time, but all these little rumours floating around – they can be bad for my business.'

'Come now,' Geoffrey said. 'If you have a clear conscience . . .'

'My dear fellow, a clear conscience is a quite negligible asset in business, I assure you. You are arguing: Shane-Hamilton came to Kilimani with some diamonds (you are sure of that, I suppose?); he rang up this highly dubious fellow Schmidt; he got killed. Therefore he had business with Schmidt and Schmidt had something to do with his death. And all the other Government men and commercials will follow the same line of reasoning when the facts leak out – as they will do. I can assure you that the whole affair had nothing to do with me; I can brandish my clear conscience in your face – but will you believe me? Will the others?'

'But if you did not even know the fellow . . .'

'Ah, but since I spoke to you last I have been doing some thinking. I believe I did meet the man once.'

Geoffrey smiled a little grimly. 'I remember you said the name sounded familiar . . .'

'Exactly. It was a trifling acquaintance. To be precise, I ran into him in a bar in Dar es Salaam, rather a shady bar if I remember aright, about two or three years ago. We got talking about shipping, moving goods up the coast, and so on and so on, and he sounded me out on a proposition that did not appear too healthy to me. If I remember, it had something to do with moving goods by a small boat from Dar es Salaam to one of the less conspicuous ports, something to do with defrauding the customs. . . . But I need not go into the details. Needless to say I did not follow it up, and that was all I saw of Mr Shane-Hamilton. I am sorry I can give you no more information about the man, but no doubt you have other sources. . . .'

'You will have gathered as much last night.'

Schmidt gave a little exclamation of disgust. 'Ah, now you think I was being tactless! That was not my meaning at all. Your wife knew Shane-Hamilton – good. But being the charming person she is, I am quite sure she knew nothing of shady deals to bilk the customs, or whatever else the young gentleman got up to.'

A little trickle of moisture was running down the outside of Geoffrey's glass. He followed it with one finger. 'No. I have heard some other things that bear out what you say, though. Chambers knew him in Nairobi.'

'Ah yes. Extraordinary how everyone knows everyone else in this part of the world. Well, I have put my side of the case to you, Hallden, and that is all I can do.'

Geoffrey smiled and stood up. 'And I have listened to it. That is all *I* can do. Thanks for the beer, Schmidt. It was very welcome.'

'It is a pleasure. But there is one other thing. I want you to do something for me, Hallden, if you will.'

'Certainly. If I can.'

'Do not look alarmed. It is not difficult. Today is my birthday, you know. I am giving a small party tonight at the club. I would be delighted if you and your wife would come.'

Whatever Geoffrey had expected, it was not this.

'Thank you. That is very good of you. But I don't think it will be possible.' ('God, no! Not the club – after last night!') 'The baby, you know . . .'

Schmidt's eyes wrinkled up in friendly amusement. 'I thought you would refuse, but let me ask you to think again. It will be quite a small dinner-party. The little group we were with last night, but including Mr Chambers, who I understand is quite recovered from his illness.'

Geoffrey started to refuse again, more firmly, but Schmidt stopped him. 'Listen, my friend,' he said, 'I think it will do both you and your wife good to come. I should really have given the invitation to her in person, but anyway, do me a favour, ask your wife, and if she says you cannot come, I will accept it. But I think it would be interesting, and, as I say, good for you.'

Geoffrey had to agree, though he was quite persuaded that Mary would refuse equally emphatically to return to the club after last night, particularly as Pauline Chambers was to be one of the party. He realised that Schmidt had the idea they would be better to face it out right away, but he did not think either he or Mary could enter the club until the Shane-Hamilton affair was settled and the gossip and speculation had a chance to die down.

12

GEOFFREY got back to the Boma, very hot and tired, to find Derek Shotter in his office with a microscope and a small collection of bullets.

'I say, Geoff,' he began without preliminary, 'this is more difficult than it sounds. According to all the books you examine the sample bullets beside the original under a microscope, and can see at a glance which is the right one. I can't seem to get it to work.'

Geoffrey leaned over to have a look. 'You never will with that instrument. Where did you get it?'

'I got Tom to send it up from his lab. Phew!' He wiped sweat off his brow. 'That was a lousy job you gave me! William sent one of his dimmest askaris and we've been most of the morning digging bullets out of that sand bunker at the back of the Boma, right in the blazing sun.'

Geoffrey grunted. While Derek was talking he had taken a magnifying glass out of a drawer and was studying the labelled bullets one at a time through it.

'Well, I'm not an expert,' he said at last, 'but it looks to me as if none of these have markings anything like the one out of the body. We'll let William have a look at them and then keep them for the C.I.D., but I think we can take it that we've drawn a blank.'

'All that sweat for nothing! Oh well, it's what I expected. I mean, no one would be ass enough to shoot a man and then keep the gun handy for the police to collect.'

'No. I expect there are several .22s around that never got licensed. And it's on the cards that Shane-Hamilton was carrying one himself and somebody used it against him. . . .'

He did not mention the other gun – the one that was missing from his own house. That was something that could be thought about later.

At about the time Geoffrey reached the Boma Mary was driving down to the main street of the town and edging the car into a space in front of Messrs Efficiency Stores. It would have been much simpler to telephone her order or send a note down with one of the servants, but she had decided she must make the trip in person. If she once let herself be frightened into staying at home by the thought of what people might be thinking and saying in Kilimani, she felt she might as well give up altogether. So she had changed into a fresh cotton frock and given a little extra care to her face and hair, and it was with an outward air of calm assurance that she walked into the cool interior of the shop.

Efficiency Stores was almost indistinguishable from the half dozen other Asian-owned grocers and general stores that battled for Kilimani's trade along the central street of the town: a rather gloomy interior, shaded from the sun by the roofed colonnade over the street outside, and packed with goods of all kinds from floor to ceiling. She made her way through the glass-topped display stands to the long counter at the back and sat down on one of the high stools, glancing quickly round her. She had known that Sunday morning would be one of the worst times to come, as most of the memsahibs did their shopping then, but with a sinking heart she saw that the shop was even more crowded than she had expected. She nodded to the Greek woman next to her, who was disputing fiercely with one of the assistants, then said a polite 'good morning' to two women seated further down the counter, drinking Coca-Colas and smoking. The Greek woman was too busy to notice her, but the other two, she realised, had already stopped talking to watch her come in. Mrs Jillson, the stout one, wife of an insurance agent, gave an effusive, 'Hullo, dear. How are you?' and Mrs Beynon, the thin one, a bank clerk's wife, smiled meagrely and turned back to her drink. Both of them had been at the club last night.

Mary turned with relief as the proprietor of the store himself came forward, waved away one of the young Indian assistants, and prepared to take her order.

'It is a pleasure to see you, Mrs Hallden,' the elderly Hindu assured her, beaming. 'And how is the district commissioner? And the little girl? You will have a drink? A cigarette?'

He accepted Mary's refusal unwillingly, but at last was resigned to licking his pencil and preparing to take her instructions. As they worked through the list each item was shouted out in Swahili and one of the Africans lounging around the back quarters fetched the goods and packed them into a large box on the counter. Automatically Mary discussed the merits of rival brands, deplored the shortages of goods that usually came by road, and examined the various new items the shopkeeper wanted her to try. The list was nearly finished when they came to a brand of baby powder Mary wanted for Lois, but which was temporarily out of stock. She said it did not matter, another brand would do, but the Indian was an enthusiast at his work, and that was not good enough. One of the young lads serving behind the counter was despatched immediately to a rival store down the road to buy what she wanted. While they were waiting Mary accepted a cigarette and pretended to concentrate on a display of packaged soup on the counter in front of her.

She could sense the approaching bulk at her back before the cosy voice greeted her.

'Finished the shopping, dear? That's right.' Mrs Jillson eased her stout hips on to the stool at Mary's side. 'And how is the baby, dear?'

'Very well, thank you.'

'Cut any teeth yet?'

'Not yet. She's a little young.'

'Mine all started theirs at two months. But there, as I always say, they can't all be forward. You're looking a bit tired, dear. Not overdoing it, I hope?'

Mary met the sharp gaze of the eyes in the chubby, smiling face. 'I've had some disturbed nights with Lois,' she said. 'That's all.'

Mrs Jillson smiled. 'I thought when I saw you at the club last night, I said to myself, she'll be overdoing it a bit, going out to parties with a young baby to care for . . .'

'I've got quite a good ayah . . .'

'Well, of course, I always say you can't trust these African women too far. Just savages, after all, aren't they? We can't expect too much from them. But there, you're not a real gadding type like some I could mention – that Mrs Chambers, for instance. Always at the club, drinking with the young men, and not even her husband with her last night . . .'

'He was ill,' Mary broke in, hoping to check the flow.

'No doubt, dear. But it's not quite the thing. You can't be too careful in a little place like this. People do talk so. Quite shocking, I call it.'

Mary tried to interrupt again, but Mrs Jillson had something to say and nothing was going to stop her saying it. She leant forward, her motherly bosom nearly touching Mary's shoulder.

'There's a lot of talk about, dear. I think you ought to know. Of course, those of us who are your friends would never hear a word against you, as I was saying just now to Mrs Beynon . . .'

Mary looked desperately round. The proprietor was serving another customer, and there was no sign of the youth who had gone to fetch her powder.

I don't think . . .' she began weakly.

Then a hand reached over her shoulder and selected one of the packets of soup.

'Which do you recommend, Mrs Hallden?' a deep voice said in her ear. 'Mushroom? Asparagus?'

Mary had jumped, then swung round in relief. 'Mr Schmidt! I didn't expect to see you here!'

Schmidt laughed. 'I have to eat, even if I am only a solitary bachelor!' He turned to Mary's neighbour. 'Ah! Mrs Jillson! What a pleasure to see you!' He placed a hand on her plump shoulder. 'Now I am sure you are the best person to advise me. What are your views on soup?'

Mrs Jillson coloured unbecomingly and edged away from the hand on her shoulder. Schmidt was a foreigner, and therefore suspect, and she had heard all about the doubtful ménage down by the jetty. 'I was just going,' she said hurriedly. 'I must get home for my man's lunch. Good-bye, dear. Remember me to your husband.'

'Good-bye,' Mary said.

There was silence for a moment.

'Thank you,' Mary murmured at last.

'Not at all. I would want to rescue anyone from that female. She looked as if she was afraid I was going to make what I am sure she would call "improper advances" – did you notice?' Schmidt's hearty laugh echoed round the shop. Mary found herself joining in.

'I loathe the woman,' she admitted. 'I know I oughtn't to. I'm sure she means to be kind, and she's a most respectable female . . .'

Schmidt chuckled. 'Even you don't manage to make that sound much of a compliment. But tell me, are you coming to my party tonight?'

'A party? Why, I didn't know . . .'

'You have not seen your husband, then? He came to have a drink with me this morning, and I told him I was giving a little party at the club tonight – for my birthday, you know.'

'Oh, many happy returns – if it *is* your birthday.'

'Well, at my age, you know, a birthday is a movable feast. But tell me, you are coming?'

'I should like to.' Mary hesitated. 'Did Geoffrey accept for us?'

'No. He did not seem to think much of the idea, to tell you the truth. But I told him to talk to you first, and then let me know. I hope I can rely on you to persuade him.'

Mary stubbed out her cigarette. 'Who else is to be in the party?'

'Just a small gathering. The Chambers, Shotter and Griffith.'

'Oh.' Mary hesitated again, then decided to be frank. 'I expect Geoffrey is afraid things may be awkward at the club. But I think we should go. Thank you for suggesting it.'

Schmidt looked at her shrewdly. 'You have a good deal of courage, my dear lady. And so has your husband – but of a different kind. You persuade him, won't you? I think he will find it interesting when he gets there.'

The Indian shop assistant had arrived at last, breathless, with the right brand of powder. An African shouldered the box of provisions and they moved out into the blazing heat of the road.

'Didn't you want to buy anything?' Mary asked Schmidt.

'I can go back in a moment. Let me help you.'

His own car was parked behind Mary's, and as she passed it she glanced into the back. A still figure was seated there, the face half hidden in the bright *kanga* draped over the head, but Mary had the idea that the woman was watching them.

Schmidt unlocked the car door for her, saw the box of goods securely placed, and tossed the African a couple of coins. Then he paused, holding the door open and looking down at Mary.

'Don't let it distress you, Mrs Hallden,' he said quietly. 'You have a lot to contend with, eh? This business is worrying, your husband is upset over it . . . and you must be sorrowing for your friend, too.'

'For Patrick?' Mary looked up, startled. 'No. No, to be honest, I can't say I am grieving for him. Except perhaps, for a moment, at the funeral yesterday, where it seemed a dreadful thing for him to have died, and in such a way. He was still young, and so much of his life was wasted. . . . But, you see, Patrick and I hadn't been . . . friends for a long time. In the end I grew to dislike him, and, this last time, almost to hate him. He wasn't a very noble character, you know. I . . . I was almost glad when I heard he was dead.'

'Then you did see him?'

'Here?' Mary met his eyes, narrowed against the sunlight. 'I suppose there is no harm in telling you. Yes, he rang up from Ismael's *duka* and came to see me.'

'Ah. That is interesting.' Schmidt rubbed one square hand over his chin. 'Forgive me if I seem to be meddling in a matter that is none of my concern, Mrs Hallden. You know Shane-Hamilton rang me as well, and I have a considerable curiosity to know why he wanted to see me. Your husband thinks he knows – that he came by arrangement to sell me some stolen diamonds. . . .'

'He said they were mineral samples . . .' Mary checked herself. 'I suppose I shouldn't be telling you all this.'

Schmidt shrugged. 'I am not a gossip, Mrs Hallden. You know that. You did not actually see these . . . mineral samples?'

'No. I am sorry, Mr Schmidt, but I mustn't say any more. Geoffrey will probably be angry with me for telling you so much.'

'Then don't tell him, my dear lady. Never invite unnecessary trouble, especially with husbands, eh?'

She slipped into the driving seat of the car and he closed the door for her and leaned in at the window. In the shade of the car his eyes were wide open now, and it struck her what a curiously cold grey they were.

'But don't forget, Mrs Hallden. You probably know more about what brought Shane-Hamilton to Kilimani than anyone . . . and that knowledge might be dangerous.'

Geoffrey reached home feeling tired and discouraged. The idea of going to any party that night was thoroughly distasteful to him, and he was astonished when Mary insisted that they must go to Schmidt's gathering at the club.

'Willy Schmidt is quite right, and I am grateful to him for giving us this chance. Don't you see, Geoffrey, if we stay away everyone will think the worst? I won't cower in our house, refusing to see or speak to anyone in case they are thinking things about me! We've got to go; and if it is with the same crowd it will make people wonder if perhaps the gossip is true after all. I'm damned if I will let Pauline frighten me away!'

'And have her creating another scene?' Geoffrey demanded, losing his temper. 'Dragging out some more of your past in public and then saying she is sorry but she thought I knew?'

Mary went white and her eyes darkened with anger. 'There isn't any more that you don't know, but I suppose it is no use my telling you that. I know I have made a mess of things, Geoffrey, for you as well as for myself, but going round saying "I'm sorry, I'm sorry" and apologising to people for my mere existence isn't going to help. We've got to face people now, together, whatever we may feel, if we and Lois are to have any future in Kilimani, or anywhere else in Tanganyika – that is, if you think there is a future for us?'

Her voice broke a little at the end, and Geoffrey answered more quietly.

'Even if all that is true, how can I in my position go publicly as the guest of someone I know is mixed up in this business?'

'In your position! That's all you think about. What do you think you are, God in Kilimani?' As he started to interrupt she swept on. 'Oh, I know you are the representative of the Queen, the voice of authority, the cock of this little dunghill – but can't you forget it sometimes? Can't you be a human being as well as a district commissioner? But if it is your job you are thinking about, you had still better go tonight. Think of all the clues you may pick up from Willy Schmidt! He's not just throwing this party for our sakes!'

'He's probably just fishing for information. He had one go at me, and a more successful go at you. . . .'

'Well, what did I tell him that could do any harm?'

'I don't know. That's just the devil of it! I don't know how far he is mixed up in this business or what he is really after. It may be the diamonds. If he knows you saw Shane-Hamilton he probably thinks you've got them.'

'I more or less told him I hadn't . . .'

'That's just it! Can't you realise that Schmidt is on the other side in this? We can't go on acting as if he was simply a pleasant social acquaintance.'

The argument went on with both of them goaded into saying more and more hurtful things, and each refusing to give an inch to the other. In the end Mary settled it by saying she would go alone if he still refused.

'And that would really give the club something to talk about!'

13

'MY DEAR, you look tired,' was Pauline's greeting to Mary. 'Should you have come?'

Mary was tired. Her face was stiff from smiling to all the people sitting on the veranda, and trying to look relaxed and normal. But she merely smiled at Pauline and raised her eyebrows, knowing that would annoy her more than anything she could say, then turned to greet her host.

The group was settled at the bar almost as it had been the night before, but otherwise this party bore no resemblance to the other. They were all quite sober and rather subdued, and if it had not been for the host there might have been an uncomfortable silence. Perhaps Dudley Chambers' presence acted as a damper. He was standing at the end of the bar, a little apart from the others, and greeted Mary and Geoffrey warmly, as if their arrival was a relief to him.

'Well, we are all here,' Schmidt said, beaming round at the ill-matched group as if he could not imagine a more ideal gathering. 'There is only one thing wrong – too many men. For a real party I should have asked two – no, perhaps one – more woman, don't you agree?'

'Nonsense,' Pauline asserted. 'I can easily cope with three men, and Mary at any rate with two.'

'Which two will you spare me?' Mary asked. Without waiting for an answer she moved forward between Dudley and Derek. 'Will that do?'

Pauline patted the stool at her side. 'Here you are, Geoff. You see she has given you up to me.'

Geoffrey had given the others the barest of greetings. The row between Mary and him had flared up again just before they left home. It had started over a missing button on his shirt, but had gone on to comprehend all the grievances of the morning's argument and a number of new ones. As a result they were late, and he felt exhausted physically and emotionally. He had not even the energy to resist Pauline's invitation, and there was a certain satisfaction in knowing his acceptance would annoy his wife. He took the empty stool and applied himself to the glass Schmidt set beside him.

The drink helped a little. He could even get a wry amusement from watching the others trying to behave like a normal social gathering. Derek Shotter was talking earnestly to Mary, keeping his back half turned to Pauline, but it was obvious that he was acutely conscious of every word or movement Pauline made. Tom Griffith was looking more sombre than ever and barely raising his eyes from his glass to respond to the efforts Willy Schmidt was making to draw him into the conversation. Dudley seemed more relaxed now and was joining in the talk with Mary and Derek. He became almost animated on the two subjects of his illness and the rains. Pauline was unusually silent, for which Geoffrey was grateful. She was smoking one cigarette after another, and whenever she thought she was unobserved her eyes would stray past Geoffrey to where Schmidt and Tom Griffith were standing.

The group were at one end of the bar, and although the club was fairly crowded, an empty space lay between them and the other members. It was, Geoffrey thought, typical of the atmosphere of the place that night. Everyone had hastened to greet Mary and himself as if to prove that all was normal, but no one had made any effort to talk to them, and as they passed through the veranda to the bar a moment of silence had followed them. But now they were settled with their party speculation could have free rein. Bates of the public works department was drinking with the Beynons and another bank clerk and his wife at the bar beside them.

Every now and again they would shoot sidelong glances at Willy Schmidt's party. The men looked carefully unconcerned if they caught anyone's eye, but the women were less cautious. Mrs Beynon stared openly at Mary, then at Geoffrey, and whispered earnestly to her neighbour.

'To hell with them!' he said to himself, and took another drain at his glass.

The only person who seemed to be enjoying the evening was Schmidt, who talked and smiled as if this was indeed just a birthday party, and kept the glasses replenished like a good host. What the devil was he at? Geoffrey thought, watching the German's bland brown face. He was making a special effort with Tom Griffith, whom he had never noticed much before, but moved round regularly among the others, dispensing drinks, cigarettes and charm. And gradually, under the triple influence, the party began to thaw a little.

It was not until they moved out to the veranda for dinner that the talk turned to the murder. Willy Schmidt had reserved a large table at one end, overlooking the sea and cut off from most of the other diners. It was a relief to get away from the crowded bar and the feeling that all the other people in it had one eye and one ear spare from their own conversation to note what went on in the Schmidt party.

There was some confusion at first. The heavy rain earlier in the day had brought out a swarm of flying ants, who hurled themselves in waves at the lights on the unscreened veranda, fluttering into drinks, shedding their wings in the food, and crawling round the necks and hair of the guests. Pauline screamed as the first ant fluttered into her face then crawled down her bare shoulder.

'Loathsome things! Take it off me, someone!'

Dudley leapt obediently to his feet, but Derek Shotter, who was sitting next to her, got there first, and flipped the insect off her with his napkin. He caught her earring a glancing blow at the same time and she turned on him sharply.

'You clumsy idiot! Do be more careful.'

Derek flushed and drew back as if she had struck him.

There was an uncomfortable silence for a moment. Schmidt broke it by calling for the Goan steward.

'Can't you do something about this, D'Souza?'

'I am sorry, sir. It is always the same early in the rains. Perhaps if we put the lights on outside?'

'We'll try it. At this rate we shall not eat much but ants for our dinner.'

There was an outside dance floor of concrete, used occasionally in the very hot weather, and the strings of light bulbs that illuminated it were turned on and the lights on the veranda extinguished. The result was a little gloomy, the diners eating mainly by the glow from the bar inside, but at least the ants diminished in number, and there was a certain intimacy now about the party gathered round the oval table.

Schmidt had put Mary on his right and Derek on his left, with Pauline between him and Geoffrey. Tom Griffith sat next to Mary, and Dudley was between him and the D.C. It was quite a tactful arrangement for a difficult party, Geoffrey thought.

As the wine circulated — and it was an excellent vintage supplied by Schmidt himself — the party warmed up a little. Tom Griffith was still rather silent and drinking a good deal, but Mary occasionally got a few words out of him. Dudley became quite jovial, and Pauline, as if to make amends for her rudeness to Derek, was very animated and divided her attention among Schmidt, Derek and Geoffrey. To any outside observer it might indeed have been merely a birthday celebration by a group of close friends.

When they had finished eating and were sitting back with their wine Geoffrey roused himself to propose Schmidt's health and to wish him many more active and happy years. The German bowed deeply in reply.

'We none of us can tell what the future will bring with our next birthday, especially an old man like me. But to all of you, my guests, let me wish you all the happiness you deserve.'

He raised his glass with a flourish and drank to them.

'Now that was not a very friendly wish, Willy,' protested Pauline, who had been doing justice to the wine.

'No indeed,' Geoffrey agreed. 'Let us have a little more than we deserve, for heaven's sake – all of us, including you, Schmidt.'

Schmidt gave a mischievous look. 'Perhaps you have something there! You mean I might be wishing one of us a happy birthday in jail next year, eh?'

There was silence, then Derek giggled uncertainly. 'Oh, I say, that's a cheerful thought, I must say!'

Schmidt waved his glass blandly. 'I assure you I have no intention of celebrating my next birthday at Her Majesty's expense. But *I* have an alibi. What does our Shakespeare say? "Let the galled jade wince . . ." eh?'

His quick grey eyes moved round the faces of his guests and fixed on Geoffrey. 'You and I, Hallden, our withers are unwrung.'

'Nonsense!' Pauline cried. 'I expect we all have an alibi . . . or–' with a glance at Mary '– most of us, anyway. I know I have. I was at home.'

'How do you propose to prove it?' Tom Griffith asked, looking directly at Pauline for the first time that evening.

'I say now,' Dudley protested. 'Don't you think . . . ?' He looked appealingly at Geoffrey.

But his intervention was all that was needed to make Pauline determined to pursue the subject.

'Of course I can prove it,' she said angrily. 'I was at home all evening. The houseboy will know. And you, Dudley, you found me there when you came in about nine.'

'And where was Dudley?' Schmidt interposed.

Pauline shrugged. 'Oh, out looking after his precious pawpaws.'

Dudley looked uncomfortable. 'I went up to see if the walls of the dam were holding. All this rain up-country was coming down the stream and there was a weak section I meant to have built up. My foreman and I patched it up.'

'Good. He has a witness.' Schmidt turned to Derek and fixed him with a stern eye. 'And how about you, Shotter? Have you got a witness?'

Derek giggled, then glanced uncertainly at Geoffrey. 'Well, no, as a matter of fact. Tom was out, and our boy as usual had sneaked off before I got back from the club about seven-thirty. I had some food and then I developed photographs till about nine. You were in then, Tom, weren't you?'

'Yes, if it is anyone else's business,' Griffith said in a surly tone.

'Oh, come!' Willy Schmidt laughed. 'This is all quite light-hearted among friends. You don't object to telling where you were?'

'Tom objects to everything on principle,' Pauline cried. 'Don't pay any attention to him!'

'If I were asked in the proper manner by the proper authority I would be quite ready to say where I was,' Griffith retorted.

'Come now, suppose we change the subject,' Dudley Chambers put in hastily. 'This is just a friendly . . .'

'Friendly!' Tom's anger now turned on the older man. 'A fine lot of friends!'

'Oh, shut up, Tom!' Pauline broke in. 'Stop behaving like a child!'

Griffith flung round on her with such a furious look on his face that she drew back as if expecting a blow. 'Keep out of this, you double-crossing cheat! I've taken enough from you!'

He got clumsily to his feet. 'I'm going . . . and I am not

saying thank you for a nice party either, Schmidt!'

He tried to make his exit with dignity, but he was not too steady on his legs. His jacket was rucked up at the back and his hair on end where he had run a hand through it. He looked very young as he stumbled for the door, and Geoffrey felt a twinge of pity for him. Schmidt got up quickly and went after Griffith and they could see him trying to reason with the furious young man.

Dudley had made an irresolute move to get up and go after them, and Geoffrey caught his wrist.

'Don't, Dudley. Leave him alone.'

Dudley sat down, not too unwillingly. He cleared his throat as if he was going to say something, but instead looked helplessly at his wife and remained silent.

'The idiot!' Pauline said through her teeth. 'What an exhibition!' Her hands were shaking as she picked up her glass.

Schmidt came back alone, shrugging his shoulders expressively. 'I suppose making a fool of oneself is sometimes the beginning of wisdom,' he said coolly. 'He is young. He will grow out of it. In the meantime, let us talk of something calming, eh?'

'You haven't asked for my alibi yet,' Mary said.

Schmidt smiled at her. 'I don't need to. You were at home all evening, weren't you? But enough of this game. Let us talk of – what? Shall we tell sad stories of the death of kings, eh?'

He did not wait for Mary to reply but leant forward to refill the wine glasses.

Griffith's departure had shattered the precarious ease of the dinner party, and soon they all moved back to the bar where they could separate into twos and threes as they chose. Mary and Geoffrey were at opposite ends of the group, by common consent. Pauline had again insisted that Geoffrey stay next to her, and was exerting herself to be entertaining. Tom Griffith's going seemed to have released her from the strain she had been under earlier in the evening. She could be amusing in a malicious way, and was making Geoffrey and Willy Schmidt laugh by her scandalous stories of some of the other club members. This chimed in exactly with Geoffrey's mood. He had drunk enough to soften the edge of his own troubles and was beginning to think it was not such a bad party after all.

Once or twice Mary tried to catch his eye, but he refused to respond. At last she broke off her conversation with Dudley Chambers and came over to the group.

'I must go and feed Lois, Geoffrey,' she said. 'I am sorry to break up the party.'

Geoffrey raised his brandy glass to show that it was still half full. 'In a moment,' he said, not too graciously.

'But Geoff!' Pauline protested. 'You don't have to feed the blessed baby! And I'm sure Mary wouldn't be so selfish as to want to drag you away just when you were enjoying yourself for once! Dudley can see her home.'

Dudley got up with his usual punctilious politeness. 'Of course, my dear, if you are ready to leave.'

'Oh, I don't want to go yet, but you know what you are over late nights. . . . With three strong men here someone can see me home. You needn't worry.'

'There's no need for anyone to come,' Mary said, not looking at her husband. 'I can drive myself home, and one of you can drop Geoffrey when he is ready.' She sounded perfectly calm but, knowing her as he did, Geoffrey could sense that her quick temper was simmering underneath.

'Wait just a moment, Mary, until I finish my drink,' he repeated. 'I'm sure Lois can last another ten minutes.'

'But really, my dear chap,' Dudley put in, 'I should be delighted to see Mary home. Pleasant as this has been, I am still a bit of an invalid, you know, and not so young – eh, Schmidt?'

Willy Schmidt just raised his eyebrows and smiled.

Mary looked from her husband to Dudley, then took the latter's arm. 'Thank you, Dudley. You are very kind. I don't want to drag you away, Geoffrey, if you are enjoying yourself. I'll see you later. Good night, Mr Schmidt. Thank you for the unexpected and very pleasant party.'

Schmidt accompanied them to the door, and Geoffrey watched with grudging admiration the way Mary walked out between the two men, smiling and calling good night to the people she knew as if there was nothing on her mind but the ending of an enjoyable evening.

Pauline made a little face at her husband's retreating back, then turned to the others.

'Well, now we can be cosy. Come on, Derek. Come up and join the fly-by-nights! And for goodness sake let's all have another drink and cheer up.'

They did, after a fashion. They drank a good deal of brandy and talked and laughed – though what about Geoffrey could not afterwards clearly remember. Gradually the other members drifted out. Bates and his party were the last to leave the bar, all a little mellowed from their session there. He paused on his way out to put an affectionate hand on Pauline's shoulder.

'Enjoying yourself, lass? Husband gone home and three lonely men to keep you company . . . I've half a mind to stay and make the fourth!'

'You haven't been invited,' Pauline said coldly.

There was a moment's silence as the stocky young P.W.D. lad took that in. Then Mrs Beynon tugged his sleeve.

'Come on, Fred,' she urged. 'I think you had better keep out of that company.'

Her face was sharp with malice and annoyance, and Geoffrey could feel Pauline draw in her breath to retaliate. Quickly he laid a hand on her wrist.

'Won't you join us for a drink before you go?' he said pleasantly. 'All of you?'

Bates reddened and shuffled his feet. 'Thanks, but we must be off. I didn't mean to butt in. Good night, all.'

Pauline turned back to the bar.

'Not one of my better efforts, Mr Bates,' she said lightly. 'Thank heavens they've gone! Come on, let's put the radiogram on and dance. We've done enough talking for one evening.'

Pauline had a weakness for sentimental records with a lot of string accompaniment, and the familiar tunes wafted pleasantly in from the veranda. They danced with her in turn, the two spare men talking over drinks in the bar where the quiet Goan steward waited patiently for orders, yawning occasionally behind his hand. The music drowned the background noises of the African night, the continuous chirping of insects and the occasional loud croak of a bullfrog, and the little bar with its rows of brightly coloured bottles and faded advertisements might have been anywhere, Geoffrey thought – somewhere in England, perhaps, blessedly far from Kilimani.

While Derek and Pauline were dancing he talked to Schmidt.

'You know, Willy,' he said, 'I don't believe you are half so bad a chap as you like to make out.'

Schmidt grinned. 'You think I draw the line somewhere, eh?'

'Yes.' Geoffrey considered the problem seriously. 'I don't think you are a very ethical business man, mind you, but I think you would draw lines at . . . well, let me see . . .'

'Murder?' Schmidt knocked the ash carefully off the small cheroot he was smoking.

The word was like a cold breath of air through the comfortable mist of alcohol enveloping Geoffrey.

'Murder?' he repeated. 'Must we talk about murder? No. No. I don't really think you are a murderer. . . .'

'And yet, according to your law I would probably be called one,' Schmidt said coolly. 'Oh no! Not your precious corpse in the Land-Rover! I assure you *I* had no reason to want him dead. No, you must look there for someone who hasn't got an alibi like me. . . .'

'Then . . .'

'Not in your jurisdiction, my dear D.C. Not even under your Government, so you do not need to trouble that active conscience of yours. And mine is quiet enough. It was a necessary killing. I have no ghost . . . "blood-boltered Banquo", eh? . . . to sit at my feasts!'

'That still leaves the other nine commandments,' Geoffrey insisted. 'And, to be honest with you, my dear old German friend, I wouldn't be surprised at your breaking any of them, in a . . . gentlemanly sort of way.'

Schmidt laughed with genuine amusement. 'Thank you for the qualification, at any rate! No, if I want a thing I can usually get it. It is simply a matter of making up your mind what you want . . .'

'And not letting a little matter of ethics interfere . . .'

'Good heavens!' Pauline's voice broke in behind them. 'What nasty long words you men use! Move over, Geoff, and let's talk about something gay.'

Later Geoffrey danced with Pauline. She danced so well that she made him feel, poor dancer as he was, that he was rather good himself, and they came off the floor laughing together. He was a little piqued when Pauline dropped his arm immediately and pulled Willy Schmidt to his feet for the next record, which was a waltz. He and Derek were left feeling rather flat, watching the two revolving slowly on the empty floor. There was a sort of intimacy in the way they danced, not laughing together, but talking quietly occasionally. Geoffrey wondered as he watched them whether Pauline was one of the things Schmidt wanted, and if so, whether he would succeed in getting her. Derek was sitting in silence, chewing on his moustache absently as his eyes followed the dancers.

Geoffrey wondered about Derek. He had said so often and so firmly that he was finished with Pauline, but the little incident at dinner had shown how much power she still had to hurt him. He was young even for his years, and at that age a passion for an older woman died hard. What would happen, Geoffrey asked himself, if Pauline was finished with Tom Griffith and crooked a finger to Derek again? Would he come running?

Derek turned suddenly and caught the D.C.'s glance. He smiled rather ruefully.

'Pauline does dance awfully well,' he said, as if it was an apology. 'Doesn't she?'

'Yes. Exceptionally well.'

'Well, I think she's been dancing long enough with the old man.' Derek got up with a determined air. 'I'm going to cut in.'

With some amusement Geoffrey watched the little pantomime on the veranda. Pauline and Schmidt were so deep in talk that at first they did not notice Derek hovering behind them. When at last he plucked up courage to touch Schmidt on the shoulder Pauline turned petulantly on him, and it looked as if he was going to have to apologise and retreat. But Schmidt simply laughed and shrugged, pushed Pauline towards the younger man and strolled back, smiling, to the bar.

'I have been put in my place, Hallden,' he said. 'Let us console ourselves with pleasures more suited to our advanced years. Steward! More drinks.'

When the last record was finished the steward began to switch out the lights in the rest of the building and stood waiting politely for them to take the hint.

'Lord, it's after one!' Pauline exclaimed, with a wide cat's yawn. 'I suppose we shall have to go.'

'I fear so,' Schmidt replied. 'If you like to get your wrap, Pauline, I will take you home.'

She gave him a little intimate glance under her lashes. 'Well, do you know, Willy, I don't think you had better. Dudley will probably be cross with me anyway, coming back at this hour, and if he hears your Volkswagen . . . No, I think I had better go with the old married man here,' and she took Geoffrey's arm with a laughing look. 'Dudley would never suspect *him* of putting a foot wrong!'

Geoffrey was not at all sure he was flattered at her reason, but he agreed politely enough.

'But Mary will be expecting you, Geoff,' Derek put in suddenly. 'I'll see Pauline home. It's almost on my way, really.'

'It's no trouble,' Geoffrey insisted, suddenly deciding that he wanted to take Pauline home. As Derek started to protest he added, 'You heard what Pauline said. You go straight home like a good boy.'

Derek flushed at his tone and looked at Pauline. She only shrugged. 'Run along, dear, when the man tells you. It's getting late.'

14

'YOU DON'T MIND taking me home, Geoff?' Pauline asked a little later, curled up in Mary's place beside him. 'I didn't want to be rude to Willy – he's rather a pet, isn't he? – but I'm not sure I altogether trust him on his own. And of course, Derek . . . well, I have to be polite to him in public, but he has been rather a bore. . . .' She yawned again. 'I've enjoyed this evening. Such fun to be gay for a change! You know, I don't think I am cut out to be a farmer's wife, do you, Geoff?' and she gave him a provocative look from the corner of her eyes.

'No. I wouldn't say you were exactly in your element . . .' Geoffrey replied cautiously.

'You think I am a bit of a so-and-so, don't you? I'm sure you feel I ought to settle down to being a good wife to Dudley – but, oh dear!' She sighed. 'I try, and then it gets so dull I nearly go mad. No gaiety, no money, no new clothes, no fun . . . I suppose I am just a frivolous creature. I should never really have married. . . .'

'Not Dudley, anyway.'

'No.' She sighed again. 'When I married Dudley I thought all I wanted was to be safe . . . have someone to look after me and be proud of me. And of course Dudley was just out of the army then, a Colonel . . . It all sounded rather glamorous. But it didn't work out that way.' There was genuine feeling in her voice, and Geoffrey thought that perhaps, just this once, he was hearing the real Pauline.

She sat, relaxed, looking through the windscreen at the headlights cutting out a swathe of rutted road with bush on either side. Then, after a moment, she turned towards him again.

'Geoff, I asked you to bring me home for a special reason – not that I didn't want you to anyway, but I did need to talk to you, just on our own. You're the only person I can turn to now. You see, I want your advice. I am worried, and just a bit frightened.'

'About what, Pauline?'

'It's Tom.' The words began to come now in a rush. 'He worries me stiff, Geoff. He's been so odd lately, since . . . since the murder. That night we came round to your house, the night Patrick was found, he was awfully broody and quiet, but I didn't think much about it. He's temperamental, you know, and goes into moods for no reason at all. Then, the next morning, I . . . I called round to see him. I expect you realised I had been there, didn't you? I asked him what was the matter, but he wouldn't say – just talked a lot of nonsense about my being dishonest with him and ruining his life, and how he was going to get away from the whole set-up and start somewhere else. I told him not to be stupid, but it didn't do any good. Then the phone rang. I could see, watching him, that something was really wrong. He told me about your finding the bullet and he said, "Well, that's that. They can't just write it off as an African killing now." And then he told me I had better get out quick and not come back or try to see him again. Afterwards I came round to your place to find out what was going on. I was so upset . . . That's why I was silly when you jumped on me, about my saying the man had been shot. . . .'

'You saw him again at the club that night.'

'Yes, I know. He was in the bar when I got there, and I thought it would just make talk if I didn't speak to him. And besides, there was no one else amusing. . . .'

Geoffrey braked the car and slid gently over to the side of the road. They were outside the town now, between Ismael's store and the turning to the Chambers house. He switched off the engine and immediately all the night around them sprang into life – the churring of the cicadas and the little musical chinking of the frogs in the rainwater pools beside the road. In the faint glow of the side lights the silhouettes of trees and bushes took shape gradually against the sky.

'Now, let's get this straight,' Geoffrey said. 'Just what is it you are frightened of? You think Tom killed Patrick Shane-Hamilton?'

Pauline drew in her breath sharply. 'Oh, no! Not that! How could I think that? It's just . . . just that I feel he is mixed up in it somewhere . . . that he knows something and . . . Oh, I don't know. I just don't know.'

'You mean the idea is there, but you don't like to think about it, is that it? Did he know Shane-Hamilton?'

'No. No. I had talked about him a bit . . .'

'You think he may have run into him the night he came to Kilimani?'

'Well, he was out . . . and he acted so oddly when Willy questioned him . . .'

'But what motive would he have for killing Shane-Hamilton?'

'Perhaps . . . if he found out about the diamonds . . . He was awfully hard up, you know. And he had some ridiculous idea of our running away together. I said it was quite hopeless, but he may have thought, if he had all that money . . .'

'I see. Well, Pauline, if it is any help to you, I can tell you there is no real evidence against Griffith. Personally I think the one behind it all is Schmidt . . . but again I've precious little evidence. I admit Griffith has acted a bit oddly, and I had a feeling at the time that he knew about that bullet wound before I discovered it . . . but there could be a lot of reasons why he should behave as he did short of having murder on his conscience. We'll have to find out in a lot more detail where he was on Wednesday night, but at the moment I shouldn't worry. He's probably got a perfectly good alibi but was just playing difficult. He's an awkward sort of cuss. . . .'

Pauline gave a little sigh. 'Thank you, Geoff. You've taken a load off my mind. 'I'll try and be sensible and not worry about it. But this whole business . . . I was fond of Patrick, you know, and hearing he was dead has just . . . well, shattered me completely. And I can't even talk to Dudley about it.'

'No. I don't suppose you can,' Geoffrey said rather drily.

He reached out to switch on the ignition and Pauline put her hand quickly over his.

'Don't think too hardly of me, Geoff. I do value your good opinion, whatever I may do or say.'

The hand lay there, warm and soft, for just a moment, and he found the light touch sent a little shiver up his arm. He started the car in silence, and as it swung out on to the road again Pauline swayed a little closer to him. 'Lord, I'm tired,' she murmured, and with a small sigh her head slipped down on to his shoulder and she appeared to be falling asleep.

When they reached the Chambers farm he switched the headlights off and drew up gently so as not to disturb the household. As Pauline made no move he touched her cheek. She stirred and gave a little murmur, then her eyes opened and met his, very close. He was never quite sure who made the movement, but it was made, and he found himself with his arm around her and his mouth on hers. It was a long kiss. She clung, and it was he who had to break away.

'Just hold me a moment, Geoff. You're so comforting,' she whispered.

Geoffrey's head was swimming a little, with the wine and tiredness and Pauline's nearness. He left his arm around her and felt her move closer again until her lips were against his.

At last she stirred. 'I must go now,' she said. 'See me inside, Geoff. I hate going into the house by myself in the dark.'

He smiled. 'You are a baby, aren't you? Give me your key.'

They walked slowly round to the veranda steps, brushing against a flowering bush that released a shower of raindrops and a soft wave of perfume as they passed. The veranda was in darkness, but the living-room within was dimly lit. Geoffrey felt for the lock, but when he slipped the key in the door swung ajar.

'Dudley must have left it open,' Pauline whispered. 'How stupid! Anyone could get in.' He felt her shiver against his shoulder and slipped his arm round her again as they walked into the dark veranda towards the lighted room.

Pauline moved ahead of him through the door, and suddenly stopped with a little smothered scream.

'Dudley!'

Geoffrey saw him almost at the same moment. He was sitting in an armchair beside the reading lamp, the light illuminating the slack body, the head flung back, the mouth slightly open, the closed eyes. For a second he held his breath.

Then Dudley's lids flickered and he gave a smothered grunt and woke up.

'What is it? What . . . ? Oh, Pauline! And Geoffrey. Come in, come in. Sorry I dropped off, waiting . . .'

He got up, smoothing his ruffled hair and pulling his jacket straight.

'There was no need for you to wait up for me, Dudley,' Pauline said peevishly. 'You gave me an awful shock. We found the door open – and there you were, lying back looking . . . looking ghastly. I thought someone had murdered you at least.'

'Oh, I'm all right,' Dudley said. 'I didn't think the party would go on so late. I decided to wait up to see you when you got back. You see, something rather unpleasant has happened . . .'

Geoffrey found his voice. 'What is it? Not Mary?'

'No, no, my dear fellow. Mary's all right. It's Griffith.'

'*Tom?*' Pauline had gone suddenly pale.

'Yes. Poor fellow was burgled tonight. A couple of Africans attacked him with a *panga*.'

'He's not *dead*?'

'No. No.' Dudley glanced at his wife quickly, then looked away again. 'You don't need to worry,' he said stiffly. 'It's only a bad slash on the arm. His boy was waiting outside when Mary and I left the club. The police asked him to fetch her to dress the wound.'

'Where is she? Did you take her home afterwards?'

'Of course, my dear chap. We were only there half an hour.'

'Someone should have called me. I'd better go right away and see what it is all about.' Geoffrey turned to the door.

'We wanted to, but Griffith wouldn't have it, and as the police were there . . .' Dudley accompanied him to the door, still apologetic. 'Mary said it wasn't worth bothering you; she'd tell you all about it herself.'

'All right. Don't bother to come out, Dudley. Good night, Pauline.'

Pauline was standing by the table, a lighted cigarette in her hand, frowning into space. She looked up as he spoke. 'Good night.' Her eyes met Geoffrey's for a second, a puzzled, speculating look in them, then she smiled and said again in her warm, throaty voice, 'Good night, Geoff. Thanks for taking such good care of me.'

Geoffrey set off for home as fast as he dared, cursing the slippery mud on the road. The dream-like feeling that had come over him in the club, listening to the music and dancing with Pauline, had shattered abruptly when he had first seen Dudley. For one ghastly second he had, like Pauline, thought her husband was dead. And then it was just dear old Dudley, caught having a nap, worried and apologetic, and Pauline had slipped back into focus as Dudley's wife, the woman he had always disliked and mistrusted. But, he thought, with an unusual gleam of self-knowledge, did a man ever dislike an attractive woman if he was not at the same time drawn to her? What would have happened if Dudley had been in bed and asleep instead of sitting in the armchair waiting for them? He hoped he knew – but perhaps it was as well he had had no chance to find out.

Grimly he concentrated on holding the car on the road and getting home as quickly as he could. He hoped to heaven Mary was still awake. He needed to see her, to reassure himself that he had only been dreaming for a little while. And then there was this business of Tom Griffith and his burglary . . .

As he drove up to the house he saw with relief that the bedroom light was still on. He put the car in the garage as quietly as he could and let himself in by the garden door.

Mary was asleep, lying back on propped-up pillows with a paper-backed novel by her hand, her dark hair tumbled over her brow. She woke as Geoffrey came into the room, wide awake immediately, as she always was from years of hospital training.

'Geoffrey!' She glanced at the clock. 'Heavens, it's late! I tried to stay awake to tell you . . .'

'About Tom Griffith. Yes. I've just taken Pauline home and Dudley told me about it.'

He sat down on the edge of the bed and studied his wife's face gravely. Yes, it was all right. The dream was broken and he was back to normal. She was the same Mary, a little flushed from sleep, her hair in damp tendrils from the heat, and the only person in the world who really mattered to him.

She was a little disconcerted by the intent gaze. Her hand went up to push her hair back from her face.

'What's the matter? Do I look a sight?'

'No. You look very sweet. Tell me about Tom.'

She smiled, relaxing again. 'I'm sorry about tonight, Geoffrey. It is all right, isn't it?'

'Yes, darling. And don't start saying you are sorry. I've been mainly to blame. But it's long after two and we ought to get some sleep. Tell me about Tom.'

Mary told him.

She and Dudley had said good night to Willy Schmidt on the veranda and walked across the muddy drive towards the Chambers' little Morris. It had seemed very dark in spite of the chain of lights still burning on the dance floor, and they had both been startled when a dark figure suddenly loomed out of the shadow of the cars and came towards them.

It was an African in untidy shirt and shorts, and even in the bad light he looked vaguely familiar to Mary.

'What is it?' Dudley demanded in Swahili. 'You want me?'

'No, bwana. I was sent to find the Memsahib. The police said . . .'

'The police? What has happened?'

'The police are at Bwana Griffith's house. They sent me to fetch the Memsahib. The bwana has been hurt. There is much blood. The Memsahib is to come and look after his wounds.'

As he spoke Mary had recognised the slovenly boy who worked for Griffith and Shotter at the house they shared a few hundred yards away.

'We had better go quickly,' Mary said. 'Why didn't you come inside for me? Shall I take our car, Dudley?'

'No, no. Certainly not. I'll drive you.'

They all got into the Morris, the African in the back. Mary was pungently aware of the closeness of his unwashed body, the smell of stale sweat and old clothes.

'What on earth can have happened, Dudley?'

'We'll soon find out. It's no good asking this lout.'

It took only a moment to reach the house. All the lights were blazing and the front door stood wide open.

Mary slipped out as the car stopped and she was the first into the house. The front door led straight into the living-room, an untidy, ill-cared for place at the best of times, littered with papers and photographic equipment and junk from Griffith's boat: but tonight it was even worse than usual. The contents of desk, bookshelves, and cupboards had all been turned out and flung about the floor. In the midst of the chaos stood a good-looking young African dressed in a neat shirt and well-pressed brown linen trousers.

'Good evening, madam,' he said in careful English.

'Good evening. Are you the police?'

Dudley had come in behind. 'This is the young fellow who was carrying out enquiries round the farm. Good evening, Constable. What has happened here?'

'An attempted burglary, I think, sir. Unfortunately Mr Griffith disturbed them in the midst of their work and one of them struck him with a *panga*.'

'Where is he?' Mary asked.

'In the other gentleman's bedroom.' He opened the screened door to the bedroom wing and Mary went through.

'Oh, there you are, Tom. What has happened to you?'

Tom Griffith was sitting on the bed, looking extremely ill. A bandage was tied roughly round the upper part of his right arm.

'I didn't want you bothered,' he said defensively. 'I could have managed quite well myself if it had been the other arm.'

'That's all right. I'm glad you sent for me. Have you got dressings and things? I didn't stop to go home for anything. Your boy seemed to think you were at death's door.'

'Not quite. You'll find what there is in the bathroom.'

Mary had slipped off her light stole and moved quickly and competently about the job, collecting dressings and antiseptic. The faint murmur of voices came from the living-room where Dudley Chambers was talking to the *askari*.

The cut was deep, but a clean gash in the fleshy part of the arm.

'You probably ought to have a stitch in that,' Mary said as she bathed it.

'It'll be all right. It's not worth making a fuss about.'

There was silence for a moment.

'What happened, Tom?'

'Nothing much. I walked back from the club. Didn't notice anything wrong, as we always leave the sitting-room light on when we are both out. Opened the front door and found the place upside-down. Was just wondering what had happened when two Africans burst out of here and made a run for the front door. I tried to stop them and one of them took a swipe at me. I yelled for the houseboy, and when he finally woke up and felt brave enough to come out of his quarters the men had vanished into the bush. I rang the police, and this young spiv turned up.'

'You didn't recognise the men?'

'No. Both had handkerchiefs tied over their faces and hats on. I got the idea one of them was tallish and light skinned – he was the one with the *panga* – and the other short and pretty black. That's all I can tell the cops.'

'Have you found out what is missing yet?'

'Nothing, so far. They must have been after cash. As you see, everything was turned out in the living-room, and in my bedroom too. I don't think they had got round to Derek's things in here yet. We had no money and not much in the way of valuables, so they have struck unlucky.'

'I think you've been very lucky, though. You might have got badly hurt.'

Tom looked at her grimly. 'I might indeed.'

Mary finished her dressing and stepped back. 'There. That will do till tomorrow. But you look a bit shaken, Tom. Have you got any sedatives here?'

'The real professional little nurse!' Tom smiled as he

eyed her up and down, a faintly unpleasant smile. 'No, I don't need a sedative. A hangover pill is all that would do me any good. That damned Schmidt and his rare wines! I should have stuck to beer.'

Mary bit back a quick retort. She picked up her stole and bag. 'I'd better go now. Good night.'

'I'll see you out.'

Tom got up, as if conscious that he had not been too gracious. 'Thank you for coming and fixing me up.'

Mary did not answer and they walked through to the living-room in silence.

Dudley got to his feet when they came through the screen door.

'Ah, Griffith. All right now?' He seemed ill at ease, and Mary remembered that he must not feel particularly friendly towards Tom tonight. 'Bad business, this. I was telling the *askari* here that they ought to tighten up on these burglaries. Far too many of them at the moment.'

The African's dark eyes showed no flicker of expression.

'I was also saying that I thought the D.C. ought to be informed . . .'

'Good Lord, why bother him?' Griffith demanded.

'The *askari* here seems to agree with you . . .'

'This is purely a police matter,' the African said flatly. 'There is no need to call the district commissioner in.'

There was still no change in his expression, but Mary thought she could trace a faintly insolent note in the clipped, fluent English.

'It would be stupid to bother him about a burglary,' she said quickly. 'I'll mention it to him when he comes home.'

'Oh. Well, if you think so, Mary . . . And now we must really be on our way.' Dudley turned to Griffith. 'Will you be all right on your own? I'm perfectly willing to stay if you would like me to.'

'No, thanks. Derek will be back soon to protect me.' Tom's voice was heavily sarcastic. 'The *askari* insists on staying till then. 'Good night.'

In the car Dudley gave a little snort of annoyance. 'Insufferable young fellow! Didn't even thank you for coming to look after him!'

'He did in the bedroom – just,' Mary said. 'That young man has got the biggest chip on his shoulder I have ever come across. And he drank far too much tonight. . . .'

'Mm. Don't understand these young fellows. No manners and less sense.'

They had reached the D.C.'s bungalow and Dudley got out to open the car door for Mary.

'You wouldn't like me to wait on a bit till Geoffrey gets home?' he asked diffidently. 'If there are these two rough characters about . . .'

'Thank you,' Mary replied. 'That's very thoughtful of you, Dudley. I'd be grateful if you would just come in with me. I shan't ask you to look under the beds for burglars! The house staff live very close and the ayah will be here. And you look fagged out. You'd better get home to bed.'

Dudley stood just inside the veranda rubbing his hand over his brow and hair.

'Yes. I'm not as fit as I used to be. Getting an old man, I suppose.'

'Nonsense. You are as fit as any of the young men here – probably fitter.'

'That's nice of you, Mary. You're a dear girl. I try to keep up, you know, but it gets more and more an effort. Sometimes I wonder if it is worth it.' He frowned down at his shoes, his thoughts clearly elsewhere. Mary guessed he was thinking of Pauline.

She took his arm and steered him towards the door. 'Go on. It's probably just the heat, and you haven't got over that chill yet. We're all under a strain at the moment any-

way, with this horrible business. It will sort itself out.'
Watching Dudley go down the steps she had repeated her cheerful words to herself. It would all work out – but would it?

15

GEOFFREY had listened in silence to Mary's account of the evening. The whole business of the burglary and the attack on Griffith puzzled him. Of course it could perfectly well have been just an ordinary robbery, but it was an odd coincidence that it had happened to one of the people connected with the Shane-Hamilton case.

But he was too exhausted and too muddled by all that had happened during the day to puzzle it out now. He put the thought aside and hoped that after a few hours sleep his brain would be clearer and he would see some sort of pattern emerging from the jumble of impressions he had collected.

Next morning he did not feel much better. It had rained heavily in the early hours of the morning, and though the skies were now clear everything was steaming under the sun. All the insect world of Africa seemed to have come joyfully to life with the onset of the rains. In spite of the screened windows mosquitoes had got into the bedroom and bitten him during the night. He had forgotten to take his anti-malaria pills since his return from safari, and he offered up an urgent prayer, as he swallowed a tablet, that he would not go down with fever at this particular moment. Mary found a scorpion in the bath, and there were other tiresome forms of the African genus 'dudu' creeping and flying around the house. He had a bit of a hangover, and was glad to be able to vent some of his irritation on these lawful enemies.

It did not help that Mary was almost gay this morning. He heard her laughing with Lois as she dressed and fed her in the next room and the sound gave him a sharp pang of guilt. Those moments with Pauline last night! How could he have been such a fool? All he wanted was to forget that the whole business had ever happened, but would he be able to? He had a feeling that Pauline herself would not be so ready to ignore it. She liked to flaunt her conquests, and this one would be calculated to set the whole of Kilimani talking. He shuddered at the thought of what would be said at the club if it leaked out that he had even flirted with Pauline. And Dudley? Had he noticed more than he appeared to last night?

He thrust these thoughts firmly away. There was a lot to do today, and he could not afford to hang around brooding over something that could not be helped now. So much was happening in the Shane-Hamilton case. He had got to try to keep abreast of it and not let anything be forgotten. He shouted to Mohammed to bring breakfast, but when it came he could only face a mouthful of toast and a cup of scalding black coffee. He called a good-bye to Mary and hurried off to the Boma.

The first job was to send for Sergeant William. He came in, saluted smartly and stood to attention until Geoffrey told him to sit down.

'Now, Sergeant. Any progress with enquiries?'

William shrugged and grinned sheepishly. 'We are asking questions all the time, Bwana Mkubwa. No answers.'

'It is incredible! The man must have been seen somewhere. Somebody must know what happened.'

William shrugged again. His eyes did not meet the D.C.'s and Geoffrey thought he could guess what was going on in the African's mind.

Abruptly he changed the subject. 'This burglary at Bwana Griffith's house – what do you think about that?'

'The burglary, bwana?' William seemed surprised. 'Constable Mlamu went there last night. Bwana Griffith said nothing had been taken, and he could not describe the men plainly either, so we did not think . . . We are making enquiries, of course.'

Geoffrey could not help smiling. 'Of course, Sergeant. But you did not think it was worth bothering much about?'

'I have been very busy,' William protested, 'with this murder.'

'I know, Sergeant. I know. But I am interested in this affair at Bwana Griffith's house. Have you been to talk to him yourself?'

'Yes, bwana. I went round this morning, but it seemed to be just an ordinary burglary . . .'

'Mm. I don't want to interfere in your normal police work, William, but I have a feeling that this burglary may be connected in some way with our murder. Had that occurred to you?'

William looked rather dazed. 'I had not thought, bwana . . .'

'Well, think now. In the meantime I shall try and go down to the house later to see Bwana Griffith.'

William's expression was politely wooden. 'Yes, bwana. Perhaps the Bwana Griffith will talk more readily to the D.C.'

Geoffrey shot him a look. Obviously he had not got on very well with Griffith. 'Perhaps he will. In any case I think it is worth trying.'

They discussed briefly the other aspects of the case, then William clicked his heels, saluted and strode out, his heavy boots ringing smartly on the stone floor.

Geoffrey had barely turned to the papers on his desk when Derek Shotter came in, looking as if he too had overdone things the night before. He had obviously screwed himself up to say something, and was anxious to get it out as soon as he entered the doorway.

'I say, Geoffrey, I've been thinking a lot about things

and –' he drew in a deep breath '– well, I've decided to leave the service.'

Geoffrey looked up at this bombshell but said nothing, and Derek must have read at least part of the look, for he burst out defensively, 'I know you'll think I am an ass, and am just saying this because things have been . . . well, difficult lately. But I've been thinking about it for a long time. I don't believe I am really suited to this job, and the sooner I get out and start something else the better. I'm sure . . .'

'No one is really suited to this job!' Geoffrey exploded. 'How can they be? It requires all the qualities of a saint, an orator, a lawyer and a civil servant with forty years' experience behind him . . . not to mention a nanny, a white hunter and a few other odds and ends. I'm not surprised you don't think you are suited to it, but I am damned if you are worse than a lot of the characters who get by all right.'

'But you don't understand, Geoffrey! I must get out! I . . . I've written out my resignation. Here it is. I am sorry to leave you in a hole, but . . .'

'What hole? You realise you have got to give three months' notice?'

'Three months? Good Lord!'

'And how much money have you got? You are only back from leave a year, so you will have to pay your fare home.'

'Oh. Yes. Yes, that'll be all right.'

'Look here, be a good chap and go away, will you? And take this bit of nonsense in quadruplicate with you. I am too busy to argue with you now. We'll talk about it in a week's time. Perhaps this appalling mess will have sorted itself out by then and you will have changed your mind.'

Derek looked unconvinced, but there was no mistaking the determination on the D.C.'s face, so he backed reluctantly towards the door.

'Just a minute. What about this business at your house last night?'

Derek came back and sat down on the edge of the desk. He seemed relieved at the change of subject.

'Oh, yes. What a rotten business! Poor old Tom might have got himself killed.'

'Teach him to walk out of parties the way he did last night,' Geoffrey retorted unsympathetically. 'But, seriously, Derek, what did you think about it? Was it just a straight burglary?'

Shotter looked surprised. 'Why, yes, I suppose so. Apparently the chaps cut the screening on the back door and got in that way.'

'Have you had any trouble before – suspicious characters loitering, odd phone calls to see if you are in?'

'No. Not to my knowledge. Just what are you getting at, Geoffrey?'

'It seems to me yours was an odd house to choose if they wanted to break into one of the Government bungalows. You haven't much in the way of valuables.'

'My cameras, I suppose . . . clothes . . . radio . . .'

'But none of these things were touched, were they?'

'The chaps were interrupted. They hadn't even got round to my room.'

'Yes. But I gather everything in the sitting-room and Griffith's bedroom was turned upside-down, and yet you can find nothing missing. The police think they were simply after money and small valuables – but I wonder. Neither of you had any unusual amounts of cash this week-end?'

Derek frowned. 'No. Well, I hadn't, anyway. And we usually carry all our money on us when we go out. I don't altogether trust that boy of ours.'

'You think he might be in it?'

'It's possible. Tom and I talked about that last night.'

'And what did Tom think?'

'Well, he seemed as surprised as I was over the whole business. But he was feeling pretty rotten when I got home, you know. He didn't want to talk much.'

There was silence for a moment. The D.C. fiddled with the papers on his desk thoughtfully and Shotter watched him, frowning and biting his moustache. In the end he broke the silence.

'Look here, Geoffrey, you think there is something odd about this. What is it?'

Geoffrey sighed. 'I don't really know, Derek. It's just that the whole business smells a bit fishy to me. You and Tom conveniently out, masked burglars who don't take anything, just turn the whole place upside-down, and instead of trying to escape by the back way when they hear someone coming, have a *panga* ready and rush straight for Griffith. After all that's been happening here lately . . .'

'You don't think they were after Tom? Were trying to kill him or something?'

Geoffrey looked startled. 'No, I hadn't gone quite as far as that. But suppose someone thought you or Tom had something valuable in your possession . . . Tell me, Derek, just how did you get the invitation to that party last night?'

Derek whistled slowly. 'Schmidt? Good Lord! It never occurred to me . . . He rang Tom up in the morning and made a great point of our both coming. Tom wasn't keen, but he said he would go in the end, and when he told me I rang Schmidt back to accept for myself.'

'By request?'

'You mean, ringing him back? Yes, I believe he did ask Tom to let him know if I could come.' Derek rubbed his moustache, a trick he had when he was worried. 'Then you think we were got out of the way while the house was searched?'

'Schmidt had some object in that party of his – and it wasn't to celebrate any birthday.'

'But what was he after? Not . . . not the diamonds! Good heavens, why on earth should he think Tom or I had them?'

Geoffrey shrugged. 'Why indeed? Well, Derek, I think I

had better go over and see Tom and try to find out if I am just acting like a nervous spinster who sees burglars behind every bush . . . or if there really could be something in all this. And, by the way, did Griffith mention this alibi business that seemed to upset him so much at the party?'

'No. We didn't discuss it. But he *was* out that evening. I was in all the time, and he didn't get back till quite late, though I didn't notice the exact time. He said he had to go to the lab, to check on some test that wouldn't wait till morning.'

'He took his car?'

'Yes. The official Land-Rover. I heard him drive in when he got back.'

'All right.' Geoffrey made a gesture of dismissal.

But Derek seemed reluctant to go now.

'Geoffrey . . . about this diamond business. You think Schmidt is out to get hold of the stones?'

'Naturally, if he sees a chance. He'll want to lay hands on them quickly and slip them out of Kilimani before the murderer is caught or the police get down here asking too many awkward questions. He might even get them without paying for them this time.'

'I see.'

As Derek still lingered Geoffrey got up and walked over to the door.

'What is bothering you, Derek? Have *you* got the diamonds?'

Derek grinned half-heartedly. 'No. Oddly enough I haven't.'

'Do you think Tom has them . . . or had them up to last night?'

'No. No. The idea hadn't even occurred to me.'

'Well, let it simmer now. I know you feel you are a friend of his, Derek, but this is a nasty business and a lot besides friendships may have to go by the board before it is finished.

Griffith has been acting in a most peculiar manner, even for him, and I would like to get at the reason. Think about it.'

Geoffrey left Derek still standing by the door. The look of misery on his face haunted the D.C. as he went out to his car, and he wondered if he should not go back and try to get to the bottom of it and all this business of Shotter's resignation. But there was a sense of urgency mounting in him. He had got to act quickly, or he might be too late.

'Hullo. Is this an official visit?'

Tom Griffith was lying on a couch in the living-room, his wounded arm bound up in a sling.

Geoffrey took a chair near him. 'Not exactly. Semi-official, shall we say?'

'Oh yes, let's.' Griffith gave an exaggerated parody of the D.C.'s tone, then switched back abruptly to his usual irritable voice. 'Listen, I've had the police, black *askaris*, sergeants, the lot, and I am fed up with it. They've had all the help I can give. Now let them go and catch the blokes who did this. I'm sick of the whole business.'

'I'm not so interested in catching the blokes who did it,' Geoffrey said quietly, 'as in finding out why they did it.'

Griffith looked at the D.C. sharply. 'What do you mean – why? Isn't it as plain as the nose on your face?'

'I've been talking to Shotter . . .'

'Oh. Derek! Well, you won't get much sense out of him.'

'He told me that a lot of trouble was taken to make sure you and he came to the club last night. . . .'

'Go on.'

'If you hadn't walked out during dinner the burglars would have had time to get what they were looking for and leave.'

'And what do you think they were looking for?'

'Diamonds.'

The word dropped into a silence. Geoffrey sat still, waiting, watching the expression on the younger man's face. There was no surprise, only anger and then a sort of grim amusement.

'So that's what you are after!' Griffith said at last. 'You think I had Shane-Hamilton's diamonds?'

'I think Schmidt believed you had them. Was he right?'

Griffith's smile faded. 'I suppose you think I killed Shane-Hamilton to get them, is that it? Well, what do you expect me to say? No, I didn't kill him. I didn't take his adjectival diamonds. I've got nothing to do with this business, do you hear?'

'You didn't seem very surprised when I suggested the thieves were after the diamonds.'

'Look here, just because you are the D.C. don't think you are the only one with any brains in Kilimani! I can put two and two together as well as you. Schmidt didn't ask me out for the pleasure of my company. I knew he was up to some game, and I thought I'd go along and see what it was. Pity I got fed up with his little charades, wasn't it, and walked in before the coast was clear?' He gestured with the arm in the sling.

'And what do you suppose gave Schmidt the idea of looking here for the diamonds?'

Tom shrugged. 'Even wily bastards like Schmidt can make mistakes. I don't know, and I don't much care. He didn't find them here, anyway. That's quite definite . . . unless they were in Derek's room, of course. That wasn't searched.'

Geoffrey looked at him sharply. 'Do you mean that? Do you mean you think they were in Derek's room?'

'He'd as much reason to expect to find them in Derek's room as mine. You can take your pick.'

Geoffrey wished he could make the young veterinary officer out. He did not sound like a man afraid of something. He was belligerent, almost jaunty, as if daring the D.C. to get anything out of him. He decided to try a different line of attack.

'Where were you the night of the murder, Griffith? You remember you said to Schmidt that you would be willing to tell the proper authority? Suppose you tell me now.'

Griffith looked him straight in the eyes. 'I went down to the lab. I had an experiment going that had to be checked that evening.'

'You went to the lab. Where else?'

'Nowhere else.'

'Have you any witness to prove it?'

'No. I haven't. And if you think you can bluff me into admitting anything the way you did that wretched Indian, you are mistaken.' He got awkwardly to his feet. 'Now I think that's enough. You go and check my alibi, have my house searched, bully my servant, try any of the other Gestapo methods you fancy . . . but, by God, when you are proved wrong I'm going to create such a stink that you'll be out on your ear, Bwana Mkubwa D.C., that I promise you!'

16

GEOFFREY got back to the Boma, his thoughts in confusion. He was certain now that Griffith did know something about the murder, or the diamonds – but was he the actual killer? In the back of his mind all morning had been the things Pauline had said about Tom Griffith the night before. Perhaps, he thought, they had coloured his judgment, and the veterinary officer was in fact just a young man who could not keep his temper and had to fight back wherever he saw even the shadow of an attack. But perhaps, again, that was the explanation of how he had got into trouble with Shane-Hamilton. Could he have met him somewhere, started a row, got involved in a struggle, got hold of a gun and fired the shot in blind anger? Hallden could see it happening that way, but how was he going to prove it?

What he needed was an hour to sit down and try to work the whole thing out, but today that seemed to be the one thing he was not to be granted. Barely was he back at his desk again when his African clerk came in and announced that the Jumbe was waiting to see the district commissioner. Geoffrey groaned. Anyone else he could have refused to see, but it was impossible to turn the Jumbe away. Unwillingly he told Rashidi to send him straight in.

Abdul was as dapper and as smooth as ever, but there was a little restraint in his manner today. Geoffrey smelled trouble, and it was a real effort to go through the deliberate exchange of greetings and polite chat that occupied the first five minutes. But at last the Jumbe leant back in his chair and prepared to get down to business.

The town had been much exercised, he said, about the

arrest of the Indian trader, Ismael. Opinion was divided on whether he was guilty of the murder or not, and there was a lot of talk about it. Geoffrey explained exactly what the charges were, and Abdul shrugged and smiled, implying that between two administrators of their seniority there was an understanding beyond these little matters of charges. The D.C. and the police had been making many enquiries since the Indian's arrest. Did this mean they were still looking for the actual killer?

Geoffrey said bluntly, 'Yes.' All they could prove against Ismael was what he had admitted himself – that he had slashed the body and moved it out to the bridge. And, he added, the further enquiries which might lead to proving that Ismael had done the murder, or indicate who else was responsible, were getting very little co-operation from the African population.

Abdul shrugged again. The D.C. knew that the more uneducated among the people did not like to get mixed up in these affairs. It was regrettable, but understandable. The police were not always tactful. But, knowing the seriousness for the town of having an unsolved murder among them, he himself had been making enquiries. The murdered man had been seen by a number of people before his death, and his car had been noticed parked on the hill above the Boma. Did the D.C. know this?

Reflecting that at least Shane-Hamilton had been tactful enough not to park outside the D.C.'s house, Hallden admitted that he had not known that particular bit of information.

'But we do know he paid a visit in the town – possibly two. Was the car seen anywhere else?'

Unfortunately, Abdul replied, it had not been noticed again until it had been seen travelling towards the bridge with Ismael driving it, some time later.

'But there are many cars like this,' he said.

Of course there were. Half the Government Departments in Kilimani used Land-Rovers, besides a number of private persons.

'Is there anything else?' Geoffrey asked, restraining impatience as best he could.

The Jumbe spread his hands out in a gesture expressive of emptiness. 'No more. No. If there were, I should have known it.'

'You think if the killer were known . . . ?'

'If the killer were an African, yes.' Abdul clasped his hands carefully over his stomach, examining the interlocking fingers with apparent concentration. 'According to the talk of the market and the *pombe* shops this was not an African murder. They shrug their shoulders and say "the affair of the Europeans".'

'They think a European killed the man?'

Abdul shrugged. For once his ready tongue hesitated. 'It is said . . . that the man who was killed came here to see a European. Many people talk. Many people say wild things . . .' He paused again, then raised his eyes briefly to the D.C.'s face. 'It would be well, Bwana Mkubwa, if the affair were cleared up quickly.'

There was silence for a moment. The African was clearly worried and ill at ease. He had said as plainly as he dared that Mary's connection with Shane-Hamilton was known. Geoffrey could imagine the rest. He got up and walked over to the window, where he stood for a moment with his back turned to the Jumbe. If all the African population of the town knew that Mary was mixed up in the case, probably, with their innate scepticism of their rulers, at least half of them would believe by now that he himself was involved, or at least suppressing the truth for family reasons. For nearly thirty years the British had been trying to build up the tradition that justice was absolute, and applied to strong and weak, governed and Government. But this was a new idea in Africa. Against that thirty years was ranged an age-long history of government by tyranny – the right of the strong, of petty native chiefs and foreign invaders alike, to make their own rules. The whole basis on which Hallden's position rested was the belief that the district commissioner was above fear or influence, and he did not need to remind himself how quickly the old ideas could rise again and how dangerous that could be for his whole job, and – less important – his personal future.

He turned round slowly. 'And what do you think, Abdul?'

The Jumbe smiled uncomfortably. 'It is very difficult. I know the police are asking questions, are trying to find out things . . .'

'But you don't think they are trying very hard, eh? You know the European police from Dar es Salaam will be coming soon? That I have sent for them?'

Abdul shrugged. 'It will be a long time . . .'

'I hope not.' Geoffrey rubbed a hand across his aching eyes. He realised that what he said now to the Jumbe was vitally important, but he seemed to have lost his touch. His mind was too confused with thoughts of Mary, of Griffith, of Schmidt, of Pauline – of all the tangled personal relationships that bedevilled this affair.

'There are a lot of things we know that cannot be made public yet,' he said. 'Not who the killer is – once we know that it will be simple enough. But I . . . we . . . think we know why this European came to Kilimani and what his business was. We hope that will lead us to the person who killed him; and when that person is found I assure you he will be arrested and charged, whoever it is. I agree with you that this is not an ordinary crime by an African for money or revenge, and frankly, investigating it is beyond the police force in Kilimani at the moment. We shall have to hope the police from Dar es Salaam come very soon. . . .'

The Jumbe agreed politely, but he was obviously not convinced. He left Geoffrey with a depressing sense of failure. If even this man, whose interests lay with authority, could not be brought to believe in him and trust the integrity and ability to govern of the administration he represented, what hope had he of the uneducated mass of the people of Kilimani?

With these thoughts turning over in his mind he paced the floor of the office, up and down, trying to forget the nagging headache and his own personal problems in the interests of this greater one.

One thing was plain. He had got to clear up the mystery of Shane-Hamilton's death as soon as possible, and preferably before the police arrived to take matters out of his hands. Only by succeeding in that could he re-establish his position in the town. He had to find the killer.

Where did the choice lie? He tried to clear his mind of all the accumulated suspicions and emotions of the past few days and think of the facts calmly, as an exercise in logic, as an outsider might see them. Obviously the killer must be among the people who had known who Shane-Hamilton was, and that he was worth killing. There might be any number in Kilimani who had connections with the dead man that he knew nothing about; but he had to go on the facts as he knew them. In his mind he listed the possible contacts.

Mary. He believed her when she said she had told no one about Shane-Hamilton and the mysterious parcel, but one of the servants at the D.C.'s house might have overheard something and passed the news on. If it had been Mohammed or his wife, the baby's ayah, then the channel of information led straight to Fatuma and Schmidt.

The Chambers. They both knew Shane-Hamilton. Dudley disliked him and Pauline had had an affair with him. If he had known Pauline was alone Shane-Hamilton might well have gone to her to ask her to look after the diamonds when Mary refused him, but would he have risked Dudley's presence? The Chambers had no telephone in their house, so he could not have found out beforehand who was there. Pauline said she had talked about Shane-Hamilton to Tom Griffith. She might also have talked to her other men friends, Derek Shotter, and even Bates (though he could hardly regard the P.W.D. man as a likely candidate for the murder).

Schmidt. It was probable that he had been warned that Shane-Hamilton was coming. He had expected to be back in Kilimani in time to meet him, but would he not have left some instructions behind in case he was delayed? He might have told Fatuma something at least about the man and what he was carrying, and she might have passed the information on to others.

That was as far as he could get at present.

Two of his three lines of possible contact led straight to Schmidt or his household, and all his instinct led him the same way. He had given serious thought to Tom Griffith as the killer, but apart from his own behaviour since the murder and the burglary at his house there was really no direct evidence to connect him with the case. The diamonds seemed to offer the only reasonable explanation for Shane-Hamilton's murder, and the man with the most obvious interest in them was Schmidt. If his suspicions were correct, Schmidt had wanted the diamonds badly enough to send men to burgle a house, armed with *pangas* which they were ready to use if they were interfered with. Might he not, therefore, have arranged something similar for Shane-Hamilton – only this time including murder? Geoffrey remembered what Mary had said about Patrick's anxiety not to keep the diamonds on his person. That seemed to fit. Or perhaps there had been an argument over terms which had turned into a fight, and Shane-Hamilton had been shot by accident.

And yet, the evening before Schmidt had not seemed seriously worried by Tom Griffith's departure before the search of his house was likely to be complete. He had gone through the motions of asking him to stay, but had accepted his failure quite calmly, and had given the impression during the evening that, whatever the object of the party was, he had achieved it. Geoffrey had the irritating feeling that some vital clue had been presented to him during the evening but that he had missed it. And now his memories were confused beyond hope of sorting out by the complication of Pauline and his own idiotic behaviour.

All he was sure of was that Schmidt had chosen that group of guests with a purpose, and therefore some or all of them must be connected with the case. But which? The first thing obviously was to check more thoroughly on alibis. He had made only the briefest of investigations so far, and he decided that he must get the police to look into the question properly. He sat down at his desk and wrote out in his own hand an instruction to Sergeant William – he dared not let anything like this go through the Boma staff now. The police were to trace in detail the movements of all the guests at last night's party, excluding himself and Mary, during the evening of Shane-Hamilton's murder.

Then there was the Schmidt angle. If someone had been deputed to get the diamonds from Shane-Hamilton he or she must be close enough to the German to be trusted by him. Fatuma? Or the men who had carried out the robbery at Griffith's place? Carefully Geoffrey drew up a further instruction for all members of Schmidt's household and any men known to work closely with him to be investigated, their movements on the night of the murder and the previous evening to be gone into thoroughly. He visualised with grim amusement what William's reaction would be to a search of this magnitude, but it had to be done. He could not see any other way round the problem.

Writing the instructions and sending them out for despatch had given Geoffrey some illusion of action, but when it was done he drifted back to his post at the window and depression settled on him again. From where he stood he could just see the roof of Schmidt's house and the curve of beach to the jetty where the dhows were moored. The ships were too small for any details to be visible, mere shapes cut out against the morning brightness of the sea. He could identify the smaller one with the blue prow, however, and he studied it carefully, wondering if the graceful shape held the answer to at least part of his problem – the disposal of the diamonds.

The telephone broke in on his thoughts. With one of those moments of telepathy he was instantly certain that the call was connected with the case, and he reached impatiently for the receiver.

'Yes?'

'It is the customs, sir.'

'Customs?' The disappointment must have sounded in his voice. Rashidi was at once apologetic.

'Mr Padar said it was urgent, sir.'

Padar! Of course! 'Put him on.'

The precise voice came over the line very clearly. Geoffrey could almost see little Mr Padar bowing at the other end.

'Many apologies for troubling you, sir. You asked me to let you know . . .'

'Yes. Yes, of course. Just hold on a moment.'

Swiftly Geoffrey made for the outer office.

'Rashidi!' There was a brisk click as the receiver of the telephone went down. Rashidi leapt to his feet.

'Go round to Mr Shotter's office and get from him the file on the import statistics, will you? Bring it straight in to me.'

Geoffrey knew this was a file Derek kept in the bottom of a cupboard, hoping that out of sight would prove out of mind. It would take the clerk at least five minutes to dig it out.

'Go ahead, Mr Padar. I am listening.'

'I have learnt this morning that the . . . er . . . vessel of which we spoke is making ready to leave. She has taken on water, and all her crew are aboard.'

'The captain?'

'Not yet, sir. I think they are only awaiting him to go . . . and for the wind, of course.'

'Of course.' At this hour of the morning there was usually a flat calm. A little later the breeze would get up and the dhow would be able to use her sails to get out of harbour.

Geoffrey was thinking hard. 'Have you seen Mr Schmidt go past this morning?'

'No, sir. I have not myself. I will ask my assistant.' There was a pause, then the gentle voice continued. 'No. He has not seen Mr Schmidt. I think we would have noticed if he had come into town.'

'Thank you.' Geoffrey had made up his mind while Padar had been consulting his assistant. Now he gave the customs officer precise instructions, made sure that he understood them, then rang off.

Rashidi came in just as he finished. 'Your file, sir.'

'What? Oh, yes. Thank you. Is Mr Shotter there?'

'Yes, sir.'

'All right. I shall be going out for some time, Rashidi, and I do not know when I shall be back. Take any messages for me. I shall probably ring through later in case there is anything urgent.'

Geoffrey arrived at the house just as Mary was finishing Lois's morning feed. He had for the moment forgotten all that had happened the night before, but it came back to him with a jolt when he saw her face. She looked startled, naturally enough, at seeing him home at this hour, but also there was a trace of apprehension in her eyes as they met his.

'You are home early. Is something wrong?'

'I've come to ask your help, Mary.'

'*My* help?'

'Over this business of the diamonds. I need someone I can

trust absolutely, and you are the only one. Can you hand Lois over to the ayah for a few hours and come with me? It's urgent. I will explain it all on the way.'

She looked at him for a moment, searching his face as if for something concealed behind the words. Then, apparently satisfied, she picked up the baby.

'I'll call ayah now. Do you want me to bring anything?'

'No. Just come as you are.'

Inside five minutes they were in the car, and Geoffrey was pouring out as fast as he could his ideas and his plan. He was banking everything on his hunch that the diamonds were to leave Kilimani in the dhow that day, and that they were not yet aboard her. He was assuming that if the gems had been in the hands of Schmidt or the dhow captain all along the boat would have left at the earliest opportunity, and therefore the delayed sailing meant that someone was expected to take them aboard in the next few hours. He told her briefly of his talk with Griffith that morning and his belief that Schmidt had organised a search for the diamonds during the party at the club.

'If I am right, and they found the diamonds there, Schmidt will probably be carrying them himself and will hand them over just before the dhow sails.'

'And if they didn't find them?'

'Schmidt must know where they are or he would have held the dhow up another day or so. If Griffith didn't have them, somebody else must be going to hand them over. So we have to watch Schmidt, see who goes into his house, or, if he goes out himself, follow him. If we are spotted it will give the whole game away, so we have got to be careful. I daren't put any of the police on to watch the house – they are far too well known – or do it myself. I have sent old Swedi down . . .'

'What, the Boma messenger?'

'Yes. I don't suppose anyone will bother about seeing him loitering around. He often takes letters and messages into town, and I don't suppose he always hurries back. Derek and I will wait in Derek's Morris on that turning that leads off the quay just before Schmidt's place. His car isn't so well-known as mine, and there shouldn't be many people around there anyway. Swedi will give us a signal if anyone goes into Schmidt's house or if he comes out. We can follow him in the Morris if he leaves by car – which I think is the most likely thing to happen.'

'And me?'

'I want you to stay in the customs office. From there you can see who passes along the quay and also keep an eye on Schmidt's office in case the contact is made there. I have briefed Padar, and he will give me a message if anything happens.'

'But couldn't Derek do that part of it?'

Geoffrey frowned, and for the first time hesitated. 'Yes, he could, but . . . well, Derek came to me this morning and gave in his resignation.'

'Good heavens, why?'

'That's just it. He says he is fed up with the job and will never make a go of it. That is probably all it is, but I've a feeling there is something else behind it. He was obviously upset and unlike himself. It might just be the old trouble over Pauline, but I can't ignore the possibility that it could be because he has got himself mixed up in this business.'

'Not Derek, surely! He seemed quite happy last night. I suppose nothing happened after I left?'

'With Derek? No. No, I didn't notice anything.' Geoffrey did not want to dwell on what had happened last night. 'He's not a strong character. He might have got involved in something without meaning to. Also he says he can afford to pay a hundred or so for his fare home, and you know how hard up he always is. Oh, I know that it is the remotest chance that he is involved, but I can't afford to take any risks. This whole expedition is a wild gamble, but it might just come off, and I can't risk anyone giving a hint to Schmidt or whoever has got the diamonds. So Derek stays with me. I haven't told him yet what it is all about – just asked him to drive down to the godowns and wait till I come.'

He stole a glance at Mary's profile. 'You don't mind doing this?'

Mary was silent a moment, then she turned and smiled, her old warm smile. 'No, I don't mind, Geoffrey. I am glad you asked me.'

17

IT WAS STUFFY in Mr Padar's office. An ancient fan creaked and swayed in the ceiling, but it did little except ruffle the papers on the desk and disturb the flies that plagued the whole harbour area. Mary had dropped Geoffrey near the godowns and seen him hurry off towards Derek's waiting car, then she had taken their own car on to a quiet area a few streets away, locked it up and come here on foot. No one seemed to have paid much attention to the district commissioner's wife taking a walk along the sea front, and she thought she had slipped into the customs office without being observed.

Mr Padar had made a great fuss about settling her comfortably in her chair by the window, and had already sent out for a stock of bottled drinks and cigarettes to cheer the vigil. He was a dear little man, she thought, so nervous and polite, but she wished she could persuade him to ignore her and settle down to his own work. He would make a few entries on a form and then leap up to swat a fly or apologise for the heat. The door of the room had to be kept shut so that the occasional visitor to the outer office would not see her, and he kept protesting that it was a great pity; normally the room was very cool.

'But soon the breeze will come,' he assured her. 'Then you will be comfortable.'

He was bursting with curiosity about the whole affair, she could see, but being a gentleman he would not even mention the reasons for her presence, and stuck firmly to platitudes about the heat, the rains, the flies and the amenities of the office.

Mary's position was a good one. The road here followed the curve of the beach, and from her seat by the window she had a good view of the harbour and the sea front almost as far as Schmidt's house. And a short distance away she could see the blank front of the German's office and warehouse, and watch anyone entering or leaving. The window was fitted with an expanded metal guard and mosquito netting, and effectively screened her from the view of passers-by.

She had arrived there at about ten thirty. Eleven o'clock came. Padar lifted his head from his papers.

'See. The breeze is coming now.'

She could see the blue silk surface of the harbour become flawed and ruffled here and there, and hear the waves beginning to lap on the beach, where before the whole surface of the sea had just seemed to sway gently, like a brimming cup. Movement began on the dhow. Men were working on the great spar that carried the sail, and the smoke of a cooking fire behind the matting screens on the deck dwindled and disappeared. And still nothing happened.

Half past eleven. Mary caught a glimpse of Swedi's shambling figure strolling across to the beach and spitting leisurely on to the sand. He took off his round red cap and rubbed his poll, then strolled back out of sight. There had been no movement from the warehouse yet, but the door stood half open, so someone must be inside.

Then she heard the sound of a car. Not many passed that way, and this one was coming from the far end of the harbour, where Schmidt lived. A moment later a drab-coloured Volkswagen came into sight and she drew back instinctively from the window. But Willy Schmidt's eyes were fixed straight ahead, and he looked so normal and unconcerned that she found herself wondering if this whole scheme of Geoffrey's was not based on sheer imagination. Then a black Morris Minor came out from the side turning and followed the Volkswagen.

Mary became aware of Mr Padar hovering behind her. His eyes gleamed with interest.

'So Mr Schmidt has gone?' Then he pulled himself up with the air of one who has just avoided a social howler. To excuse his presence at the window he produced a packet of cigarettes and begged Mary to take one.

She got up to stretch her stiff limbs.

'Won't you smoke too, Mr Padar?'

He smiled and bobbed. 'Thank you, but no, madam. With five children to educate, you understand, I cannot afford to smoke.' And as he fussed about lighting the cigarette and finding an old tin lid for an ash-tray, he told her about the three sons and two daughters: the eldest boy who had done so well at school and was going to follow his father into the customs, and the second who was not quite so satisfactory and wished to be a telephone engineer ('An artisan almost, is it not?') and the third who was delicate . . .

Mary listened and smiled and wondered what was happening to Geoffrey. Her heart lightened as she remembered his voice saying, 'I want your help . . . I needed someone I could trust absolutely . . .'

At the back of her mind she must have heard and noted the footsteps some time ago – quick, sharp steps, out of place in this area accustomed to shuffling sandals or bare feet. She swung round to the window, but was just in time to see the back view of a woman, slender, elegant in a black blouse and boldly patterned skirt and high-heeled black sandals. She was walking quickly, picking her way over the rough paving. Mary leaned forward with her face almost against the dusty screen to make sure she was not mistaken. But the figure had hesitated, then turned into the door of Schmidt's warehouse.

Pauline Chambers!

She turned to Padar.

'Is there any way I can get closer to the warehouse without going into the street?'

Padar was clearly at a loss. 'I don't think . . .'

'What about the back? Is there any way of getting behind the buildings here?'

'There is a . . . a kind of lane, for loading, you know, but it is not very clean . . . not suitable for a lady . . .'

'Oh, never mind that! Can I get out that way?'

'Yes. Yes, I will show you. But you will permit me to come with you?'

Mary was at the door already. 'I shall be quite all right. You must be here in case my husband telephones. Quick, Mr Padar!'

They hurried through the outer office, where the clerk behind the counter gaped in undisguised amazement, and through a dank passage to a store-room full of unclaimed goods awaiting disposal. There was a double door, which Padar unlocked, and they stumbled out into the blaze of noonday sun, half blinded. It was hardly a lane, just a stretch of sandy ground between the row of buildings on the sea front and the godowns behind. Not a soul was in sight; only a brace of black and white carrion crows were picking among the litter of broken crates and refuse, and hopped angrily away, wings outspread, at their approach.

'Which is Schmidt's warehouse?' The backs of the buildings all looked alike to Mary.

'The third one. The green doors.'

There was no difficulty about that. The doors were the only ones with any paint on them in the row.

'All right. Thank you. You go back now, Mr Padar. I'll be perfectly all right.'

She left him standing in the open doorway saying, 'But madam . . . !' and wringing his hands. She hoped he would have the sense to do as she said, but had no time to make sure he did. She picked her way quickly through the litter, looking up at the flaking walls with their barred, dusty windows and sealed doors. It looked as if the whole place were dead – shuttered houses only waiting for a gust of wind to fall down into heaps of rubble.

She had only twice been in Schmidt's warehouse, and the last occasion was months ago. She tried to picture the inside of the building now, in relation to this blank wall at the back. She remembered the office section had been at one side, near the front entrance, and the rest of the place had seemed to consist of a dark cavern stacked with crates and bales, and stretching heaven knew how far back. She looked up at the windows, several feet above her head and closely barred. Even if she could reach up to them she could never hear or see what went on in the front of the warehouse.

The double doors were, as she had noted, freshly painted and stout. They had a smaller door cut in one side, with a businesslike Yale lock on it. Trust Schmidt to protect his property! She gave it a push just to test its firmness, and not in any hope of finding a way in through it. But to her astonishment it swung open with a faint creak. A waft of cold, damp air, smelling of musty packing, spices and tar, came out to her. Her mind registered the thought that Geoffrey had made a blunder in forgetting the back of the building, while her body had already made the decision and stepped inside. She glimpsed a pile of crates like a wall in front of her, with a small gap to the left, then pulled the door to behind her and was plunged suddenly into what seemed at first like complete darkness. For a moment she paused, while a trickle of sweat stole down her spine. She had always from childhood disliked the dark, and now there was just enough light in the warehouse for her to make out the bulk of crates and bales without being able to see into the shadows behind them. Then, faintly, she heard a voice. It was a fretful voice, husky and reassuringly familiar, but too far away for her to make out the words. In her anxiety to hear she forgot all about the darkness and the sinister possibilities of the stacked crates, and began to feel her way forward towards the front of the building.

Mary could make out the words before she could see the speakers. Pauline was saying, in a petulant voice, 'How do I know you are the right person? *I want to ship some stuff to Dar* – do you hear? I was told that a responsible person would be here.'

She sounded rather as if she was berating an inefficient shop assistant – the nagging plaint of the memsahib. Mary's triumph at getting at last within earshot was short-lived. Had she gone to these lengths just to hear Pauline dickering about some luggage?

The other voice was only a murmur. Mary thought it, too, was feminine, and decided it must be Fatuma, for whose presence Geoffrey had prepared her.

The murmur was brief, and Pauline was starting again.

'Well, I don't like it. I think I will wait for Bwana Schmidt.'

The reply came more firmly this time, but still Mary could not catch the words. She edged forward behind a pile of musty bales and found that a crack between them would just let her see the small part of the warehouse set apart as the office.

In the dim light from the door and a few high windows she could see Pauline standing on one side of the table and on the other an African woman in a red and black *kanga* and ornaments that glinted gold when she moved her head. The two women were staring at each other, Pauline defiantly, biting her lips and fidgeting with her black handbag. Fatuma was quite still, but Mary had, in spite of Pauline's bluster, the feeling that the African woman was the stronger of the two.

At last Fatuma made a gesture to a chair. 'You had

better sit down,' she said in slow, correct English. 'Mr Schmidt may be late.'

Pauline hesitated, looked down at the hands wrenching the clasp of her handbag and then back at the other woman.

'He should have told me,' she began petulantly, then shrugged and seated herself, her bracelets jangling as she adjusted the folds of her full skirt.

There was silence for a moment. But Pauline could not seem to sit still. She fidgeted again with the bag, and shot quick glances under her eyelashes at the quiet woman standing behind the table. She took out a cigarette, fiddled with it, then lit it. Watching her Mary became aware that this was more than Pauline's usual butterfly restlessness. She had not simply come to see Schmidt on business. Either this was a move in the flirtation game she had been playing at the club, and she was not sure of her reception, or after all she was the unknown who had the diamonds.

Mary concentrated furiously, leaning forward till the loose strands of jute from the bale tickled her cheek, watching every move.

Pauline stubbed out her cigarette on the floor and glanced at her wrist watch. 'How much longer will he be?'

'Bwana Schmidt? I do not know. A long time, perhaps. But he gave me instructions . . .'

'How do I know I can trust you?'

'Bwana Schmidt trusts me.' There was simple pride in the soft voice.

Pauline laughed. 'He trusts you!' she repeated mockingly. 'In his business, perhaps, but you should hear the way he talks at the club, about his dusky little bit of stuff!'

Mary knew that was untrue – Schmidt would never dream of mentioning Fatuma – but it caught the girl on the raw. Her hands gripped the edge of the table and her whole body tautened. It was the measure of her anger that she forgot her careful English and lapsed into Swahili. In the familiar tongue her voice sharpened and became almost shrill.

'You! You, the fine Memsahib, truly! You think he likes you, that he trusts you? He makes use of you, you understand. That is all. And when that is finished –' she flung out her hands '– then you finish too! I never liked this affair. I do it because he wants me to – that is enough. As for me, you can go, go! You can tell the bwana why, afterwards, when it is too late. He will be very angry, and when he is angry he is not a good man to deal with. I warn you.'

'*Bas!*'

Pauline got up. Mary knew her Swahili was rudimentary, but she could not have mistaken the gist of the African girl's words.

'That is enough. I didn't come here to argue with you. This is a matter of business . . .'

Pauline's indecision was plain. She would have liked to walk straight out, and actually made a move towards the door, but then she hesitated. She looked again at her watch, then glanced at Fatuma. The African woman was standing quite straight behind the table, her face expressionless. Pauline took a step back towards her and said, half contemptuously, as if the matter was of little importance:

'Have you got it – the money?'

Mary was holding her breath. So Pauline had got the diamonds! She waited tensely for Fatuma's answer.

At the back of the warehouse a door creaked.

Mary stepped back instinctively, looking for cover. The bales and crates were all arranged in haphazard piles, but from where she was standing there was a wide, irregular lane along which she had groped her way from the back door. She realised that anyone coming in that way was almost bound to pass her. Quickly she moved towards the wall of the warehouse furthest from Pauline and Fatuma, feeling her way with her hands and listening intently for another sound. There was nothing. The warehouse might have been completely deserted. Had she imagined the noise?

Then there came a sharp click. She recognised the sound as the catch of the Yale lock being released. Someone had come in and closed the door after them. She was seized with a moment of panic that almost paralysed her. Should she wait and see who it was, or should she try to get out by the back door? Geoffrey would be waiting for a message. The most important thing was surely to warn him that the diamonds were here before it was too late. If only he had noticed that back entrance!

She started to move again, very quietly, towards the rear. Her own breathing sounded terribly loud. She could hear nothing from Fatuma and Pauline. Were they listening too? It was very dark at this side of the warehouse. Her hands were her only guide. They moved over the rough corners of packing cases, touched a stack of timber that trembled alarmingly, then found the yielding softness of bales of some sort of fibre. Then there was nothing, and she stepped cautiously into the gap and almost stumbled over a heap of something on the floor – goat hides or wild animal skins by the feel and smell – and there was a faint rustle as the pile shifted. She edged round it, praying she was keeping her sense of direction in the darkness. Then dimly, high up, she saw a gleam of light from one of the rear windows. Was the man still waiting by the door? Dare she advance into the light and see?

She heard nothing, but suddenly there came to her nostrils a new smell that made every nerve tighten with a sense of danger. It was an animal smell, a sharp tang of sweat and the musty odour of stale clothes. It was very close.

She turned round desperately to try to locate it.

There was a sudden swish of movement. A hand came round her throat and another was over her mouth.

Geoffrey was cursing fluently. They had got Swedi's signal clearly enough and managed to pick up Schmidt's Volkswagen as it passed the turning. They had followed at a distance along the sea front into the main part of the town, where Schmidt had left the car and walked into a grocery store. With difficulty they managed to park on the crowded street a little further up and Derek kept the engine running while Geoffrey watched. It seemed a long time, and Geoffrey had wild ideas of Schmidt holding a rendezvous in Efficiency Stores. In the meantime a surprising number of people recognised the D.C. and the D.O. in the little black Morris, and their presence there at that time of day was obviously causing some speculation.

But at last Schmidt came back to his car, followed by two boys carrying a box of groceries and a crate of beer. He started up leisurely, swung out into the road and passed the Morris without a second look. He took the turning which led up the hill and they had got half way up after him when Geoffrey started to curse – oaths that he had not used since army days. Abruptly he told Derek to stop.

'I thought so! Guess where the so-and-so is going!'

'Well, it looks like the Boma,' Derek answered cautiously.

And so it was.

'He's going to sit on his backside in my office establishing an alibi while things are fixed up elsewhere, I'll wager a fiver! And I bet he is enjoying laughing at us.'

But it was no good just swearing at Schmidt. He had to think quickly.

'You had better run me back to the warehouse area, Derek, then go to the Boma and see what he wants. If he leaves before I get back try to follow him without being too conspicuous.'

Derek hesitated. 'Are you sure? Don't you think you had better just see what he wants first?'

'While things are happening elsewhere? No, that's just what he will be hoping for.'

'But . . . what shall I say?'

'Just tell him I am out and you don't know where. Then let him do the talking.'

'What are you going to do?'

'I must see Swedi and Padar. I guess if the diamonds are being handed over this morning it must be either at Schmidt's house or the warehouse. Come on, Derek, don't argue! Step on it!'

Swedi was still at his post and came up beaming as the D.C. climbed out of the Morris and beckoned him over. But he had no news. No one had entered or left Schmidt's house.

Geoffrey looked along the curve of the sea front. There were few people about, as it was getting too hot for loitering out of doors. The dhow was still there, he noticed, apparently empty of life, at the quay. The door of Schmidt's warehouse was closed and it appeared deserted. Swedi, however, swore that no one had come out recently, and Geoffrey was sure the door had been open when he had followed Schmidt past it, half an hour earlier. To make sure of not being seen passing the warehouse he detoured around the block and approached the customs house from the other side. He was hoping devoutly that Mary and Padar had something to report, but the feeling was growing on him that the whole thing was a wild goose chase.

Padar leapt to his feet as the D.C. came in. It was the measure of his excitement that he did not even say 'good morning'. He clasped his hands before him in a gesture of appeal.

'Your wife, sir! She is gone!'

Geoffrey had taken in her absence in the same second.

'Where is she?'

As Padar began to stumble through his story he grabbed him by the arm.

Quick, man! Tell me as we go. Which way is it?'

Almost running behind him Padar related Mary's insistence on his returning to his office, and his own doubts at leaving the D.C.'s wife to go alone on such a venture.

'But she was very definite, sir!' he panted. 'Most definite!'

'Yes. Yes. She would be. What then?'

'I waited here, sir, for a little time. Then I decided I must go out and see if she was still there. I went – but there was nothing, nothing at all. The warehouse was all shut up and I could see nobody to ask. I went round to the front as well, but the door was closed and I could hear nothing inside . . .'

'How long ago was this?' Geoffrey rapped out.

'About . . . ten minutes, perhaps? I thought you would phone at any minute, and I must be here in the office.'

Geoffrey did not curse this time. A cold knot of fear had suddenly formed just under his diaphragm. And it was he who had brought Mary into this wretched affair! He tried to convince himself that she had gone off on some wild chase without having time to notify Padar. Perhaps she had followed the woman she had seen going into the warehouse and was unable to get to a telephone. But in the meantime he had to make sure. They had reached the warehouse by now, and he tried the door of the loading bay. It was locked. He looked up at the windows, and as Mary had done a little while before, dismissed them immediately as useless.

'I wish to heaven you had told me about this back lane, Padar. Anyone could have got in or out here.'

'Yes, sir. I am sorry, sir. But you did not ask me.' Padar's voice was faintly injured.

'Oh well, never mind. We shall have to try to get in the front way. Go back to your office, Padar, and collect a couple of your men. Wait in the street outside Schmidt's place. I'm going in. If I need you I will shout. If you don't hear anything in, say, five minutes, ring Mr Shotter at the Boma. Tell him what has happened and ask him to get the police down here. Then you come in, with your men. All right?'

Padar fairly ran back down the lane while Geoffrey hurried on through the narrow archway into the street, to reach the front entrance of the building by the shorter route.

The door was still closed, and when he tried the handle gently he found it was locked. He hesitated. Could Swedi be mistaken in thinking no one had left the building? Or could they have gone out by the back entrance and so been missed? Was he about to make the biggest blunder of his career as a district officer? He could imagine the trouble Schmidt could make if the D.C. broke into his premises on such flimsy evidence, and how thin the whole story would sound in court or in an official memorandum.

He drew a deep breath, then banged on the door.

'Open up! Open this door at once! This is the district commissioner.'

There was a sharp cry inside – a woman's voice, he thought, then complete silence.

He flung himself at the door. 'Open this door at once! In the name of the law!'

Padar and two excited customs clerks were pelting up the street to join him.

'Get something to break the door in, Padar! And you, go round and see no one gets out the back way. Quick!'

The younger clerk dashed off, full of excitement, while Padar, civil servant to the last, detailed the other to fetch a weapon from the office, and then hovered behind the D.C. saying, 'What is it, sir? . . . Is your wife there? . . . What shall we do? . . .'

Geoffrey, ignoring him, banged again and shouted, 'Open up at once or we shall break in!'

The customs clerk came panting up with a big tyre lever used for opening packing cases. 'Here, sir! Here you are!'

Geoffrey reached for it, but before he could grasp it a

swarthy hand stretched past him and he glimpsed the red fez and grinning features of old Swedi.

'Wait, bwana! Here's the expert at this!'

He hefted the lever in a business-like way, then drove the flat end into the crack of the door by the lock and flung his weight against it. Geoffrey had a moment to wonder just where Swedi had become so expert at forcing doors before, with a tearing noise, the lock gave and the door shot back on its hinges. They all plunged into the dimness inside.

Geoffrey stopped in the middle of the room. Standing on either side of the office table, in attitudes of astonishment, were Pauline Chambers and Fatuma. Pauline's mouth was half open and she started to say something, but with a swift movement Fatuma was out from behind the table and between her and the D.C.

'Did you wish something, Bwana Hallden?' The cool words, spoken in Swahili, held a touch of insolence.

'Yes. First I wish to know why you did not open the door when I ordered you to.' He nodded to Padar. 'Search the place, Padar.'

'Wait!' Fatuma's voice rang out clearly. 'What is this? You are the D.C., I know, but have you the right to search this place without Bwana Schmidt's permission?'

The customs men hesitated.

'Go ahead, Padar,' Geoffrey said more quietly. Then to Fatuma, 'We have reason to believe some contraband goods are being handled here. These customs officers have the right to search on my authority.'

'What are you looking for? Bwana Padar knows we have nothing here but goods paid for when they land!' Her voice was rising to a shrill argumentative pitch. 'It is not justice! You must wait until I can fetch Bwana Schmidt.'

'Go on, Padar.'

'Just a minute.' Pauline stepped forward quickly. 'This is all most unpleasant for me, Geoff. I just happened to be in here seeing about some stuff I wanted shipped to Dar. Then when all the noise started I was frightened. I didn't dare call out or move. I don't want to be mixed up in some customs *shauri*, and I'm late meeting Dudley already. You don't mind if I go, do you?'

She had moved closer to Geoffrey and now put her hand on his arm, smiling her most melting smile. But he noticed her eyes were strained and over-bright and the hand on his bare arm was cold and moist. He moved instinctively away from her touch and his voice was icily official.

'Please stay here, Mrs Chambers.'

Her eyes hardened and the smile faded. 'That's not very helpful, Geoff. I thought we were . . . friends.' The emphasis on the last word was unmistakable.

Geoffrey had realised at once that Pauline must be the woman Mary had followed to the warehouse, and if she was mixed up in this affair he was not going to allow her to blackmail him, however politely, into letting her go.

'This is a matter of business,' he said coldly. 'We are investigating a suspected crime and I am afraid no one can leave. Please sit down in that chair.'

Pauline could not mistake the note of determination in his voice. Her eyes moved briefly towards the door as if measuring the chances of calling his bluff, but the way was blocked by Swedi, standing very erect and soldierly with the tyre lever sloped over his shoulder. His ancient cloudy eyes were missing nothing of the scene before him.

'Thank you,' Pauline said angrily. 'I would rather stand.'

Padar and his clerk had been watching the drama with breathless interest, but now at a sign from the D.C. they started moving towards the bales, slowly, as if not at all sure of their ground.

'Start from the back and work forward from the back door,' Geoffrey said.

He had almost forgotten about Fatuma in the exchange

with Pauline, but something in her attitude now caught his attention. She had moved back to the table and was bracing herself against it with her hands. Her clear, coppery skin had faded to a muddy colour and for one unguarded moment her eyes flashed towards the pile of bales to her left.

'Watch them, Swedi!' Geoffrey shouted in Swahili.

He whipped past Fatuma and round the stack. The others heard a cry and then confused sounds of struggle behind the swaying bales.

Pauline screamed.

Padar and his clerk dashed forward, and emerged a moment later dragging a cursing, struggling figure. It was the dhow captain, his splendid turban awry over his greasy curls, his coat pulled half off his arms. He was swearing volubly in Arabic and trying to get his hands to the curved dagger at his belt. The two Indians hung on grimly. Then Geoffrey appeared with his arm round Mary. Her hair was ruffled and her lipstick smeared, but her eyes were brilliant with anger. She pushed away Geoffrey's supporting arm and wiped her mouth vigorously with her handkerchief.

'That devil!' she fumed. 'He crept up behind me and grabbed me. He and that woman were arguing.' She flung a glance at Fatuma. 'I couldn't understand all they were saying, but I think he wanted to kill me and dump me in the harbour. I am sure Pauline would have been delighted! Then we heard you outside. I got out one yell, then he put his filthy hand over my mouth and nearly wrenched my arms off to keep me quiet.'

'What had happened? How did you get here?' Geoffrey demanded.

'I got in the back door. It was left open – for this creature, I suppose. Pauline and the African woman were arguing. Pauline wanted to deal with Schmidt . . .'

'I wanted to see him about some baggage,' Pauline broke in angrily. 'I've got nothing to do with all this.'

'No,' Mary retorted. 'You didn't even think to mention to Geoffrey that I was here!' She turned back to her husband. 'The Arab came in at the wrong moment. Pauline had just said, "Have you got the money?" . . .'

'I said "*I* have got the money!"' Pauline cried. 'You're twisting everything round, Mary. I . . . I was frightened and upset. It was natural to try to get away. You were all right. Your precious husband was here to rescue you. I didn't want to get mixed up in a fight. After all, it's none of my business . . .'

Just then the dhow captain got an arm free and made a grab for his knife. There was a loud outcry from his captors and a moment of confusion with both Geoffrey and Swedi rushing to the rescue. Pauline saw her chance and made a dash for the door.

Mary was the only one who noticed her. She was further from the entrance, but she was wearing flat sandals to Pauline's three-inch heels. They reached the door in the same instant. Mary did not attempt to touch Pauline but grabbed for her black handbag. For a moment the two struggled in the doorway, Pauline uttering little screams of rage and refusing to let the bag go. Then her grasp failed. Mary stepped back out of reach, holding the bag, just as Geoffrey came up to them. She snapped open the catch and pulled out a small, heavy packet in a linen envelope.

'I thought it was there,' she said, suddenly quiet. 'That's the package that Patrick was carrying.' Her eyes came up to Pauline's face. '*You* were the one who killed him!'

18

AT LAST Geoffrey and the police got the party sorted out. The Arab captain, who had relapsed into a brooding silence when his dagger was taken away, was removed to the police station to join Ismael in the cells until he was in a more receptive mood for questioning. The three women were driven to the Boma.

Pauline had thrown a storm of hysterics at Mary's accusation and renewed her screams every time she was asked a question. Fatuma had refused to say a word, except to spit out a few well-chosen phrases in Swahili when the African police tried to hustle her out to the car.

As they drove into the Boma yard Geoffrey noticed that Schmidt's car was parked there. Rashidi told him the German was still in the D.O.'s office, and Geoffrey devoutly hoped he would not hear the commotion of the party's arrival and come out to see what was going on.

The Boma was not really adapted for dealing with crime on this scale. Geoffrey had to turn a couple of clerks out of an office to house Fatuma and Pauline while he talked to Mary and tried to get the story straight. He kept Sergeant William beside him to add a flavour of the official to an unorthodox interrogation, and one of the constables sat at a side table to take notes when it became necessary.

'Is it all over now?' Mary asked when her story was told. 'Are you going to arrest Pauline?'

'For the murder? Do you think she did it?'

Mary hesitated. 'I would like to think so,' she said honestly, 'but I can't quite see it. For one thing Pauline is too fond of her own skin to risk it. She'd cheat to get money, but I don't think she would kill for it. Of course,' she added, 'she probably wouldn't draw the line at getting someone else to do it for her if she thought she could share the proceeds without any danger . . .'

'I think we shall get her on the diamond-dealing charge,' Geoffrey said, 'but the other . . . I don't know.'

It had seemed quite conclusive from Mary's story and the discovery of the diamonds that Pauline had brought the stones by appointment to the warehouse and that Fatuma was there to buy them from her. But when Fatuma was brought in for questioning she seemed quite unperturbed by the evidence against her. She sat coolly on the edge of her chair listening to the D.C. and casting an occasional glance of contempt at the constable writing it all down.

Then she repeated her original story, word for word. Mrs Chambers had come simply to see about some baggage. They had heard a noise, and the captain, arriving on business, had caught Mrs Hallden hiding in the building. He had been a little rough with the Memsahib, but then what was she doing there, in such a place? The Arab had ordered her to close the door and she had been too afraid of him to open it when Mr Hallden arrived. Yes, there was a large sum of money in her possession, but it was usual for Bwana Schmidt to keep a lot in the office during business hours. It was his affair and she did not interfere. Diamonds? No, she knew nothing about diamonds.

Unfortunately the story was, so far as Geoffrey could see, quite watertight. He tried to break it down, and the sergeant tried, with a great show of anger and threats, but Fatuma's black eyes continued to regard them calmly and mockingly and she would not alter a syllable of her story.

In the end Geoffrey dismissed her, under guard, and had Pauline brought in.

She had apparently decided that hysterics were no longer any good to her and had made some effort to pull herself together. But her handbag was still in the D.C.'s possession and she had had no chance to mend the ravages to her looks. For the first time since Geoffrey had known her she looked her age. Her mouth was set in a tight line that made unsuspected wrinkles and hollows form in her skin. Her make-up had vanished and her hair was straggling round her face. And with the outer shell of beauty she had lost all the tricks of the good-looking woman – the conscious charm, the confidence that she will get her own way by a smile or a soft look. She was sullen now, and when she spoke her voice had lost most of its husky warmth.

A gleam of anger came into her eyes when she saw Mary sitting beside the D.C.'s desk. 'What is she doing here? She has no business here!'

Geoffrey had been shaken in spite of himself by the change in Pauline. He answered her quietly, almost gently. 'Mary is an important witness. I want her to hear what you have to say to see if it tallies with what she heard this morning. I have already warned you that you are not compelled to make any statement, but if you wish to do so, you may. It will be read over to you before you sign it.'

'I told you I had nothing to do with Patrick's death . . .'

'What about the diamonds? You don't deny you had them?'

'He . . . he gave them to me. He said if anything happened to him I should keep them.' Her confidence returned a little. 'I want them back.'

'They were not his to give. You must be aware of that. And the fact that you saw him and received the stones, and withheld the information, is still a serious matter.'

'Mary saw him and withheld the information – didn't she?'

'But I didn't take a parcel of stolen diamonds and then try to sell them!' Mary retorted.

'Be quiet, Mary.' Geoffrey's voice was stern. 'I think perhaps you had better leave now. Wait outside, will you? I may want you later.'

As soon as the door had closed he turned again to Pauline. 'Do you want to make a statement?'

Pauline looked at him under her eyelashes, and for a moment he thought she was going to try some of her old tricks. But the gleam vanished.

'I want Dudley,' she said flatly.

'We are trying to find him to tell him you are being held for questioning. Do you want him to be here when you make your statement?'

She thought for a moment. 'Well . . . no, perhaps not.'

Her eyes had lighted on the black bag lying on the desk in front of her.

'That's my bag! Can I have it back?'

Geoffrey hesitated.

'You've got the diamonds,' she said sulkily. 'There's nothing else in it of any interest to you.'

Geoffrey had looked through it already and knew that was true. He pushed the bag silently across the table. Pauline pulled out a mirror and comb, then a lipstick and powder compact, and quickly touched up her face. The rest of the room waited in silence until she had restored her appearance to something like its usual finish. She gave a last glance in the mirror then sat back in her chair and crossed her legs.

'That's better.' Her confidence was visibly returning. 'May I have a cigarette?'

Geoffrey lit one for her and she took a few deep breaths of smoke.

'Look, Geoff, shall I just tell you how it all happened? I don't have to make a formal statement, do I? It sounds so alarming.'

'Tell it just as you like.'

'Patrick came to the house that evening – some time after half past seven, I think it was. Dudley was out, and he had parked down the road a bit and walked round the house to the veranda, so nobody but me saw him arrive. He . . . we had been friendly, you know, in Nairobi. I shouldn't say so, I suppose, but he had been very devoted to me. And now he was in trouble, and I was the only one he could really trust. He told me he had these diamonds and wanted to sell them to get enough money to set up in business on his own in Kenya. There was some difficulty in Dar . . . the deal was too big for them to handle, or something . . . and a friend put him on to a man in Kilimani . . .'

'Who was it?'

Her eyes widened. 'Why, Willy Schmidt, of course. Patrick seemed rather afraid of him, though. He said Willy was known to be a tricky customer, and if he had the diamonds on him when they talked terms, Willy might just take them off him and refuse to pay. So he wanted me to hold them till he had it all settled. And if anything happened to him I was to keep the diamonds – he was most definite about that.'

'He expected something to happen?'

'Not exactly expected something . . . but he seemed very worried about meeting Schmidt. That was why he said about me having the diamonds . . .'

Geoffrey looked down at the papers on his desk and lined them up into a neat pile with his finger-tips. Pauline, he thought, could talk and talk, and one never knew where fact ended and imagination or sheer untruth took over. Probably she did not know herself.

'And when did he leave you?'

'Well . . . it might have been eight, perhaps, or a bit later. He wanted to stay, as we hadn't seen each other for such ages, but I thought as things were he had better not risk meeting Dudley. They never got on awfully well.'

'Did he give you any idea where he was going when he left?'

'He didn't say exactly, but I gathered he was going straight to see Willy Schmidt.'

'But he knew Schmidt was away in Mafia.'

'If he was! Patrick didn't tell me that, anyway. But perhaps he was going to see that African *bibi* of Schmidt's. I wouldn't put it past her to cut his throat!'

'His throat was not cut,' Geoffrey said drily. 'He was shot, if you remember. Do you know if he had a gun with him?'

'He didn't say so.'

'Did you actually see him go?'

Pauline hesitated. 'I stayed on the veranda.'

'Well, did you hear the car drive off?'

'Oh, yes.' But her eyes had dropped to the bracelet on her wrist and she was fiddling with the little gold charms hanging from it.

Mary had gone into the outer office to wait, but Rashidi was ostentatiously doing some filing on the table and a number of the other Boma staff seemed to have business in the room. They held muttered conferences with the clerk, eyeing Mary with the frank curiosity typical of the African. She walked out into the corridor, looking for somewhere quiet to sit down. The district officer's door was closed. Presumably Schmidt was still there talking. The only other possible room was a small office with a very large, very black *askari* outside it. He was chatting to Swedi, and the old messenger grinned when he saw Mary and snapped to attention. Then he came forward and took Mary's hand between his two palms, bending his head in an old-fashioned gesture of respect.

'*Salamu*, Mama.'

'*Salamu*, Swedi.' Mary was touched. 'What is the news, old man?'

'Good, Mama. But what is the news of the Memsahib? That villain did not hurt you? I would like to kill him with my bare hands,' and he gestured fiercely a wringing of the Arab's neck.

Mary touched her own throat, which was still sore. 'It is good, Swedi. He did not hurt me much.'

'Ah, the Memsahib D.C. has courage. Would you be as brave, eh, big one?' and he dug the tall *askari* in the ribs.

A grin spread over the black face and he greeted Mary shyly.

'I am looking for somewhere to sit down and rest, Swedi, while the Bwana D.C. is busy. Is there anywhere?'

'Alas, Memsahib, all the rooms are full of criminals!' He grinned gleefully, showing his few worn teeth. 'Perhaps . . .' He glanced into the room behind him. 'But of course the Memsahib would not wish to sit with that one.' He gestured towards the silent figure of Fatuma sitting cross-legged on the floor, staring in front of her.

Mary hesitated, then shook her head. 'I don't mind, Swedi. May I go in, *askari*?'

Swedi waved the policeman back with an imperious gesture and led the way in. He brushed off a chair and set it beside the table, then shot a fierce look at Fatuma.

'You behave yourself, you!' he said sharply; then to Mary, 'I shall be outside, Memsahib, if you want anything.'

Fatuma looked up once then lowered her eyes without a word. The two women sat in silence for what appeared a long time. Mary studied the still figure. Fatuma seemed to have slipped back completely into her background. She might have been any African woman with nothing to do, sitting in the traditional way, hands lying palm upwards, idle, in her lap, the red and black *kanga* draped over the bent head and hiding most of the face.

Mary had been a bit frightened of the termagant in the warehouse, but she had also admired her single-mindedness and her devotion to Schmidt. And now she was deeply sorry for her. She liked Willy Schmidt, but if it came to a choice between his neck and Fatuma she did not doubt what his decision would be.

She took a cigarette case out of her bag and went over to Fatuma. 'Will you smoke a cigarette?' she asked in Swahili.

Fatuma looked up, hesitated, then took one. She drew the smoke in deeply and leant back against the wall. Her face, revealed as the *kanga* fell back, looked remote and expressionless.

'I have to thank you, Fatuma,' Mary went on quietly.

'For what?'

'For saving my life when the Arab wished to kill me.'

Fatuma's expression did not change. 'It would not have been wise, Memsahib. Killing the D.C.'s wife would make very big trouble.'

'Nevertheless I am grateful. I should like to help you if I can.'

The dark eyes looked suspiciously at the foreign woman.

'I do not need help,' she said curtly.

She jerked the *kanga* back around her face and leant against the wall, drawing hard on the cigarette. Mary went back to her chair and they smoked in silence for a few moments.

She had been dimly conscious of the murmur of voices outside as Swedi and the *askari* talked. Africans always seem to have endless things to discuss, and it was so familiar a background that Mary hardly heard it. Then suddenly she became aware of a new voice, speaking in Swahili, but with a note of authority. She got up, curious, and walked to the door. It was Mlamu, the elegant young plain-clothes policeman who had been at Tom Griffith's house the night before.

He saw Mary immediately, and acknowledged her presence with the briefest of greetings. He and the uniformed *askari* had been arguing and he turned back immediately to continue the dispute.

Then Swedi stepped forward. 'The Memsahib D.C. will settle it,' he said. 'Will you not, Mama?'

'What is it?' Mary asked.

Mlamu made a quick, contemptuous gesture with his hand. 'Be quiet, old man.' He turned to Mary. 'This is a matter of police business,' he said stiffly.

But Swedi refused to be silenced. 'You should learn a proper respect for your elders, young sprig – and your betters. The affair is this, Memsahib. This Mlamu here says he wishes to talk urgently with Sergeant Williams, and the *askari* has orders to let no one into the Bwana D.C.'s room.'

'How urgent is it?' Mary asked, speaking directly to the young man.

He began sullenly, 'I have arrested a suspect . . .'

'The fact is,' Swedi broke in again, 'he has just caught the fellow who broke into the Bwana D.O.'s house last night and nearly killed the other bwana with a *panga*. It is a young fellow who works on the Bwana Schmidt's boat – brother of that one in there.' He nodded his head towards the open door.

Mary caught her breath. 'Yes, that may be very important. The D.C. will wish to know it. Why don't you send a note in? Swedi can take it.'

It was the obvious solution. Mlamu looked as if he would like to object, but instead jerked his head for Swedi to follow him and went off without a word towards the D.C.'s outer office.

The *askari* gave Mary an apologetic look. 'Mlamu is a very educated man, very clever,' he murmured.

'Yes, I can see that,' Mary replied.

She went back into the little office. At once she realised that Fatuma had heard. She stood just inside the door, her eyes enormous in a face suddenly greyish and haggard.

'They have arrested my brother?'

'You heard the *askaris* . . .'

'I must see the bwana! Please help me, Memsahib! I must see the bwana.'

Mary knew she meant Schmidt. 'He is here, at the Boma,' she said. 'But they won't let you see him now. He will find out very soon, don't worry. Perhaps he can do something.'

She realised this was not what the D.C.'s wife ought to be saying – after all, Fatuma's brother was presumably guilty of burglary and assault – but she could not help herself.

'He is here? I must go and find him.'

'Wait . . .'

But Fatuma had already slipped past her to the open door. The big *askari* was taken by surprise, but he put out an arm and managed to catch her by the wrist. She struggled like a wild thing, spitting out curses at him, her voice rising higher and higher. He got hold of her by both arms and was gradually succeeding in forcing her, none too gently, back into the room.

In the midst of the turmoil the D.O.'s door was flung open and Derek Shotter and Schmidt appeared on the threshold.

'Good Lord! What's going on?' Derek demanded.

Fatuma saw Schmidt. 'Bwana! Bwana!'

Schmidt took it all in in one swift glance. '*Askari*, let her go!'

Astonished, the African loosed his grasp and Fatuma slipped past him. In a flood of Swahili she poured out the story of her own arrest and that of her brother.

Schmidt put up his hand in an imperative gesture. 'That is enough. Mrs Hallden, can you make sense of this? Everyone seems to have gone mad around here. Shotter! What the devil is going on?'

Derek looked helplessly from Mary to Fatuma. 'I've no idea. I don't know any more than you do, Schmidt. Perhaps Geoffrey . . .'

'Geoffrey is busy,' Mary said firmly.

'Oh, is he?' With a quick movement of his burly shoulders

Schmidt pushed Derek aside and made off towards the D.C.'s office.

'Oh Lord! Stop him, Derek!' Mary called, starting after Schmidt.

The D.O. hovered irresolutely for a moment, then came to. 'Here! I say . . . !'

19

GEOFFREY had been struggling on with Pauline, but he had got no more out of her about Shane-Hamilton's visit. When he turned to her dealings with Schmidt she was even more vague. She insisted that Schmidt had been the first to mention the diamonds, though Geoffrey found this hard to reconcile with Pauline's obvious efforts to ingratiate herself with the German during the past few days. According to her story Schmidt had tackled her the night before at the club, while they were dancing. He had said that he had learnt that she was a friend of Patrick's, and he had approached the subject of the diamonds very cautiously, saying that Patrick had some property of his which he was anxious to trace. She had shown she knew what he was talking about, and then he had tried to force her to give him the stones with some story of Patrick having been paid for them already. But she was not fool enough to fall for that one. Then at intervals, when they had a moment or two alone, he had pestered her to sell them to him for an agreed sum, and at last she had given in. A packet of diamonds in the rough were no use to her, and if Patrick had promised to sell them to Schmidt she thought it only fair to let him have them. She denied hotly that she had known the deal was illegal. She knew nothing of I.D.B. or Government regulations on buying or selling uncut stones – how should she? She had assumed Schmidt wanted the deal kept quiet because of the fuss about Patrick's death. She herself had not mentioned the stones to the authorities, 'Because,' she said, 'if it comes to lawyers and wills and things I might not be able to keep them. He meant me to have them, though. I don't care what the law says!'

At that moment the door opened and Swedi came in. Pauline watched with anxious eyes as he placed a note on the D.C.'s desk, and saw Geoffrey read it, frowning, then pass it over to William. The sergeant was slowly absorbing the contents when, suddenly, there came the sound of rapid steps on the stone floor outside. They all looked round as the door was flung open.

It was Willy Schmidt, closely followed by Mary and Derek Shotter. The German was not smiling for once, and looked quite formidable with his jaw set and his eyes hard as ice. He gave a quick glance round the room, taking in the presence of the two policemen and Pauline sitting in a chair by the desk.

'Hallden! I find you are holding Fatuma here under some pretext or other. What is it all about?'

Geoffrey had risen to his feet as soon as the three appeared. He had expected Schmidt would arrive sometime, and was thankful he had managed to talk to Fatuma and Pauline before the German got wind of what was happening. He saw Derek making agitated signals behind the other man's back, indicating that he had tried to stop him and failed. But he had no intention of trying to keep Schmidt out now. The whole interrogation was unorthodox enough anyway, and he thought he might learn more by letting the German have his say.

He said calmly, 'Come in, Schmidt. And you, Mary, and Derek, come in too and shut the door. I am holding Fatuma, Schmidt, on fairly conclusive evidence of buying diamonds illegally from Mrs Chambers. And by the way, your Arab friend from the dhow is in separate custody at the police station on a similar charge – and also, if Mary chooses to press it, of assault on her.'

Schmidt's expression of astonishment was probably genuine enough.

'Assaulted your wife? What on earth . . . ?'

'She was witness to the deal – rather an inconvenient one, it seems.'

Schmidt jerked forward a chair and sat down.

'Now what is all this about diamond buying? I know you had a bee in your bonnet about it and the Shane-Hamilton case, but this seems to be taking it a bit too far. All I know is that Mrs Chambers was going to come down to the warehouse today to see about shipping some stuff of hers.'

'That is not Mrs Chambers' story,' Geoffrey replied, watching Pauline. She was biting her lips and staring at Schmidt with narrowed eyes. 'She says you offered to buy the diamonds from her.'

'*I* did? Then where are they?'

'We found them in Mrs Chambers' possession.'

As soon as Geoffrey said it he knew he had made a mistake. Schmidt sat back in his chair and smiled for the first time since he had entered the room.

'So nobody bought them, eh? And you have just Mrs Chambers' story to go on? Fatuma's English is not very good, you know, and Pauline may quite well have misunderstood her. I don't know how Mrs Chambers came to acquire diamonds . . .'

'You devil!' Pauline was on her feet, looking as if she was going to fly at Schmidt. 'You're trying to put this all on me, aren't you? Well, I am not taking it! I swear you promised to buy the diamonds . . .'

'I deny it.' Schmidt sat back calmly and folded his arms.

It was beginning to dawn on Pauline that she had no actual proof of Schmidt's complicity, and in her overwrought state it came as the last straw that he should be able to keep out of trouble while she was irretrievably committed. She went very pale.

'At the club last night . . . you told me to come this morning . . . You said the money would be there. It was there, wasn't it?' She appealed to Geoffrey.

But before Geoffrey could speak another voice intervened. Derek Shotter, who had been standing behind Willy Schmidt, spoke, his voice harsh with nervousness.

'It's true. I heard it.'

'You heard them arranging a deal for the diamonds? And didn't say anything?' Geoffrey swung round on his D.O. in amazement.

Derek flushed deeply. 'I did try to tell you this morning, Geoff. . . . But I only overheard a few words. I wasn't sure that was what they meant. It worried me. I wanted to see Pauline and tackle her about it before I said anything. It didn't seem fair to her . . .'

Geoffrey remembered Derek's efforts to take Pauline home the night before, and his cavalier dismissal of the younger man. He also saw why Derek had tried to resign that morning.

'There you are!' Pauline said triumphantly. 'Derek will prove Willy forced me into it!'

'Will he?' Schmidt swung round in his chair and eyed the D.O. consideringly from head to toe. 'I don't think it would sound very well in court. And everyone knows he would do a good deal to get you out of trouble, Pauline. No, I don't think you'll get very far with that one. After all, *you* had the diamonds, however you acquired them!'

'Patrick left them with me . . . because he didn't trust you. He told me he was going to see you about them, but he never got there. Or did he? Anyway, you didn't get hold of the diamonds, whatever you did to him!'

'Be quiet, you little fool!' Schmidt did not raise his voice but it cracked like a whip. 'You are not doing yourself any good by trying to frame me for Shane-Hamilton's murder. I was in Mafia at the time and I can prove it.'

'Then it was that filthy Arab who tried to kill Mary . . . or that precious *bibi* of yours . . . I expect she did it. You are not even man enough to soil your fingers with your own dirty work. You get a woman to do it for you!'

Pauline was working herself up to the verge of hysterics again but Schmidt sat, apparently unmoved, waiting with tight lips until she should finish.

'It's no good trying to insult me, Pauline. You know quite well who shot Shane-Hamilton. Your gallant Welsh lover, eh? No doubt at your suggestion, so you could keep the diamonds.'

'*Tom?*'

The room had gone suddenly quiet.

'You had an appointment with him, hadn't you?' Schmidt went on grimly. 'At your house, while the old man was out of the way?'

'It wasn't Tom! He wasn't there!'

'Oh yes, he was. I can produce witnesses who saw him driving up to your house . . .'

'Why didn't you tell me that before, Schmidt?' Geoffrey demanded. 'You knew it might be vital evidence!'

Schmidt turned his shrewd glance to the D.C. 'My evidence was, shall we say, indirect, and I did not want to be brought into the business if I could help it . . .'

'For obvious reasons . . .'

'For good reasons,' Schmidt amended. 'I hoped the little comedy of alibis we played last night would give you the clue, and you could go and find it all out for yourself. But perhaps your mind was on other things?' The ghost of a twinkle appeared in his eyes for a moment. 'That was really what I came to see you about this morning – to make sure the seed had not fallen on stony ground. If Mrs Chambers had not made these rather rash accusations . . .'

Geoffrey swung round to Pauline. 'Did Griffith come to the house?'

'No. It's all lies. You can't believe this . . . this creature!'

'Were you expecting him?'

Her eyes flickered momentarily. 'No. No, of course not.'

'Well,' Schmidt put in coolly, 'if you deny it all so hotly,

Pauline, the poor D.C. is going to think either that you and Griffith did the murder together or you did it alone. Take your choice!'

Pauline gave him a look of sheer hatred. Then she turned to Hallden.

'Geoff!' She stretched one hand out to him appealingly. 'Don't listen to him. You know I had nothing to do with Patrick's death! I . . . I was fond of him. Hearing he was dead like that was the most awful shock to me. . . .'

The D.C.'s face was grimly unresponsive. She looked round the room, at Mary, at the motionless sergeant, at Derek, who dropped his eyes as they met her gaze.

'All right,' she said at last. 'I . . . I had asked Tom round for a drink that evening . . .'

'Did he come?'

'No. He said . . . afterwards . . . that he came as far as the drive and saw a Land-Rover parked there. He thought I had company so he went away again.'

'I see.' Geoffrey frowned down at his desk. 'Why didn't you tell me this last night?'

Pauline shrugged. 'That wouldn't have been very bright, would it? You had no idea Patrick had been near me.'

'And you hoped I would never find out? Derek!'

The D.O. jumped. 'Yes?'

'Will you go and fetch Griffith here at once? I don't care what excuses he makes, he has got to come. Do you want William to go with you?'

'No. No. That would upset Tom. I'll go alone.' He turned to the door.

'Derek.'

'Yes?'

'Don't tell him anything on the way, will you?'

Geoffrey got up and walked over to the window. The skies were darkening and Kilimani lay in a yellowish light. The sea was dead as stone, and the palms along the shore stood black and motionless against it. There was something unnatural about the stillness outside. It was not only that the wind had dropped: every bird and insect had suddenly fallen silent. Inside the room it was so still that the creak of the fan sounded unpleasantly loud.

Then the constable at the table shuffled his feet and coughed. Geoffrey swung round.

'Schmidt, who are the witnesses who saw Griffith going up to the Chambers farm?'

Schmidt crossed his legs and leant back, quite at ease. 'One is a female known as Bibi Nene – no better than she should be, I understand. She lives near Ismael's *duka* and was walking back home when she saw Griffith's Land-Rover turn off to the Chambers place.'

'You know her, William?'

'Yes, bwana.' William was emphatic. 'She has been in court for brewing *moshi*, and other things.'

'I admit she is not a very reliable character,' Schmidt said smoothly, 'but the other witness is a thoroughly respectable gentleman called Selemani, who I understand is Chambers' foreman and lives actually on the estate. He saw the car going up towards the house.'

'But he was questioned,' William protested. 'He said he knew nothing at all.'

Schmidt shrugged. 'Naturally. It was wiser to know nothing at all. But when he realises the story is out he will be ready enough to give evidence.'

'How did you get on to this?' Geoffrey put in. 'Is this genuine information, Schmidt?'

'Perfectly genuine, Hallden, I assure you. As for how I got on to it . . '

Suddenly the telephone rang sharply. Geoffrey gave an exclamation of impatience and picked up the receiver.

'What is it, Rashidi? I thought I told you not to interrupt me?'

There was an apologetic murmur from the instrument and Geoffrey's lips tightened as he listened.

'All right. Thank you. Put in a call for me to the C.I.D. headquarters as soon as the line is open.' He put the receiver gently back on the rest, his brow creased with thought.

'The line is through?' Schmidt asked.

'Yes. The engineers are just testing it. We should get a call through to Dar in the next hour or so.'

This was what Hallden had been praying for ever since the murder, but now that the outside world was almost within reach he felt nothing but dismay. He had wanted to have the case settled and tied up first, and now time was so short, so very short.

He swung back to face Schmidt. 'You know another of your employees has been arrested?'

'Quite an epidemic, isn't it? Yes. Fatuma told me. Her brother.'

'He is one of the crew of your schooner?'

'Yes.'

'What do you know about it?'

'About what, my dear fellow? I understand he has been arrested for burglary . . .'

'And wounding Griffith . . .'

'Quite. But what he does in his free time is none of my business. He is a good seaman, but not a very reliable character. He has been in jail already, you know. Some little peccadillo a few years ago . . .'

'And that is all you have to say about it?'

Schmidt met the D.C.'s eyes squarely. 'He knew the risk he ran in attacking a man with a *panga*. I have no taste for unnecessary violence. I shall get the chap a good lawyer. I owe him that.'

'You do indeed,' Geoffrey replied grimly.

They all heard the car draw up outside. Two pairs of footsteps echoed on the stone floors.

Griffith came in first. He looked round the room.

'So the vultures are gathering. . . . I understand you insist on seeing me, Bwana D.C. Well, here I am.'

'Sit down.' Geoffrey had gone back to his seat at the desk. 'I thought you had better hear some new evidence that has come up. Mrs Chambers has admitted that Patrick Shane-Hamilton came to see her between seven thirty and eight on the night he died, and that you were invited for a drink about that time. Mr Schmidt says he can produce two witnesses who saw you going towards the Chambers' house. What have you to say about it?'

There was silence for a moment. In the last few minutes the sky had darkened, and now a gust of wind brought a sudden chill into the room. Then the rain came, in a burst of sound, the drops falling straight as small bullets on the ground. In a moment the eaves of the Boma were pouring water in cataracts. But no one in the room even turned to look. They were watching Tom Griffith.

Griffith was looking at Pauline. It was a long, bitter look, as if he was seeing her as he had never done before. She met his eyes defiantly, but her colour paled a little and her lips tightened.

When he spoke it was directly to her, as if none of the other people in the room existed.

'So you got caught out in the end, did you? And now you think you will throw me to the wolves – you and the Hun together . . .'

'I only told the truth,' Pauline exclaimed angrily. 'What do you expect me to do?'

'You weren't so keen on my telling the truth earlier, were you? You were frightened of your own precious skin then. And like a fool I believed you when you said nothing had happened while Patrick was at your house . . . that it would shatter your pretty little nerves if you got involved in this shocking scandal! So I stuck my neck out, tried to get the fellow buried before our noble D.C. spotted he had been shot, lied right and left . . . and got this –' he gestured at the sling on his right arm '– for my pains because your dear friend Schmidt thought *I* had the diamonds! Well, I've finished with that. Yes. Let us have the truth – all of it.'

He swung round to face the D.C. 'Pauline asked me to drop in for a drink and a chat. I went. Got there about eight o'clock. There was a strange Land-Rover parked a bit away from the house, under the trees. I didn't feel like facing company, so I beat it back to the lab. And that's the lot – whatever Pauline may say. She was there with him alone. Let her lie her way out of that one!'

'Are you trying to make them think I killed him?' Pauline demanded. 'Because you know now you don't matter a damn to me, you think you'll get back at me this way – is that it? I let you hang around making a fool of yourself over me, because there was no one better to amuse myself with but a common fisherman's son from the Welsh backwoods! You thought I would run away with you . . .you! And live in a hovel while you doctored cows, I suppose!'

'You said you would!'

'Yes. I said I would. It was the only way I could see to get out of this god-forsaken dump. Anything was better than Kilimani – even you!'

Tom's dark skin had reddened slowly as she spoke. He seemed to be controlling himself only by an enormous effort. 'So you thought when you had the diamonds you didn't need me . . . you could get out alone. And you decided it would be nice if I was disposed of – didn't you? If you said Patrick left you while I was there, that you heard us arguing and then a shot . . .'

'Did you, Pauline?'

20

THERE WAS a sudden hush as the D.C. spoke. Geoffrey's eyes were on Pauline. She looked, he thought, like some cornered animal, her eyes bright and narrow, her lips drawn slightly back from her teeth; her brain calculating desperately the best chance for her own safety – whether to throw Tom Griffith to the pursuers or not. Neither considerations of the truth, or her own feeling for Griffith would weigh very much in the calculation, of that he was sure. Schmidt, with his back to the door, was watching her too, his eyes inscrutable. Derek was staring at the floor as if he could not bear to look at her.

Only Mary had seen the door swing open and Dudley Chambers stand there listening. She felt a pang of pity for him. He looked more than his age today, no longer dapper and alert, but seeming to have shrunk into himself. Over his usual white drill he wore an old Army raincoat, stained and shabby, his hands thrust deep into the pockets. The coat was dripping with rain, and his hair straggled damply over a face still pale after his recent illness.

He took a step into the room and Pauline saw him.

'Dudley!' She went over to him and caught his sleeve urgently. 'Darling, you've got to help me! They are accusing me of the most dreadful things.'

He did not remove her hand but seemed to draw back from it a little. 'Yes, I heard.' His voice was very tired. 'Aren't you going to answer the D.C.'s question, Pauline?'

She looked at him as if a pet dog had suddenly turned and bitten her, and snatched her hand away.

'You don't believe them? You don't think I had anything to do with Patrick's death?'

'No. I don't think you would go to the length of killing, Pauline, even for diamonds. But suppose you try telling the truth now. *Did* you hear an argument and a shot?'

She dropped her eyes from his gaze – a remote gaze, singularly unlike her husband's usual expression when he looked at her.

'No. No. I only said that to frighten Tom. But I can explain all this, Dudley . . . about the diamonds, and getting mixed up in poor Patrick's murder . . .'

'I am sure you can. But that can wait.'

Dudley turned to the D.C. 'I don't have to tell you I knew nothing about these diamonds? If I had they would have been handed over to you at once.'

'I realise that.'

'Dudley!' Pauline's voice was appalled. 'You can't just . . . just abandon me like this! You've got to help me. I've got no one else to turn to. I didn't realise it was wrong to keep the diamonds. . . .' She started to cry, not hysterically this time, but quietly, the tears running out of her eyes. She moved closer to her husband.

'You know what a fool I am about things like that, darling. You've always said I needed someone to look after me or I would get into trouble, haven't you? You must tell Geoffrey I didn't mean to break the law or anything. He won't listen to me.' She darted a sudden glance at the D.C. and her eyes were no longer tearful. 'He's your friend, isn't he – whatever he thinks of me? He'll believe you . . .'

Geoffrey was aware of the hint of a threat in her glance and in her words. He met her eyes squarely.

'Friendship has nothing to do with this, as Dudley is fully aware.'

'Of course.' Dudley's voice was still lifeless, and he looked at the D.C., not his wife. 'Pauline has taken these things and apparently tried to sell them to . . . to Mr Schmidt. What share of the blame is his I do not know. But you must have realised, Pauline, the diamonds were not yours to keep or sell.'

'Patrick meant me to have them!'

'They were almost certainly not his to give. He was never very fussy about other people's possessions . . .'

'You've no right to say that! I did all this in good faith . . . for you!'

'But you didn't think of telling me about the diamonds?'

'No! Because I knew you would have stupid ideas of giving them to the Government! They were worth thousands, Dudley – enough to buy us out of this awful place and let us go somewhere civilised and really live! You could have done whatever you wanted to do . . .'

'On stolen money? You didn't really think I would accept that, did you, Pauline?'

'Oh, you!' She drew away from him. The contempt of years curdled her voice. 'You deserve to be a broken-down failure! You've never gone out and taken anything you wanted in your life. You've always fussed about honour and doing the right thing – and look where it has got you! Of course I knew you would never touch the money! I was going to leave you, do you hear?'

'Yes. I heard. You were going away with Griffith.'

'Yes, I was! But with the money I could get away on my own and start a real life again before I'm too old to enjoy it! Patrick was twice the man you are. I could have been happy with him. He knew what he wanted out of life and took it!' She started to sob angrily. 'Oh, go away! Go away and leave me! You haven't even the guts to stand by your wife when she is in trouble.'

'That's enough, Pauline.' Geoffrey had watched Dudley's face as his wife's tirade went on, and he could stand it no longer. 'Dudley, do you want to stay? I don't think there is anything you can do here now.'

The older man raised his eyes to the D.C.'s face. He looked grey and drawn, as if the life had seeped out of him in the last few moments, and he seemed to fumble for the words to reply.

'No . . . I suppose not. I suppose not.'

He paused, and then with an obvious effort roused himself to speak again. 'Are you arresting my wife for this murder?'

Geoffrey hesitated. 'No. Not at present, at least. We have still no evidence that Shane-Hamilton did not leave your house alive, and meet his killer somewhere else. But we shall have to hold her on the charge of trying to dispose of stolen diamonds.'

'I see.' Chambers pulled his raincoat around him as if he was suddenly cold. 'She didn't kill Shane-Hamilton, you know.'

Geoffrey met his eyes. 'No,' he said slowly. 'I know she didn't.'

There was a pause.

'Thank you Geoffrey – for all you have done.'

Dudley nodded once briefly to the D.C. then turned and, without a glance at his wife, walked out of the room. Pauline made a movement to follow him, then checked. The others sat there waiting for the D.C. to speak, but Geoffrey remained motionless, staring down at his desk, listening to the roar of the rainstorm gradually dying away.

The crack of the gun sounded very loud in the silence. Shotter and the two policemen leapt for the door, but Geoffrey stopped them with a gesture.

'There is no hurry,' he said.

They found Dudley Chambers sitting at the wheel of his

car with Hallden's gun in his hand and a bullet through the temple. Neatly folded in the breast pocket of his shirt was a letter, addressed in his small, precise handwriting, to G. Hallden, Esq., M.C. It was to be delivered 'in the event of the Indian, Ismael, standing his trial for murder', and had obviously been written just after Ismael's arrest.

'How did you know Dudley killed him?' Mary asked that night as they sat on the veranda of the D.C.'s house.

'It is difficult to say exactly,' Geoffrey replied slowly, trying to relive the flashes of knowledge that had brought him to a conviction of Dudley's guilt. 'There was something about him when he came in. . . . He looked as if he had gone through an experience that had finished him . . . he just wasn't interested any more.'

Mary nodded. She had felt that herself most poignantly.

'With Pauline,' Geoffrey went on, 'he wasn't angry or heart-broken, as I would have expected him to be. He didn't care. She wasn't really important. Whatever he felt for her must have died soon after he killed Shane-Hamilton. I suppose he began to see at last what she was really like – shallow, incapable of any real feeling, selfish to her bones . . .' He checked himself, realising how bitter the words sounded.

'These were all just impressions, but there were two tangible things that convinced me. Did you notice he did not take his hands out of the pockets of his raincoat all the time he was in the room? It occurred to me suddenly that he reminded me of those gunmen in American films who keep their hands on their guns, ready to fire.

'Then there was a paper on the top of the pile on my desk. Somehow when all that madhouse was going on with Pauline I must have read it without realising it and taken in what it meant. It was Sergeant William's summary of the information he had already collected on some of the alibis I asked him to check this morning. He had assumed Chambers was covered till about nine, when he admitted arriving home, by the foreman he took with him to look at the dam on his plantation. The African was vague about the time, as they always are after the sun goes down, and if the bwana said it was nine he was not going to contradict him. But Schmidt had said earlier that one of his witnesses was Dudley's foreman, and he saw Griffith drive up to the house before eight. So there was an unexplained gap of about an hour, and we know Shane-Hamilton was at the house during that time.'

'And Dudley ran into him?'

'He must have arrived soon after Tom Griffith came and went. He had gone to one of the out-buildings to lock some tools up, and walking back he saw the Land-Rover parked by a tree, where it could not be seen from the house, and thought it was Griffith's. He hadn't been so indifferent to Pauline's affairs as we thought, and was apparently pretty worked up at the idea of Tom sneaking in while his back was turned. So when he saw a vague shape coming towards the car he tackled him. Shane-Hamilton panicked and pulled the gun, but Dudley was quite tough, you know, with all that cult of fitness we used to laugh about, and he managed to get hold of the gun . . .'

'But surely then it was self-defence?'

'If Dudley had been a different sort of chap he could have claimed it was and got away with it. But apparently it did not occur to him. He himself knew it was murder, you see. He said in the letter that he flashed a torch on Shane-Hamilton and recognised him. He had always hated the man, who I gather was Pauline's first serious affair since their marriage. Seeing him there he just went crazy for a moment and shot him, deliberately. If Shane-Hamilton hadn't stolen my gun and pulled it on Dudley he would almost certainly still be alive and out of the country with his ill-gotten gains . . .'

Mary shivered. 'If Patrick hadn't come to me . . .'

Geoffrey put his hand quickly over hers. 'Don't think that

way, darling. It's no good. These things happen, heaven knows why: a chain of events apparently hangs on something small. But I can't believe it is all accident. Patrick Shane-Hamilton had been preparing for his own death ever since he started stealing diamonds and other men's wives, just as surely as if he had fired that gun himself. You must believe that.'

'Dudley would be alive too.'

'Yes, poor devil. But no one forced him to kill. It was his own act. And, do you know, he said that the only thing he really regretted about the whole business was dumping the body at Ismael's. He wasn't to know Ismael had any connection with Shane-Hamilton, of course. He only wanted to get the evidence away from his own house, partly to protect Pauline, and also because he didn't see why he should hang for a rotter like Shane-Hamilton if he could possibly avoid it.'

'Was it all worth it, I wonder . . . for her?'

'A creature like Pauline? God, no! And he obviously realised that at the end.'

Mary was startled at the explosive anger in his voice. Knowing him well she had guessed some of the truth during the day. But this was not the moment to probe into her husband's feelings about Pauline Chambers.

'It's a horrible business,' she said. 'I liked Dudley.'

'Yes. So did I. You know, he said an odd thing at the end of his letter. "A man must have his pride." I suppose that sums up Dudley and his code of life as well as anything. Pauline was his wife. What he really felt about her we shall never know, but she must have put him through hell the last few years.'

'I never really thought he was aware of what was going on.'

'I know. The old figure of fun – the complaisant elderly husband, worrying about his health and his sport and his appearance . . . and underneath . . .' Geoffrey's voice died away. He was thinking, 'Thank heaven Dudley did not know of his wife's last little escapade.'

Mary's quiet voice broke in on his thoughts. 'He is better out of it all now.'

'Yes. I thought so. Having all the history of Pauline's amours dragged out at the trial would have been torture for him. . . .'

There was silence for a moment, a peaceful silence.

'And Pauline?'

'She'll stand trial – and thoroughly enjoy it, I expect. She will probably swing the minimum sentence for suppressing evidence and keeping the diamonds, if she gets a susceptible judge and a good counsel. She may get away with trying to sell them altogether if Schmidt can't be brought to trial. And I don't think he will be. Derek's evidence is the only outside proof, and I don't think it will be worth much.'

Mary smiled. 'I liked Schmidt's nerve, saying he hoped to have the pleasure of entertaining us to dinner soon, in happier circumstances!'

'Yes. And I would probably be tempted to accept.'

They stayed there peacefully, looking out over the quiet bay. The thundery clouds had gone tonight, and the moon made a slender pathway of light across the water. Near the beach a reddish glow showed where a fisherman was wading through the shallows with torch and spear. A scattering of lights along the shore marked the town, and a faint throbbing of drums told them that Kilimani was still awake.

Mary asked the question that had been in her mind all evening.

'And what about you, Geoffrey?'

'About me? The C.I.D. should get here by boat tomorrow and they will take over tidying up the loose ends. My guess it that I shall be officially congratulated for bringing a difficult case to a conclusion with speed, drive and initiative, in the absence of the regular police. Then, in about a month's time,

I shall be transferred to a small station very far up-country and left there until the whole thing is forgotten.'

'Will you care much?'

Geoffrey pondered. 'No. I don't think so. I have done all I can for Kilimani, and I think it has done all it can for me. We have exhausted our use for each other and it is time I moved on. And none of it will matter very much,' he added, turning to smile at her, 'so long as we are in it together.'

50 Classics of Crime Fiction 1900-1950

1
Classic Stories of Crime and Detection.

2
Margery Allingham. *Dancers in Mourning.*

3
H.C. Bailey. *Mr. Fortune: Eight of His Adventures.*

4
E.C. Bentley. *Trent's Last Case.*

5
Nicholas Blake. *Minute for Murder.*

6
Ernest Bramah. *Max Carrados.*

7
Gerald Bullett. *The Jury.*

8
Miles Burton. *The Secret of High Eldersham.*

9
Raymond Chandler. *The Lady in the Lake.*

10
G.K. Chesterton. *The Innocence of Father Brown.*

11
Agatha Christie. *The Murder of Roger Ackroyd.*

12
G.D.H. and Margaret Cole. *The Murder at Crome House.*

13
Edmund Crispin. *Buried for Pleasure.*

14
Freeman Wills Crofts. *The Box Office Murders.*

15
Arthur Conan Doyle. *The Hound of the Baskervilles.*

16
Helen Eustis. *The Horizontal Man.*

17
Kenneth Fearing. *The Big Clock.*

18
R. Austin Freeman. *The Singing Bone.*

19
Erle Stanley Gardner. *The Case of the Crooked Candle.*

20
Andrew Garve. *No Tears for Hilda.*

21
Michael Gilbert. *Smallbone Deceased.*

22
C.W. Grafton. *Beyond a Reasonable Doubt.*

23
Anna Katherine Green. *The Circular Study.*

24
Cyril Hare. *When the Wind Blows.*

25
Matthew Head. *The Congo Venus.*

26
Georgette Heyer. *A Blunt Instrument.*

27
James Hilton. *Was It Murder?*

28
Elspeth Huxley. *The African Poison Murders.*

29
Michael Innes. *The Daffodil Affair.*

30
Thomas Kindon. *Murder in the Moor.*

31
Thomas Kyd. *Blood on the Bosom Devine.*

32
Lange Lewis. *The Birthday Murder.*

33
Ross MacDonald. *The Drowning Pool.*

34
Pat McGerr. *Pick Your Victim.*

35
Paul McGuire. *A Funeral in Eden.*

36
Ngaio Marsh. *A Wreath for Rivera.*

37
A.A. Milne. *The Red House Mystery.*

38
Dermot Morrah. *The Mummy Case.*

39
Oliver Onions. *In Accordance with the Evidence.*

40
Marco Page. *The Shadowy Third.*

41
Virginia Perdue. *Alarum and Excursion.*

42
Eden Phillpotts. *"Found Drowned."*

43
Dorothy L. Sayers. *Strong Poison.*

44
C.P. Snow. *Death Under Sail.*

45
Rex Stout. *Too Many Cooks.*

46
Arthur Upfield. *The Bone Is Pointed.*

47
Henry Wade. *The Dying Alderman.*

48
Henry Kitchell Webster. *Who Is the Next?*

49
Ellen Wilkinson. *The Division Bell Mystery.*
50
Clifford Witting. *Measure for Murder.*

50 Classics of Crime Fiction 1950-1975

1
Frank Arthur. *Another Mystery in Suva.*
2
Alex Atkinson. *Exit Charlie.*
3
John and Emery Bonett. *Not in the Script.*
4
Fredric Brown. *The Deep End.*
5
Leo Bruce. *Furious Old Women.*
6
Joanna Cannan. *The Body in the Beck.*
7
A.H.Z. Carr. *Finding Maubee.*
8
Glynn Carr. *Death Finds a Foothold.*
9
Philip Clark. *The Dark River.*
10
K.C. Constantine. *The Man Who Liked to Look at Himself.*
11
Amanda Cross. *In the Last Analysis.*
12
Elizabeth Daly. *Death and Letters.*

13
Thomas B. Dewey. *A Sad Song Singing*.

14
Stanley Ellin. *The Key to Nicholas Street*.

15
Nigel Fitzgerald. *Suffer a Witch*.

16
Dick Francis. *Dead Cert*.

17
Edward Grierson. *The Second Man*.

18
Bruce Hamilton. *Too Much of Water*.

19
M.V. Heberden. *Engaged to Murder*.

20
Tony Hillerman. *The Fly on the Wall*.

21
S.B. Hough. *The Bronze Perseus*.

22
P.M. Hubbard. *High Tide*.

23
Michael Innes. *One-Man Show*.

24
P.D. James. *Cover Her Face*.

25
Carlton Keith. *The Crayfish Dinner*.

26
Henry Kuttner. *Murder of a Wife*.

27
Christopher Landon. *Stone Cold Dead in the Market*.

28
Emma Lathen. *Murder Makes the Wheels Go 'Round*.

29
Norman Longmate. *Strip Death Naked*.

30
John D. MacDonald. *Dead Low Tide*.

31
J.J. Marric. *Gideon's River*.

32
John Miles. *The Night Hunters.*

33
William Mole. *Small Venom.*

34
Patricia Moyes. *Johnny Under Ground.*

35
Simon Nash. *Killed by Scandal.*

36
Ellis Peters. *Never Pick Up Hitch-Hikers!*

37
J.B. Priestley. *Salt Is Leaving.*

38
Maurice Procter. *The Pub Crawler.*

39
Ruth Rendell. *A New Lease of Death.*

40
Helen Robertson. *Swan Song.*

41
Jean Scholey. *The Dead Past.*

42
Frank Swinnerton. *On the Shady Side.*

43
Julian Symons. *The Narrowing Circle.*

44
Josephine Tey. *The Singing Sands.*

45
Simon Troy. *Swift to Its Close.*

46
Walter Tyrer. *Such Friends Are Dangerous.*

47
Robert Van Gulik. *The Lacquer Screen.*

48
Colin Watson. *Just What the Doctor Ordered.*

49
Hillary Waugh. *The Missing Man.*

50
Classic Short Stories of Crime and Detection. Selected by Jacques Barzun and Wendell Hertig Taylor.

DATE DUE

DEC 3 '84

PR9399
.9
.S36D4
1983

Scholey

The dead past

Due Date | 1st Ren. | 2nd Ren.

PR9399
.9
.S36D4
1983

Scholey

The dead past